Roper held his breath and went down on his heels beside the body. He carefully hooked a finger around one of the corpse's chill ones and lifted it. It was loose and rubbery, so rigor mortis must have occurred then gone again. Days ago, probably.

"She's been dead three or four days," said Dr. Hall, watching him. "It looks like a classic."

Roper made no answer. Suicides, in his book, were never classic.

"And there's one more thing, sir," said Weekes.

"What's that?"

"The gas-tap, sir," said Weekes. "When Sergeant Crisp came in and turned it off, it was barely turned on at all. About a quarter of the way at most."

"Odd," agreed Roper.

"Meted out in Hart's understated, highly effective prose..."

—*Publishers Weekly*

"...a well-developed plot with all the clues in the right places."

—*Booklist*

Also available from Worldwide Mystery by
ROY HART

A PRETTY PLACE FOR A MURDER

ROY HART

A DEADLY SCHEDULE

W✪RLDWIDE.

TORONTO • NEW YORK • LONDON
AMSTERDAM • PARIS • SYDNEY • HAMBURG
STOCKHOLM • ATHENS • TOKYO • MILAN
MADRID • WARSAW • BUDAPEST • AUCKLAND

A DEADLY SCHEDULE

A Worldwide Mystery/June 1996

First published by St. Martin's Press, Incorporated.

ISBN 0-373-26205-1

Copyright © 1993 by Roy Hart.
All rights reserved. No part of this book may be reproduced or transmitted in any form or by any means, electronic or mechanical, including photocopying, recording or by any information storage and retrieval system, without permission in writing from the publisher. For information, contact: St. Martin's Press, Incorporated, 175 Fifth Avenue, New York, NY 10010-7848 U.S.A.

All characters in this book are fictitious, and any resemblance to actual persons, living or dead, is purely coincidental.

® and TM are trademarks of Harlequin Enterprises Limited. Trademarks indicated with ® are registered in the United States Patent and Trademark Office, the Canadian Trade Marks Office and in other countries.

Printed in U.S.A.

A DEADLY
SCHEDULE

ONE

'OH WELL DONE, Madam,' Roper murmured appreciatively, shielding his eyes from the bright sunshine with the postcard he had just written. A keen justicer himself, rarely had he seen retribution follow so swiftly upon the heels of the crime.

Sitting on the second-floor balcony outside his hotel bedroom, he had had a bird's-eye view of the entire business from start to finish. And so certain had he been that a villainy was about to be perpetrated that when it did happen it unrolled beneath his gaze in a predestined slow motion.

Firstly, he had observed the older of the two olive-skinned youths, jeaned and black tee-shirted, skulking furtively in the shadowed alley between the souvenir shop and the seminary, with one foot poised above the kick-starter of his rust-riddled Lambretta moped. His equally suspicious-looking colleague had, for several minutes, been leaning over the rickety handrail at the top of the wooden steps that led down from the promenade to the beach. He too was wearing a pair of tattered blue jeans. But his tee-shirt was a dirty white, and around his neck he wore a white polka-dotted red bandana. And if Roper was interpreting his body language correctly, the latter youth was the lookout man for his partner on the moped.

Then it had erupted. The lookout had blown a shrill whistle between his teeth, flicked down his Polaroids from his hair to the bridge of his nose, then doubled back past the souvenir shop and flung himself astride the pillion seat of the Lambretta, which his accomplice had already kicked into noisy life.

And as the moped had swung into action so two women's heads appeared as their owners came up the stairs from the beach, English Lady Number One and English Lady Number Two, both of them returning to the hotel for lunch and their afternoon siesta after a morning's sunbathing. It was to English Lady Number One that Roper had taken a markedly serious fancy, despite the fact that she had dumped a heavy suitcase on his foot when they had boarded the ferry at Piraeus. They had shared the same hotel for a week now and still he didn't know her name.

The two women started to cross the stone sets of the promenade, a light breeze off the sea flapping their beachwraps around their knees. Apart from them the street was almost deserted, the locals and most of the wiser tourists well inside by now out of the heat of the noonday sun. Then with an ear-splitting roar of its exhaust the Lambretta leapt from the shadows and headed straight for them. The pillion-passenger's arm was already outstretched, his target plainly English Lady Number Two's shoulder bag, she being the nearer as the Lambretta bore down on them.

English Lady Number One, however, in the split-second she had to anticipate what might be going to happen, got it exactly right. She was carrying her own beach-bag in her hand and swung it like a flail. And timed her reaction so beautifully that it swept the pillion-passenger, together with English Lady Number Two's beach-bag, backwards off the Lambretta—which was when Roper had muttered his approval—so that, after seeming to hang suspended in the air for an interminable time, the bandana'd youth landed heavily on one twisted foot and a shoulder.

Probably unaware that he had lost his passenger, the youth driving the Lambretta made off in a cloud of stinking blue smoke, although by then English Lady Number One was kneeling on the pillion-passenger's chest and opening his fingers to release her friend's bag from his grasp.

Only when she had done that was the youth allowed to scramble to his feet and hobble off, limping, on a route that took him straight into the radiator grille of a police prowl-car that stopped just in the nick of time with a squeal of rubber.

THE TWO ENGLISH LADIES were not at lunch. A half-hour had passed since the incident with the Lambretta. Roper had been on the point of going down to the street and offering himself as a witness when the lunch gong had sounded. He waited a minute or two to see how the two women fared with the officer who had been driving the car, but it was fairly obvious the policeman didn't understand a word they were saying. But he must have seen something of what had happened for himself because he slapped a pair of handcuffs on the errant youth and bundled him into the back of his car. He had then driven off again, at which juncture Roper, famished after a morning's hard labour at the dig, had gone down to the dining-room and tucked himself into his corner by the window where, as always, he minded his own business while he tackled his charcoaled lamb chops with a side-plate of salad and *feta*, the local goat-cheese.

Over a couple of cups of sweet black coffee and a cheroot, he spread a well-used road-map over the cloth and planned his route for the tour he would take after his siesta this afternoon. One of the Germans along at the dig had told him that there was an interesting Minoan site over at Káto Zákros, at the eastern end of the island, which was well worth a visit, and with some spectacular scenery on the way.

There was still no sign of the two English women when he folded his map, pushed back his chair and headed for the reception lobby and the stairs to his room. He heard their voices first. They were standing beside the huge potted palm tree near the door to the street and English Lady Number One was protesting vociferously that she and her friend had acted in self-defence. Their listeners were two shirt-sleeved police officers—a capped, moustached and sweaty-looking sergeant with a beer belly hanging pendulously over his pistol belt, and a crisply white-shirted, dapper little man with a pencil moustache and gold-rimmed sunglasses. The latter had enough pieces of metal on the epaulettes of his shirt to denote that he was a very big wheel indeed in the local constabulary.

'—And that was exactly the way it happened,' said English Lady Number One. '*They* were going to grab *our* handbags. All *we* were doing was crossing the street. For pity's sake, man, I *took* my friend's bag out of his hand!'

'But there are no witnesses, you see, *Despinida* Carmody,' explained the senior officer patiently.

'But there was! The policeman who came up in the car!'

'He saw only the end of the affair, I am afraid, *Despinida* Carmody,' said the senior officer, in impeccable English. 'Which was you kneeling on the young man's chest before you released him.'

'But the policeman arrested him!'

'True,' agreed the senior man. 'Because it was more likely that a teenaged youth was the cause of the incident rather than an English lady tourist. But when he was questioned as to what the incident was about, he insisted that he and his friend on the moped were merely driving past you when you stepped forward and swung your handbag at them.'

'Well, they're liars,' insisted English Lady Number One fiercely.

'Yes, they are,' agreed English Lady Number Two more timidly. 'It was exactly the way my friend told you it was. Honestly, it *was*.'

At which juncture Roper decided he just had to butt in. 'The two ladies are dead right,' he said as he came up behind them. 'I was sitting on my balcony and watched the whole thing happen. A couple of young muggers on a moped. They snatched this lady's handbag.'

'And you are ... ?' asked the little man, staring up inimically at Roper through his Polaroids.

'The name's Roper. I'm a guest here. And the ladies are right. That's just what happened.'

The little man smiled shrewdly. 'And you are English, *Kyrios* Roper, of course?'

'You can forget the of course,' said Roper tartly. 'I don't even know the names of these two ladies. And who might you be, exactly?'

'Major Ioánnis Spiridakis,' said the sleek little man, unperturbed. 'I am the Deputy Chief of Police of this district of the island.' His softly spoken English really was very nearly perfect, and Roper even thought he heard an occasional inflection of suburban London creep into it from time to time. Spiridakis reached up to the bridge of his Polaroids, plucked them off, folded them carefully, then tucked them into the pocket of his beautifully ironed shirt. 'So, *Kyrios* Roper, your story of what happened outside in the street this morning, please.'

And Roper began at the beginning, with the one youth waiting astride a moped in the shadow of the seminary and the other hanging over the handrail while he selected his prey, and finished with the arrival of the roving police car.

'Can you describe these two young men, *Kyrios* Roper?'

And Roper did, right down to the polka-dotted bandana and the grubby white sneakers they had both been wearing.

'And the Lambretta?'

'Metallic blue, with red seats. A lot of rust. And half the rear number-plate had been broken off.'

Spiridakis had listened to all this with a lessening hostility that finally turned to frank satisfaction. His moon-faced sergeant, who probably hadn't understood a word, had simply stood by and continued to sweat.

'Thank you, *Kyrios* Roper,' said Spiridakis. 'I do not think I could have asked for more than that. Do you wish me to charge the young men?' he asked, turning to the two women.

'No, we don't,' said English Lady Number One, now revealed as Miss Something or Other Carmody. English Lady Number Two merely shook her head.

'Good,' said Spiridakis. 'Here on Crete that will save a lot of paperwork. And I would have had to ask you both to stay on the island until the case came to court. And that takes a long time here.'

'And I presume we can expect an apology of some sort?' enquired Miss Carmody, who seemed to be a spirited lady as well as an attractive one, giving Spiridakis the kind of icy glance that ought to have levelled him where he stood.

Spiridakis shrugged. The French may have invented the shrug but the Cretans have turned it into a language all of its own. 'Of course, I am sorry, *Despinida* Carmody, but a serious allegation was made and I was obliged to look into it.' A world-weary smile fleeted under the little black moustache. 'It is not always easy being a policeman—sometimes judge, sometimes jury—keeping everybody sweet as you English say. So far as I am concerned, the affair is now closed.' He inclined his head towards Roper and touched the visor of his cap to the two women. '*Kalispera,*' he said. He started to go, the sergeant following, but then he stopped and turned back again. 'And by the way,' he said, 'the two young men, they were not Cretans. They came from the mainland, and tomorrow they will be sent back there. I thought you should know that.' He inclined his head again. 'Please enjoy the rest of your holiday. *Kalispera.*'

'*Kalispera,*' said Roper.

'Thank you very much, Mr Roper,' said Miss Carmody as Spiridakis and his sergeant went out to their car. 'We really are very grateful.'

'Yes, we certainly are,' agreed English Lady Number Two.

'Glad to be of help,' said Roper, and left it at that. Had Miss Carmody been alone he might have pursued the acquaintance, but he had already guessed that English Lady Number Two was the clinging kind and would be lost without someone to lead her about.

'WELL, HE CERTAINLY saved our bacon this afternoon,' said Miss Carmody.

'So he did,' agreed her companion, with a disapproving purse of her lips behind her coffee cup. 'But I still think he looks so incredibly dour.' She leaned closer. 'And I'm very suspicious of middle-aged men who go on holiday alone. It makes you think...well, that they're looking for...well, you know. And where does he go each morning in that awful little motor-car? This morning he went off just after six o'clock. Yesterday it was five o'clock. I think that's *very* suspicious.'

'How do you know he shoots off that early?' enquired Miss Carmody, who was beginning to find Mrs Gribo so tedious that she wished she had taken her holiday somewhere else. 'I didn't think you were up and about much before seven.'

'I'm not. But I can't sleep for the heat. I hear him creeping down the stairs every morning.'

'It could be anybody.'

'No, it's him. Because a few minutes afterwards I hear his terrible little car start up. And there's something else I ask myself: why does he always come back covered in dust from wherever he's been?'

'I haven't the faintest idea,' said Miss Carmody wearily, briefly burying her nose in her coffee cup.

The subject of their conversation sat in the lounge at the far end of the hotel's little bar, a copy of yesterday's *Daily Telegraph* spread over the counter in front of him. So far as Miss Carmody was concerned, the man in question had the not inconsiderable quality of keeping himself to himself, but not unsociably so. He always had a quick ready smile and always a polite good-afternoon, good-evening or good-night; but not a good-morning because, as Mrs Gribo had noted, he was never about the hotel in the mornings. And if he had not come up trumps at lunchtime today, she and Susan Gribo might be languishing in a police cell by now on bread and water.

'Well, I think he's definitely a shady character,' said Mrs Gribo, who didn't seem to like anybody very much and was always most particular about having the last word.

'*KALISPERA, KYRIOS* ROPER,' said a smooth voice at Roper's shoulder. 'May I join you, or would you rather be alone?'

It was Major Spiridakis, as dapper at night in a civilian tropical suit as he had been in uniform that afternoon.

'Be my guest, Major,' said Roper. 'Can I buy you a drink?'

'No, it is my shout,' said Spiridakis, his hand already in his hip-pocket and drawing out his wallet. 'No, please, I insist,' he added as Roper beckoned the barman. 'It will be my pleasure. I have come looking for you, and I have found you.' As the barman approached, Spiridakis pointed to Roper's glass, then ordered a light beer for himself. That done, he climbed on to the stool beside Roper's and took a packet of cigarettes from his jacket.

'Thanks,' said Roper, as Spiridakis proffered them, 'but I only smoke cheroots.'

'But otherwise you go Greek on holiday,' said Spiridakis, as he leaned over the lighter Roper had struck for him. 'Since you are lodging in *Kyrios* Krasakis' modest hotel and since also I see you are drinking *ouzo.*'

'Well-watered *ouzo,*' said Roper, tucking his lighter away again. 'I have to get up early in the morning.'

'To work on the archaeological dig at Kázis, I believe,' said Spiridakis, with another of his smiles. Even his teeth were perfectly tailored.

'You're very well informed, Major.'

Spiridakis shrugged. 'It is my business to know what is going on at all the digs in this corner of Crete, *Kyrios* Roper. Too many of our island's treasures are already in your London museums. We prefer what is left to stay here.'

'Acting suspiciously are we, Major?'

'No, of course not,' protested Spiridakis. 'It is flattering to us that foreigners want to come to our island and

uncover our history. But you, I think, are not an archaeologist.'

'I'm not,' said Roper. 'I just go up there each day and
do a bit of labouring.'

'Which seems to me to be a strange way to have a holiday. You enjoy that kind of work?'

'I like old things. This morning I was scrubbing down a
Minoan pot. About so high.' Roper held his hand six
inches or so above the counter. It had been something close
to a mystical experience holding that pot. 'Something that
nobody's seen in a couple of thousand years. Damned near
priceless, I should think. I don't often get a chance to do
that.'

'Now, you see, *Kyrios* Roper, that makes you even more
interesting to me,' said Spiridakis, picking up his beer.
'*Stin iyassou.*'

'*Episis,*' said Roper, taking a sip of his well-watered
ouzo. Across the room, the two Englishwomen were gathering up their handbags. From what he had seen of them
so far they liked to turn in early. Miss Carmody rose to
bring their used coffee cups back to the counter.

'You speak some Greek,' said Spiridakis. ''So I assume
you have been to Greece before. Yes?'

'Often,' said Roper. 'But to Crete mostly. It's quieter.'

'True,' agreed Spiridakis. 'But things are changing fast.
Tourists, concrete hotels, thieving boys on motor-cycles. I
have seen most of these changes in my own lifetime. It is
very sad, I think. Tell me, *Kyrios* Roper,' he said, abruptly
changing the subject. 'What do you do when you are not
washing pots on a dig?'

'I'm a civil servant,' said Roper.

Spiridakis smiled again. 'That is what it says on your
passport, I suppose?'

'You want to see it?'

'No, of course not,' said Spiridakis. 'I would not be so presumptuous. But I do not think you are just a civil servant any more than you are an archaeologist.'

'Does it matter?'

'To me, yes,' said Spiridakis. 'And it matters because of a spotted red bandana and a broken number-plate—and that you have no fear of policemen. I think,' he said, knowingly tapping the tip of his nose with a forefinger, 'that you are also a policeman. It is something here.' The forefinger rose and circled Spiridakis' eyes. 'The eyes. You know?'

A brief distraction was a good-night spoken by Miss Carmody as she and her friend passed behind them on their way upstairs.

'Good-night,' said Roper, over his shoulder.

'*Kaliniktah*,' said Spiridakis, over his. Turning back again he said, 'Well, *Kyrios* Roper, am I right or not?'

'Oh, you're dead right, Major,' said Roper. 'And you didn't learn English like that on this little island.'

'True,' agreed Spiridakis. 'Where, do you think?'

'London,' suggested Roper.

'Hounslow,' said Spiridakis. 'I was in lodgings there. For two years I was a student at the London School of Economics. I had grand ideas about saving the world from itself. But we Cretans are like your English seaside rock; cut us wherever you like and you will find *Kriti* printed in red. So I came back, and to the despair of my father I became a policeman. You are from London also, I think?'

'Originally,' said Roper. 'But these days I live in Bournemouth.'

'Coincidence,' said Spiridakis. 'Your Miss Carmody is also from Bournemouth.'

'Small world,' said Roper. 'And Bournemouth's a big place.'

'Please,' said Spiridakis, raising a placatory hand. 'I was insinuating nothing. It is merely that I am fascinated by coincidences. Like traffic accidents. If one or the other of the vehicles had not been in a very specific place at a very specific time, then the accident could not possibly have happened . . .'

AT ONE O'CLOCK in the morning, to the patent despair of the barman, Roper and Spiridakis were still in the bar, and even his sweeping the floor around them had failed to make an impression. Their current discussion concerned the criminal mind.

'Take those two lads this morning,' said Roper. 'Say what you like, they're a pair of dyed-in-the-wool villains. And they got away with it. And for the next twenty years they'll probably get away with it some more, until they end up killing somebody. And they'll probably get away with that, too.'

'I would say that is very likely,' agreed Spiridakis gloomily. 'And to be honest, they lied to me so beautifully that I was almost tempted to believe that your two English ladies were a couple of homicidal maniacs I would have to lock up. Until I met them, of course.'

'But it was such a bloody stupid lie,' said Roper. 'Why did they bother?'

'*Philotemo*,' said Spiridakis. 'What you English call machismo. Pride. Young Greek men set a lot of store by their *philotemo*. To be knocked off a motor-cycle by a crazy Englishwoman, that is just about sufferable. But to try to steal her handbag and not only fail but to be bested in the process, that, my friend, is a loss of *philotemo* that no Greek man could live with—and could certainly never tell his friends.' He shrugged. 'So, in case there might have been a witness, they told their little lie. And, after all, it was *almost* the truth, wasn't it?'

ROPER SURFACED the next morning at eight o'clock, with a head that felt as if someone had buried an axe in it. A cold shower helped, but not entirely, and when he bent to strap his sandals the floor took on a definite tilt that took several long seconds to right itself. He and Spiridakis had finally parted company round about two o'clock in the morning and the water the barman had left on the counter had run out long before the *ouzo* bottle. Not that the *ouzo* bottle had been full in the first place, but half full or half empty the end result was much the same.

Already an hour and a half late at the dig, he locked his bedroom door behind him and padded briskly towards the stairs. He had just reached the first-floor landing when a door clicked open behind him and a woman's urgent voice called after him: 'Excuse me, Mr Roper, can you help me, please?'

A worried-looking Miss Carmody hurried towards him. 'Good-morning,' she said. 'Look, I'm dreadfully sorry to trouble you, Mr Roper, but I'm terribly worried about Mrs Gribo—that's the lady who was with me yesterday. I've knocked on her door several times, but I just can't rouse her.'

'Perhaps she's gone out,' suggested Roper.

Miss Carmody shook her head. 'No, I don't think she'd do that. She doesn't like going anywhere on her own. And I think I can hear water running in her bathroom. I wonder if she's slipped in the shower, or something.'

'Tried your key in the lock?'

Miss Carmody shook her head and began digging into her handbag for her key. Roper tried his. It sprung a couple of wards but was then brought up short before it com-

pleted the full circle. Given some jiggling about it might
have worked but Miss Carmody had by now produced
hers. After a bit of rocking it up and down and shoving it
backwards and forwards, there was a satisfying click and
Roper carefully edged the door open. The sound of running water was louder. That the bed was made up and the
lights were switched on were the first things he noticed.
That Mrs Gribo's wardrobe and suitcases had been ran-
sacked and their contents tossed all over the floor at the
bottom end of the bed was the second. The curtains were
closed to all but a narrow slit that let through a single shaft
of morning sunlight. But by the time he had taken all that
in he was already knocking on the bathroom door.

'Mrs Gribo,' he called loudly. 'Are you there?'

'Something terrible's happened,' whispered Miss Carmody at his shoulder. 'I just know it has.'

He knocked again, but there was still no reply. He tentatively tried the door handle. Whoever was in there hadn't
used the bolt.

'Do you want to look,' he said, 'or would you rather I
did?'

'Frankly, I'd rather you did.' Her tanned face had gone
distinctly pale. 'If she's slipped and injured herself I don't
think she'll give a damn about the proprieties, do you?'

With the door open a scant half-inch, he called Mrs
Gribo once more, just to be certain, and, still meeting only
the sound of running water, he went in all the way. Saw
first the thin white bony hand dangling from its wrist over
the edge of the shower tray between the shower curtain and
the tiled wall, saw second an ominous stain that looked like
diluted blood close to the bottom of the curtain, saw third,
when he drew it back, the gaping-mouthed and wide-eyed
face of Mrs Gribo staring up at him as she sat there hud-
dled in the shower tray, her naked back to the tiles and her

knees drawn up, wearing ear-plugs, a split in her yellow shower-cap and a wound across her scalp that she could never have got from simply slipping in the shower.

Mrs Gribo had been brutally and efficiently battered to her death.

TWO

HE STEPPED BACK into the bedroom and drew the bathroom door to after him.

'She's dead, isn't she?' said Miss Carmody. 'I can tell by your face.'

'I'm afraid she is, Miss Carmody,' said Roper. 'I'm deeply sorry.'

'Oh, it's all right,' said Miss Carmody, then added hastily. 'No, of course it isn't all right. What I really mean is, she's only someone I met on the flight to Athens and got stuck with. Other than that we scarcely knew each other. What do you think we ought to do now? Get Mr Krasakis up here, I suppose.'

'Later,' said Roper. From what he had observed of Mr Krasakis, the hotel owner, that gentleman was likely to wax inordinately hysterical and turn the entire place into a bedlam in a matter of minutes. 'We go out, we shut the door behind us, you go back to your room, then I'll go downstairs to phone the police. Are you going to be all right?'

Miss Carmody nodded. 'Sure,' she said. 'I'm okay. Just a bit shaky, that's all.'

Roper saw her back across the passage to her room and went downstairs to the reception desk, where Mr Krasakis himself was signing out an American couple who stood amidst their pile of elegant matching suitcases. Roper waited patiently for them to finish. There was, after all, no immediate hurry. From the looks of her, Mrs Gribo had been dead for some considerable time and whoever had killed her would be well away by now.

'I'd like to make a phone call, Mr Krasakis. The local police-headquarters. No, it's all right,' he added quickly as Krasakis' eyebrows arched in fright. 'It's about the business outside yesterday. The two boys on the moped. The name's Roper. Room Twelve.'

He went across to the medieval phone booth on the other side of the lobby and waited with the receiver to his ear while Krasakis juggled feverishly with jacks and sockets and the tangled spaghetti of black wires that served as the hotel's switchboard.

A muffled growl then at Roper's ear. Greek and sleepy. *'Astinomya.'*

'Milata Anglika?' asked Roper hopefully, doubting very much that he would have the luck to find an English-speaking policeman at this hour of the morning.

'Oki,' the muffled voice denied curtly. *'Perimeno.'* And with that instruction the owner of the voice dropped his receiver noisily on to a desk. Then receding footsteps, a door closing. Then silence, a long, long silence.

'Hello,' another muffled but brisker voice said at last. 'This is the central police post at Agios Nikólaos. How can I help you?'

'My name is Douglas Roper,' said Roper, enunciating each word carefully. 'I am speaking from—'

'My dear *Kyrios* Roper!' the voice cut in. 'How are you on this extremely bright and sunny morning?'

There was no mistaking that voice now. It could only be Major Spiridakis with immaculate English like that.

'Well, Major, thank you,' said Roper. 'Look, I've just walked into a spot of trouble here at the hotel. Remember Mrs Gribo? The English woman who had her handbag snatched yesterday?'

'Indeed,' said Spiridakis, a note of wariness creeping into his voice. 'Do not tell me she has had it snatched again.'

'She's dead,' said Roper, turning away as he met Krasakis' interested gaze through the glass of the booth. 'She's presently sitting in her shower with her skull broken. Been dead since last night, at a guess.'

'Accident?'

'No,' said Roper. 'Definitely not.'

'You, of course, have touched nothing?'

'Just a couple of door handles. Couldn't get in otherwise.'

'You have told no one at the hotel?'

'Not yet.'

'Good,' said Spiridakis. 'And do not, please.' He broke off for a moment and called to someone in Greek. Whoever it was replied and Spiridakis was quickly back on the line again. 'I will be with you in a quarter of an hour. Which room is the poor lady in?'

'Six,' said Roper.

'And where will I find you?'

'Don't worry, Major,' said Roper. 'I won't be far away. Across the passage, probably.'

MISS CARMODY opened her door to his knock, her eyes falling gratefully on the cup of tea he had brought up to her from the dining-room, where most of the other guests were at breakfast, blissfully unaware of the drama that was slowly unfolding above their heads.

'I'm afraid it's only a tea-bag on a string,' he said. 'Umpteen thousand years of culture and they still can't make a decent cup of tea.'

'So long as it's wet and warm,' she said, opening her door wider to take it from him. 'I'm absolutely gasping. Thank you. Have you had one?'

'I had a quick coffee while they were hunting for the tea-bags.'

'Did you manage to contact the police?'

'Yes,' he said. 'I had a bit of luck and got through to Major Spiridakis.'

A beat or two of silence. 'He seems a nice sort of man, Major Spiridakis,' she said.

'He is,' said Roper. 'A bit of a philosopher, too.'

There was another hiatus, a feeling of discomfort between them, a slight heightening of tension. He seemed to be on the point of going. She hoped he wouldn't.

'If you need anything else,' he said, 'I'll be up in my room. Room Twelve. Spiridakis says he'll be here in fifteen minutes.'

'Would you mind very much staying with me?' she asked, and hoped she didn't sound as if she were importuning the poor man. 'I've been going absolutely barking mad the last few minutes, with no one to talk to. I'll leave the door open, in case anybody gets ideas. Please?'

'Sure,' he said. 'I could do with someone to talk to myself.'

She opened the door wider still and went to sit on the end of her bed with her cup of tea. He took the creaking wicker armchair in front of her dressing-table. The room smelled womanly—a hint of perfume, make-up, soap. Very tidy.

He watched her take a couple of sips of her tea. 'How d'you feel now?' he said.

'A bit shattered,' she said. 'But improving.'

'Good,' he said.

'You seem very cool about the whole business,' she said, having taken another sip and setting her cup back on its saucer.

He smiled. 'It's just a front,' he said. For a second or two in that bathroom, he'd had a sour aftertaste of last night's overdose of *ouzo*. He had held it back only with difficulty.

'Have you told them downstairs?'

'No,' he said, 'not yet. I'd rather Spiridakis was here when Mr Krasakis gets his attack of the vapours.'

'Oh, he'll definitely do that,' she said, with a small smile. She sipped again. 'This is really the most awful tea, you know.'

'Isn't it just,' he said.

She almost laughed. So did he. It was the moment that broke the ice.

'Where did you and Mrs Gribo first meet up with each other?' he said.

'Gatwick. On the aircraft. She came up the aisle behind me and sat down next to me. And she'd latched on to me ever since.'

'You sound as if you weren't very keen on the idea.'

'I wasn't,' she said. 'To be honest, I'd banked on a holiday on my own. But in a way I felt sorry for her.'

'Sorry?'

'She was very nervy. On the night we arrived, she managed to get her room changed so that she could be near me. In fact I'm surprised she decided to take a holiday on her own in a place like this. She was the sort a coach tour would have suited better. With lots of people about, you know?'

'All right for cash, was she?' Because what that mess in Mrs Gribo's bedroom looked like was a break-in-and-robbery job.

'She seemed to have pots of the stuff. Wherever we went, she insisted on paying for everything. I was beginning to find it very embarrassing. She just wouldn't take no for an answer.'

'Have much jewellery, did she?'

'Yes, a fair bit. Good stuff too, most of it. I suggested she ought to put it in the hotel safe, but she wouldn't.' At which point it suddenly occurred to her that she was being quietly but thoroughly quizzed, almost as if Mr Roper were a policeman himself.

'Husband alive, is he?'

'Yes, I think so. I gather he's a doctor. A general practitioner.'

'Is he on Crete, too?' Because in Roper's book, when you find a murdered wife, the first person to put the squeeze on was the husband. And more often than not you were justified.

'No,' she said. 'Scotland. I think he's having a fishing holiday.'

'Get on all right, did they?'

'She never said otherwise. Not that she talked about him all that much.' She took a longer swallow of her tea, draining the cup. She was about forty-two or -three, he judged. Particularly nice eyes, frank and honest, brown. Well-built, but the sort of woman who would fight to the last inch not to run to seed. Over the last week, he had watched her build up a tan. Mrs Gribo had stayed as pale and wan as when she arrived here. But what he had liked most about Miss Carmody was her aura of independence, which was probably why she was still a Miss. Or maybe she was widowed or divorced and had reverted to her maiden name. In either event, she was the first woman that he had been drawn to in a long time. Not that it could go anywhere. He had seen too many other coppers' marriages fall by the wayside to take up the state himself. There had been several women in his life, but there had been too many cancelled meetings, too many late nights and early mornings and the telephone calls that came in the middle of dinner and called him out somewhere on a job. There weren't many women who could stand a hodge-podge life like that, nor did he blame them.

'What do you think the chances are of getting a flight home tomorrow?' she said.

'Rough, I should think,' he said, with a tinge of disappointment that he hoped hadn't showed. 'Unless you sit around the airport and wait for someone to cancel a seat. We're right in the middle of the season.'

'Only I can't stay here,' she said. 'Not now. Not after all this.'

'You could always move to another hotel,' he suggested.

'Yes,' she agreed, brightening a little. 'I hadn't thought of that. But she's left a terrible hole, even though I didn't like her all that much. It makes my holiday feel sort of doomed. You know? On the other hand, I've quite got used to this place—despite Mr Krasakis flapping about. I hate the thought of moving into one of the awful high-rise concrete barracks along in the main town.'

'How about moving up to the next floor?' he proposed then. 'Those Americans went home this morning. Their room could still be vacant. I'll go down now and ask Krasakis, if you like.'

'Oh, don't worry,' she said, suddenly feeling a lot better. 'I'll go down and do it when the police have been.' A nice man all round, she decided. And he really did seem interested. She still recalled that awful moment on the ferry when she had dumped her two-ton suitcase across his feet and blurted, 'Oh, I'm so sorry,' and he had flashed that incredibly unexpected smile and said, 'It's all right, I'll

live.' What attracted her to him now was his quiet gravity.
It had calmed her down even more than that terrible cup
of tea. The word reliability kept coming to mind. Her luck
with men had not been good. Her one and only husband
had gone off with his adolescent filing-clerk and the man
she had later lived with for a year or more had gone to
work one morning and never returned. She still didn't
know what she had done wrong, or even if she had done
something wrong, but of late she had stopped worrying
about it—and until now had relished the feeling that independence had given her. Not that she was going to throw
it away now unless she was absolutely certain of the man
in question. But he really did seem keen that she should
stay on here, didn't he? And he had a sense of humour,
thank God—droll, but it was certainly there. And at the
moment she was greatly in need of a good laugh. But not
a holiday romance, she was too long in the tooth for that
sort of thing . . .

'Been around the island much?' he asked her.

'Hardly at all,' she said, trying to sound innocently unaware that she was being propositioned. 'A couple of
coach trips. Iráklion, and round the coast to Ierapetra,
only they whizz round so fast you hardly get a chance to
see anything. But that's all Susan wanted to do.'

'Susan?'

'Mrs Gribo.'

'Ah,' he said. Their eye-contact was broken for a moment as he leaned forward in that awful creaking chair and
hung his clasped hands between his knees. 'You haven't
been up in the mountains, then?'

'No, I haven't,' she said hopefully.

'That's where the real Crete is,' he said. His eyes fixed
on her again. 'We could drive there this afternoon. Take
your mind off this business. I've hired an old Volkswagen

Beetle. It's a bit of a banger, but it's reliable and the inside's clean.'

'Yes,' she said, to his surprise—and her own, come to that. 'I'd like that very much. Thank you.'

'And perhaps we could have lunch together.'

'Yes,' she said. 'That would be nice.' A bit too forthcoming, that, but he didn't seem to notice, perhaps because of the voices and footsteps coming up the stairs. The noisiest voice was that of Mr Krasakis.

And with a sinking feeling in his gut—because he had lived through too many moments like this before and seen too many broken bodies all too often—Roper got up from his chair and went out to the passage to meet them.

Krasakis was leading the way, protesting volubly and rubbing his hands together in that unctuous way he sometimes had. Major Spiridakis was hard on his heels and behind him were two young men in summer suits, one of them carrying an aluminium suitcase and a camera and tripod.

'She's in there,' said Roper with a nod of his head towards the door of Room Six. 'The bathroom.'

'Thank you,' said Spiridakis, staying Krasakis with a tug on his sleeve, then going into the room followed by his two detectives.

Krasakis gazed up at Roper anxiously, almost in tears. 'They will not tell me what is happening. It is something with *Kyria* Gribo, yes?'

'Yes, it is, Mr Krasakis. She's had some kind of accident.' Roper put his finger to his lips, seeing Krasakis open his mouth to exclaim just as a couple of guests passed by at the end of the passage.

'But why are *they* here?' whispered an anguished Krasakis, after a glance over his shoulder. 'It is twice in two days. They come here like Turks. As if it is theirs. It is bad for my hotel. And why is she not in *hospital?*'

Roper was saved from replying by the reappearance of Spiridakis. He said something to Krasakis in Greek, too much and too quickly for Roper to take in much of it, but presumably he was asking Krasakis to go in and look for himself because Krasakis looked as if he might faint away altogether as he furiously shook his head. Then Spiridakis called out one of his two plain-clothes men to take a statement from Krasakis, and the two of them went off to another room, Krasakis stumbling along on legs that were no longer able to fully support him, and in such a state that his hands seemed to have locked together permanently.

'Who found her?' Spiridakis muttered softly to Roper. In the room beside them, the other detective was bolting his camera on to its tripod.

'I did,' said Roper. 'Apparently, Mrs Gribo and Miss Carmody take breakfast together. Miss Carmody knocked a few times on Mrs Gribo's door, couldn't get a reply, then heard the sound of running water, which got her worried, and she asked me the best thing to do. End of story.'

'I see,' said Spiridakis. 'The shower is still running a little. Did you turn it down from full, or was it like that?'

'It was like that,' said Roper. 'I didn't touch it.'

'And the time?'

'About eight-fifteen, as near as I remember.' Roper, who had asked that question himself so many times and got equally vague answers, had forgotten to look at his watch, to his irritation.

'The room is in a mess,' said Spiridakis. 'So we could be looking at a robbery, and whoever it was was interrupted by Mrs Gribo—except, of course, that she could hardly have done that without leaving the shower. Do you know if she kept the door of her room locked?'

'It was certainly locked when I tried to get in,' said Roper.

'So whoever locked the door behind him must have left the hotel with *Kyria* Gribo's room-key,' proposed Spiridakis.

'Not necessarily,' said Roper. 'One key in this place seems much like another. Given the knack.'

'Thank you,' said Spiridakis. 'That will be worth remembering. Has the lady a husband?'

'Apparently,' said Roper. 'But he's currently on a fishing holiday in Scotland.'

'So he will be difficult to contact, I expect. But we shall do our best. How is Miss Carmody taking it?'

'Well,' said Roper. 'She seems a pretty hardy sort.'

'I shall have to question her, of course,' said Spiridakis.

From somewhere in the late Mrs Gribo's room came a stroke of light as the photographing detective fired his electronic flash. 'Perhaps it would be best if you join us. The lady might feel freer with a fellow countryman at hand. If you can spare the time, of course.'

'My time's yours, Major,' said Roper, standing aside to usher Spiridakis into the room opposite.

Miss Carmody was standing by the window, her empty cup and saucer on the ledge.

'Just a few questions, *Despinida* Carmody,' said Spiridakis after bidding her good-morning. 'I will try not to keep you too long. Please sit down, if you wish.'

'I'd rather stand, thank you,' she said.

'Whatever suits you,' said Spiridakis, 'so long as you are comfortable.'

For a minute or two then, with his pocket-book out and his ballpoint spilling out Greek characters across the pages, he asked almost the very same questions that Roper had.

About the husband. Was *Despinida* Carmody certain that he was in Scotland? Off-hand did *Despinida* Carmody know *Kyria* Gribo's home address? Where had *Despinida* Carmody first met her? What kind of woman had she been? Had she been carrying much money? Had she brought much jewellery with her? Would *Despinida* Carmody recognise perhaps if any of it would be missing? How had *Kyria* Gribo been—her mood—when *Despinida* Carmody had last seen her? Was she worried about anything? Was she upset? Had she met anybody else here on Crete who might also know about the jewellery? And of course the time when *Despinida* Carmody had last seen her? That was very important.

'About eleven-fifteen last night,' replied Miss Carmody, further revealed now, after giving her passport details to Spiridakis, as Sheila Margaret Carmody of 14 Dartington Close, Bournemouth, Dorset. 'We parted company in the passage outside. She told me she was going to take a shower before she went to bed.'

'You are sure about that? That she intended to take a shower *before* bed? Because, if she did, it would help us to fix the time of her death more exactly.'

Miss Carmody, clearly a woman of some intelligence, had begun to look suspicious.

'Why's the time so important?' she said, frowning. 'The poor woman's dead. She simply had an accident, didn't she?' But then she looked at Roper, hard and long, and said again, '*Didn't* she?'

'Maybe not, Miss Carmody,' said Roper.

Her face stiffened. 'Good God, you're not telling me . . . all that mess in her room . . . are you saying someone *else* did that?'

'It is possible, *Despinida* Carmody,' said Spiridakis apologetically. 'I am deeply sorry.'

Until now, her mind had been in a muddle, but suddenly all her confusion was swept away. It had been bad enough to know that Susan Gribo had died in her shower. To find out now that she might have been murdered in it put a whole new complexion on things. For instance, Mr Krasakis' quiet little out-of-the-way hotel had suddenly lost a lot of its charm. And so had that Mr Roper. Because she recalled how opportunely he had butted in yesterday afternoon after the incident with the two boys, and how buddy-buddy he and Spiridakis had looked in the bar last night, and how calm, relatively speaking, he had seemed to be when he had come out of Susan Gribo's bathroom not half an hour ago, almost as if he had known what he was going to find and had been prepared for it. And he had picked Susan Gribo's door-lock with considerable expertise; all right, so the hotel door-locks had probably been made around the time of Queen Victoria's youth, but he had appeared to know *exactly* what to do to open one. So perhaps he had done that before, too. He could even have done it last night, while Mrs Gribo had been in the shower, and that's how he had known what he was going to find when he went into the bathroom. And perhaps he and Spiridakis knew each other because the one was a policeman and the other a criminal. She had seen on television how policemen and criminals often had that strange rapport with each other. And Susan Gribo *had* remarked how shifty he looked, hadn't she? So perhaps he was, and he was going to take her into the mountains this afternoon and bump her off...

But then, amidst these seemingly clear and logical progressions, she remembered the quietly spoken questions he had asked her after they had come back to her room earlier. At the time, they had sounded like casual asides, but she realised now that they were exactly the same questions

Spiridakis had just asked her, and almost in the same order...

She eyed him narrowly. 'Are you some kind of policeman, too, Mr Roper? When you're not on holiday, I
mean?'

'Yes, I am,' he said, and probably had no idea at all
what a relief it was to her to hear him say that.

'I think that is all for now, *Despinida* Carmody,' said
Spiridakis, flipping his notebook shut. 'Thank you. You
will be somewhere near the hotel all day?'

'No, we shan't,' said Roper. 'We're driving up to
Elounda for lunch, then going across to Spinalónga. Assuming you can get along without us.'

'I think so,' said Spiridakis. 'Certainly for the time being. I will perhaps wish to speak to you both again this
evening.'

'We'll be back around seven o'clock,' said Roper.

'I shall be here.' Spiridakis slipped his notebook into his
shirt pocket and clipped his ballpoint beside it. 'Until this
evening, then. *Kalimera.*'

'I thought it might be better if we got out of here now,'
said Roper, when Spiridakis had gone back across the
passage. 'I've got a feeling all hell's going to break loose
in this place in the next half-hour. D'you mind?'

'Not at all,' she said. 'I'll be glad to get out of here myself.'

Although she would have preferred to have been told
about the arrangements for the rest of the day at first hand
rather than his telling them to Major Spiridakis. A bit
chauvinistic, that. But then she decided, given the circumstances, that he was probably doing his honest best to
stop her thinking at all for the next few hours and that it
was better to swim with the tide.

THREE

SHE LIKED ELOUNDA. Like the rest of the places she had so far seen on Crete, it was fast becoming a tourist-trap, but there was still enough of the old town left untouched to really get the feel of the place it had once been. And he had not taken her to one of the smart hotels for mid-morning lunch but to a tiled and concrete *taverna* over-looking the harbour. From the outside it had been an ugly, unimpressive place, slapped up in a few days with a con-crete mixer, hammer and nails, but inside there were hand-hewn wooden tables and chairs, and flowers everywhere, and the manager and his wife provided the kind of service that you'd be hard put to find in the middle of London. And the view from the window was incredible. An ex-panse of glittering water, as blue as the sky, and on the far side of the water the long low hump of Spinalónga island, sandy-brown and sandy-green, with a stone rampart, looking like a snake, climbing up it and disappearing over its far side.

'I can't see many houses.'

'You won't,' he said. 'The locals think it's unlucky. It used to be a leper colony.'

'Oh, dear,' she said. 'And it looks so gorgeous.'

And she had eaten her first all-Greek meal. She had eaten Greek at the hotel, but only a modified form, suit-able for the cautious palates of the tourists. What she was eating now were the local biscuits and goat-cheese, washed down with equally local wine.

'Fancy going across there after lunch?' he said.

'Yes, I do, rather,' she said. 'If you want to.'

They went across in a brightly painted row-boat of great antiquity, manned by a capped and heavily moustached old man who looked like a retired bandit and who talked all the time although neither of them understood a word. He did though, she could not help but notice, ask for his fare in very passable English.

And in the afternoon, they took the longer drive into the mountains. And she saw the kind of monastery she had only ever seen before in photographs, a little stone box with a tiled roof, stuck somehow to the side of what was virtually a precipice, several hundred feet in the air. Just hanging there amongst a few shrivelled-up bushes.

'How on earth do the poor old monks get up and down?'

'With a rope and basket, usually,' he said.

'I wouldn't care to chance *that*,' she remarked, with some feeling.

'Can't say I would, either,' he said, and flashed that smile again. He was, she had discovered, not the greatest of talkers. But on the other hand, when he did speak, it was always something intelligent that came out. His silences, too, were of the companionable kind, and he was attentive without overdoing it. When earlier in the afternoon they had climbed up to the top of Spinalónga, and it had been no mean climb, he had carried her shoulder-bag for her, and when he had helped her over the steeper parts of the climb, he had simply grabbed her hand and soon let it go again. She had several times tried to imagine him in a blue uniform and a tall helmet with a badge on the front, but simply could not make it all fit together.

AT DINNER she finally broached the subject. And it was just like getting blood out of a stone.

'I'm a superintendent,' he finally admitted, but only with the greatest reluctance. 'As from last Monday.'

'A uniformed one?' she pressed on.

'Not for the last twenty years or more.'

'A detective?'

'More or less. Serious Crime Division.'

'Like murders and things like that? You investigate those?'

'Not on my own. I've got a team of lads and lasses.'

She liked that, lads and lasses. He could so easily have been pompous about them. And then, at last, they finally got around to the subject both of them had studiously avoided since first thing that morning.

'I half guessed something really terrible had happened when you came out of that bathroom,' she said. 'More than that Susan was dead, I mean. And this place, to-night. It's like a tomb.' Which it was. More than half the tables were empty, and there had been a hasp, staple and a brass padlock newly fitted to Susan Gribo's door. Of Mr Krasakis there had been no sign. He had retired to his bed, most likely, and was still getting over his swoons.

'Are you still thinking of flying home?' he said.

'No,' she said. 'I don't think so.'

'Room Fourteen's vacant,' he said. 'That's the room the Americans had. I checked with Mrs Krasakis. There'll be no extra charge. Unless, of course, you'd rather be at the front of the hotel.'

'No,' she said. 'I don't care where. Just a bit wary about being murdered in my bed.'

'Murder's a bit like lightning,' he said. 'It doesn't often strike twice in the same place. And you can always jam a chair under the door handle.'

She still wasn't entirely convinced.

'Put it this way,' he said. 'I'm a light sleeper and I'm almost right opposite. All you've got to do is yell.'

'Damn right,' she said. 'I'll yell. And you've changed the subject. We were talking about Mrs Gribo.'

'I'm pretty sure it wasn't an accident,' he conceded cautiously.

'And if it wasn't an accident, she was murdered, wasn't she?'

He shrugged. 'I'm sure Spiridakis will tell us—eventually.'

'But you know now, don't you,' she persisted. 'And so does he. So what's all the mystery about?'

'It isn't a mystery,' he said. 'I've been doing my job a long time, and the first thing I learned was never to assume anything. But, yes, I *do* think Mrs Gribo was murdered, and so does Spiridakis. But there's got to be a post-mortem examination. Then we'll all know.'

'Are all policemen as cagey as you?' she said.

'Yes,' he said, and cracked his smile at her; then, more adroitly this time, he again changed the subject. 'Can I ask what you do for a living?'

'Antiques,' she said. 'I work on the front counter at Marr's, the auctioneers, up in London. Nothing grand. I just look over the stuff people bring in and phone for the relevant expert to come down and assess it—only if it looks like the real McCoy, that is. Most of the time it's just junk, sad to say.'

A new light had crept into his eyes, one that she had not seen before.

'That's what I plan to do when I retire from the Force,' he said. 'Start a little antiques shop. Furniture and china.'

'Do you know much about it?'

'A fair bit,' he said, far less modest now that he was on a subject that was obviously his hobby-horse. And for the

first time in the few hours she had known him, he chatted
eloquently and enthusiastically, and knowledgeably too.
Watching him as he spoke, she judged he was somewhere
in his middle forties. And he wore just the one ring, a gold
signet on his right hand. When she had first seen him, on
the ferry from Piraeus, he had been pale and tired-looking.
Now he was as brown as a nut, and she wondered how he
had got a tan like that. He certainly wasn't the sun-
worshipping type. But then they both got on to the subject of pots, upon which he waxed even more lyrical, and
he told her about the Minoan jar he had had in his hands
yesterday, and it transpired that he drove off each morning in his Beetle to a small archaeological site a few kilometres away in a village called Kázis, where he worked
from seven o'clock until the sun was too high, which was
usually around eleven-thirty. She had already guessed that
he was a Londoner born and bred and he told her that he
had transferred from the Metropolitan Police to the Dorset Constabulary some ten years before. In a smaller Force,
there were better chances of promotion and, as he suc-
cinctly put it, 'less rolled-up trouser-legs and funny hand-
shakes'. Early in the day, he had called her Miss Carmody,
and he had been Mr Roper, but now they had dropped
names altogether. And then to her mild but pleasant surprise, he dropped the fact that he, too, lived in Bournemouth. A flat, overlooking the cliffs, along at Critchley
Chine.

'It's a bit expensive along there, isn't it?'

'Fairly,' he admitted, but then added, 'but I've only got
myself to look after.' Which she immediately decoded as a
frank confirmation of his availability should she wish to
pursue the acquaintance, which she seriously thought she
might, given a few more days to get to know him better.

After dinner, they went out to the desk and arranged the changing of her room with Mrs Krasakis. Mr Roper helped her carry her things upstairs and showed her how to jam a chair under the door handle to maximum effect. Perhaps it wasn't meet and proper that she should move up to his floor, but at least she would sleep easier tonight knowing that he was within earshot.

A stroll then into the main part of the town and around the harbour and among more people than she had seen all day. The night was balmy and boats were bobbing on the water amongst the reflections of the lights from all the hotels. And taken all round, if it had not been for the death of Susan Gribo, whatever its circumstances, she would have felt more content than she had in many a long year. But of course, that had been lurking at the back of her mind all day and had taken most of the gilt off the ginger-bread; nevertheless, she felt that her life might have reached another inch-mark. Her only serious doubt was that he might have kept her company today only to take her mind off things—considering that for the previous week, apart from a good-afternoon or a good-night whenever they had passed each other in the hotel, he had uttered not a word to her, nor given the remotest sign that he was interested. And perhaps, even now, she was mis-reading the signals he was putting out.

When they arrived back at the hotel, Major Spiridakis was in the lobby with one of his detectives. They were at the counter with Mrs Krasakis, examining the register. And two more guests, a man and a woman, were coming downstairs with their suitcases and the unmistakable air of people about to check out.

Spiridakis looked along his shoulder as Roper and Sheila Carmody came up beside him.

'Any news yet?' asked Roper.

Spiridakis shook his head. Then, leaving his junior with Mrs Krasakis and the register, he joined Roper and Miss Carmody and shepherded them into the corner by the potted palm.

'We have taken her to the mortuary in Iráklion,' he said quietly. 'An autopsy has been arranged for tomorrow afternoon. A good man will be doing it. A Doctor Constanduros from Athens University.' He gave one of his small wry smiles. 'Mrs Gribo is suddenly a very important person, you see—a tourist. And since tourists are our bread and butter we cannot afford the bad press. So we have to be seen to be doing our utmost best. Already *Kyria* Krasakis is telling me that six of her rooms were vacated today and two more will be vacated tomorrow.' He shrugged. He was in full-fig tonight, grey-green twill uniform, shiny-visored cap. And, to give him his due, he looked exhausted. 'So, it is a bad thing for everybody. And this afternoon, I was called to the Mayor's inner sanctum. If I have not resolved the matter in forty-eight hours, then he will call in the police from Athens. Bad publicity for the island, you see.'

'D'you reckon you stand a chance of cracking it?' asked Roper.

Spiridakis spread his hands. 'Who knows? Perhaps, or perhaps not. The motive appears to be theft. We found her jewel-box—empty—and there is no sign of the lady's passport.'

'But they didn't steal all her rings,' said Roper. He distinctly remembered glimpsing at least a carat and a half of engagement ring twinkling on a finger that had dangled over the rim of the shower that morning. 'I wonder why that was?'

'If you'll excuse me,' said Sheila Carmody, who at this late hour had no wish to hear the gory details, 'I think I'll go to bed. Do you mind?' she asked Roper.

'No, of course not,' he said. 'I'll see you tomorrow. Good-night.'

'*Kaliniktah,* Miss Carmody,' said Spiridakis, lifting his hand to his cap. 'Sleep well.' Then turned slowly to watch her go. 'A most attractive lady,' he observed, when she was up the stairs and safely out of earshot. 'You have taken her under your wing, as they say?'

'Too soon to say yet,' said Roper. 'But I'm working on it.'

Spiridakis smiled. 'And I would say that was a very sound move. I wish you luck. May I buy you a drink? Talk a little?'

'I finished with that last night,' said Roper. 'I woke this morning without any legs. But I'll gladly share a pot of coffee with you.'

'Done,' said Spiridakis. 'I too am off the alcohol for a few days. The Mayor might take it into his head to smell my breath.'

They settled into the bar, with a bubbling percolator plugged into the electrical socket beside them.

'Have you noticed how we policemen always seem to sit in dark corners?' commented Spiridakis, taking out his cigarettes as Roper made the first pour over their cups.

'Stops people creeping up behind us,' said Roper drily, sliding a cup and saucer across the table.

'Yes,' agreed Spiridakis. 'I would say that is very probable.'

'So what's new?' asked Roper around the cheroot he was lighting.

'Too little,' said Spiridakis. He paused briefly to lean towards Roper's lighter flame. 'As I told you, we found her jewel-box. And it was empty, and I doubt very much that she would have flown all the way from England with an empty jewel-box. We must therefore suppose that whoever killed her took the contents. Her passport also seems to be missing. Situated where we are in the Mediterranean, there is a ready market for passports, especially English and American ones. Some bleaching agent here, some bleaching agent there, a substitute photograph. It is not too difficult.'

'How about entry?'

'Her window is immediately over this roof here.' Spiridakis extended a little finger from the handle of his coffee cup to point above their heads. 'This part of the hotel is a new extension. And the roof is flat. But *Kyria* Gribo's window was closed, and locked on the catch, and since it would be almost impossible to shut the catch from the outside we have to conclude that whoever killed her came in through the door. That is why you saw me with Sergeant Stepanikis looking through the register.'

'Suspect one of the guests?'

'Not particularly,' said Spiridakis. 'I questioned all of them this morning. But now we are looking into the possibility of it being one of the guests who was here last week, saw Mrs Gribo in some of her jewellery and came back to steal it.'

'If he's sensible, he'll be off the island by now,' said Roper.

'Agreed,' said Spiridakis. 'But apart from two Americans who left the island this morning—and I do not suspect them since both of them were too old to strike the kind of blow that killed poor *Kyria* Gribo—all of the other departed guests are somewhere about still. So...' He shrugged expansively.

'How about someone on the hotel staff? They have access to all the keys, don't they?'

'We questioned all the staff without exception,' said Spiridakis. 'And equally without exception they are all as horrified as Mr and Mrs Krasakis. Besides which they were all on duty again this evening; whereas Mrs Gribo's killer would be unlikely to put in an appearance. So, no, I do not think that whoever killed Mrs Gribo works here. Also, no one who was on duty for the hours in question saw anyone suspicious in or around the hotel. But then faces are always changing in place like this. So if someone walked in boldly enough and seemed to know where they were going, I doubt that anyone would see fit to stop them.'

'How about those lads on the moped?' suggested Roper.

'The first people we spoke to,' said Spiridakis. 'Both have impenetrable alibis. And anyway, they are only small-time, little boys looking for some mischief.'

'Did you find her room-key?'

'No,' said Spiridakis. 'So presumably her assailant did and took it away with him. And perhaps she forgot to lock the door on her way in, so it could be that the man was an opportunist who had come into the hotel to try his luck. He found the door virtually open, walked in thinking the room was empty. And . . .'

'From what I remember, the carpet in the bedroom was dry,' said Roper. 'So he was more likely to have gone into the shower rather than her come out of it. And he would have heard the water running, wouldn't he? So he was hardly likely to have gone in there and duffed her over like that on the off-chance. Unless he'd got his eye on that engagement ring she was wearing—which, in any case, he left behind.'

'Also true,' agreed Spiridakis. 'But what I have to ask myself is, was the lady a deliberate target, or, as I said, was the murderer simply an opportunist?'

'That was a hell of a mess he left behind,' said Roper.

'Almost too much mess,' agreed Spiridakis.

'Right,' said Roper.

'There were so many other things he *could* have taken,' said Spiridakis. 'A gold powder-compact, from Mappin and Webb, in your Regent Street. An Olympus camera—almost new, a pair of folding binoculars, and credit cards also. All these things, just lying around. And yet he did not take them. Nor the rings she was wearing.'

'Leave any prints behind, did he?'

Spiridakis sketched a shrug with a lift of his coffee cup. 'In a place like this? There would be hundreds, most probably. We shall be checking them all of course, but the chances of separating *Kyria* Gribo's killers will be practically zero, I think.'

'Any idea when she died?'

'Only very vaguely. The preliminary examination by our local man suggests some time between ten o'clock last night and perhaps three or four o'clock this morning.'

'But we saw her go up to her room with Miss Carmody shortly after eleven o'clock last night.'

'So we did,' agreed Spiridakis. 'But I was careful not to tell the doctor that. I believe in making such people tell me for themselves.'

'So she died between eleven last night and four this morning, say. How many flights have there been off the island today?'

'Over twenty,' said Spiridakis. 'Crete is becoming far too popular. And three ferries have come from Piraeus and returned again. So you see several thousand people could have come and gone from the island today. And where they all are now, who can say?'

'How about your local villains?' asked Roper. 'Checked any of those out yet?'

'These days there are too many of them, alas—families of them, in fact. And somehow I do not think it was done by a true professional because the killing is such a curious one. The question I keep asking myself is, why did the culprit go into the bathroom in the first place? He would have heard the shower running and must have realised that *Kyria* Gribo was not likely to come out until it stopped. Also *Kyria* Gribo was wearing ear-plugs, not that he would have known that, but it does preclude the likelihood of *her* hearing *him*. And then this man, who is ruthless enough to kill, stops short of stealing those rings the lady was wearing. It almost tempts me to believe that the lady herself was the prime target.'

'And if she was, how well did he know her and what was his motive?'

'Precisely,' said Spiridakis. 'Or alternatively, it was simply a robbery that was bungled. Perhaps he did think of taking the rings but, having killed her, lost his nerve. I think our main hope is to find some kind of witness, someone who perhaps saw someone else who was in a hurry leaving the hotel. And most likely leaving through the front door, because, according to *Kyria* Krasakis and the chef, the only door to the hotel that was unlocked after eleven o'clock was the main entrance. It could even be that the man in question had a vehicle parked somewhere close, or even that he left by taxi. It is also not impossible that his clothes would have been heavily bloodstained.'

'Put all these ideas about yet?'

'Oh, yes, indeed,' said Spiridakis. 'Every newspaper here and on the mainland will have the story on its front page tomorrow, and we can only hope that someone's memory will be jogged. I have also spoken and telexed to Interpol in Paris. They are currently in touch with your own police in an effort to track down the husband. Will it be easy, do you think? I have never been to Scotland.'

'Could be difficult,' said Roper. 'There's a lot of space between places in Scotland, and if he's holed up in some little bed-and-breakfast hotel on one of the lochs, it could take a couple of days. But they'll find him eventually, bet your life on it.' He reached across the table for Spiridakis' empty cup and replenished it, then his own. 'And, as for the rest, I'd say you've got your work cut out,' he said, as he slid it back again, and the sugar bowl after it.

'I know that also,' said Spiridakis, spooning brown sugar. 'But if the killer is someone from the island, we shall find him. Bet your life on it.'

SHEILA CARMODY spent the morning mooning about. She took a taxi into town, had a coffee sitting by the harbour wall, watched the boats, and on the front page of a newspaper a man was reading at a nearby table, she saw an artist's impression of a woman who looked remarkably like Susan Gribo. When she saw several identical pictures on a news-stand, she realised that it actually was of Susan Gribo and that today the poor woman was headline news. She looked at a London *Daily Telegraph* on the same stand, but it was yesterday's issue, and when it had been running through the presses Susan had been very much alive.

She bought herself a silk scarf on her credit card, returned to the harbour and treated herself to another coffee. He hadn't been at breakfast this morning, but then he never had been, so presumably he had driven out to his dig again in the wee small hours. Not that he had mentioned it last night when they had parted company, but then, in all honesty, why should he have? Except that he had said 'I'll see you tomorrow', and it would have been nice to know when, because she was beginning to find that mooching about on her own like this was thoroughly depressing, even though she had intended taking this holiday completely alone. It wasn't often you banded up with somebody, then had that somebody murdered more or less under your very nose. It did rather tend to change one's perspective on things.

IN THE LAST FEW DAYS she had learned the virtue of eating only the lightest snack at lunchtime. Even one forkful too much and the blistering afternoon heat could knock her out completely, and sleeping was certainly not what she had come here to do, at least not in the daylight hours.

And there he was.

'May I join you?' he said.

'Yes,' she said. 'Do.' And felt better at once.

He pulled out the chair opposite and sat down, lifted a hand to attract the waiter. 'Interesting morning?' he asked.

'No,' she said. 'Not particularly. I took a taxi into the town, had a wander, then took a taxi back again.'

'See any newspapers?'

'Yes, I did. Susan's picture was plastered all over them.'

He ordered some coffee, a few crackers and a large helping of *feta*. He really did seem inordinately fond of *feta*—which she knew now was goat-cheese, because she'd tasted it at the *taverna* along at Elounda yesterday and hadn't cared for it all that much, although she had been too polite to say so.

'Major Spiridakis able to tell you anything interesting last night?' she asked.

'Not a lot,' he said. 'He's making contact with the UK police to find Doctor Gribo. He'll probably know more after the post-mortem. Doing anything particular this afternoon?'

The question came so unexpectedly that it caught her momentarily off-kilter. Given notice of it she might have had time to invent an excuse—he had, after all, kept her dangling about all morning—but instead she found herself saying, with untoward promptness, 'I didn't have anything in mind.'

'That's good,' he said, and sounded as if it really was. 'You interested in old churches?'

'Very,' she said. 'Whereabouts?'

'Not far. Over at Kázis.'

'But that's where you work in the mornings, isn't it?' she protested. 'You must have seen it before.'

'So I have,' he said. 'But I want you to see it. It'll knock you sideways.'

And it certainly did that. Approached up a dusty path trodden between olive trees, it had not been all that impressive from the outside, with its whitewashed stone walls and slitted windows and a single bell hanging in an arch above the door. But inside was an entirely different matter. With the door closed behind them they were at once in a dark and blissful cool. She had never seen so much gold behind a door that wasn't kept locked, and there had been a single bright shaft of light falling across the front of the altar where a brightly burnished gold and copper ikon lay on a white cloth draped across a low lectern, and beside that stood a circular brass table, its top not much larger than a dinner plate, upon which half-a-dozen small candles burned in a sea of old tallow. At one point a bearded, capped and black-robed priest had come through a side door, regarded them for a few moments, and then retired again.

For perhaps twenty minutes then, they had simply sat in one of the hand-carved pews and absorbed the atmosphere.

'What's in that gold box with the glass top over there?' she had whispered.

The head of Abbot Nicodemus,' he whispered back. 'He's very nearly a saint around these parts. The Turks executed him back in 1866, and sent his head back to the village. They kept it. They say it cures everything. Want to take a look?'

'No, thank you,' she said. She'd had enough of all that sort of thing in the last twenty-four hours to last her a lifetime.

Going out again was like walking into an oven. She watched him stuff a fistful of banknotes into the offertory box, and asked him if he was religious.

'Just careful,' he said. 'I always believe in hedging my bets.'

They took some refreshment in a *taverna* in the village square.

It was full of old men playing cards, all of whom fell silent as the two of them went in, and eyed them suspiciously. And as they sat on a bench by the door and they drank their coffees, a goat took a fancy to her handbag, which she was able to extricate from its teeth only with difficulty. They watched the local women do their washing in a stone trough with a pump at one end, communally and with their sleeves rolled up, chattering to each other ceaselessly.

The rest of the afternoon had a similar timeless, dreamlike quality. More churches, more old villages, one of them roofless and derelict with grass and poppies growing out of the downstairs floors, boys with herds of goats, old men with herds of goats, a procession of monks chanting their way to evening prayers, a young man in front swinging a gold censer and perfuming the warm windless air for yards around.

'Getting bored?' he'd said.

'No,' she'd replied. 'Not a bit.' Nor was she.

They were back at the hotel soon after seven o'clock, and she took a bath and wrote a postcard home to her sister. At the very end of it, squeezed in at the bottom, she started to write: *I have also met a very nice*—but thought better of it, scrubbed her Biro through it until it was totally illegible and simply wrote, *love to you all, Sheila,* in the little space that was left.

The only blot on the landscape appeared at dinner, in the shape of the Heepish Mr Krasakis.

'There is a telephone call for you, Meestair Ropair,' he said, dry-washing his hands and generally doing his bowing and scraping act.

'Who is it, Mr Krasakis?'

'Major Spiridakis,' said Krasakis. 'He says he has some news for you. He is telephoning from Iráklion.'

And this, she thought, is the acid test. Will he go and answer it, or will he stay?

'Tell him I'm having my dinner,' he said. 'Tell him to give me an hour and ring me back.'

'But Major Spiridakis is the police, Meestair Ropair.'

'So am I, when I'm at home,' said Roper. 'My respects, and tell him to ring me back in an hour.'

'I expect it's about Susan Gribo,' she said, when Krasakis had scuttled off again.

'Probably,' he said.

'Aren't you interested?'

'I'm on holiday,' he said, but all the same she sensed that he spent the next half-hour on tenterhooks. But Spiridakis didn't ring back and after dinner they walked to the town again and had a couple of drinks sitting by the harbour wall. Which was when she decided that it was time to tell him that women had come of age and chauvinism was strictly out.

'It's nothing to do with chauvinism,' he said. 'It's the way I was brought up.'

'But you've paid for everything so far. Now I want to divvy in. How much were they?'

'Four hundred and twenty-five *drachmae*,' he said.

She gave him a five-hundred *drachmae* note from her wallet.

'Supposing I don't have change?' he said.

'Then I'll have to trust you until tomorrow, won't I?' she said, and he smiled, and it really was quite charming, that smile.

FOUR

HE WAS AT THE DIG early the next morning, down on his
hunkers in a shallow ditch, carefully brushing away at one
of its walls with a paintbrush and catching the débris in a
plastic dustpan. The air was sticky and humid. Storm
weather. Already, on the far side of the site, two of the
German girls were stretching a polythene sheet across the
mosaic floor that had been partly uncovered last week,
while Dieter Lange, the chief archaeologist, assisted by one
of the young American lads pegged it down. On the slope
behind them a couple of local volunteers were skilfully
cutting away a terrace with turfing shovels.

Despite the fact that he was determined to enjoy his
holiday, the murder of Susan Gribo was never far from his
mind. It was none of his business, strictly speaking, and he
was doing his best to keep it that way. But old habits died
hard and he couldn't stop himself theorising about it. He
had been up and about since five o'clock that morning,
and when he had left the hotel at half-past he had not seen
a soul on his way out. There had been no one at the reception desk and the door to the street had been wide open,
wedged open, in fact, with a corner of the coconut mat. It
had been a particularly hot night last night, so presumably the door had been left open to let some air into the
place.

But even when the door was not wedged open, it was
never locked, or at least he had never found it so. Whatever time he went out in the morning and whatever time he
returned at night, the main entrance was never locked.

And, more often than not, there was no one manning the reception desk, so it would have been easy for Mrs Gribo's killer to have slipped in and slipped out again without too much, if any, notice being taken of him.

Robbery had seemed to be the motive. But why had Mrs Gribo's room been chosen? Unless, of course, someone had spotted her wearing a particular piece of her jewellery in the street and followed her back to the hotel and then up the stairs to see where her room was. It didn't seem likely, but it wasn't impossible.

Spiridakis suspected none of the hotel's few staff. And having taken a closer look at them during the last few days, Roper himself could see none of them as a murderer, except perhaps the fly-looking young barman who came on duty in the evenings. But, as Spiridakis had suggested, if one of the staff had killed Mrs Gribo, he or she was hardly likely to be able to appear for work the next day as if nothing had happened.

But, on the other hand, if the killer had been someone from outside the hotel, why had he picked on Mrs Gribo? Had she in fact forgotten to lock her door while she was taking her shower? In which case any wandering sneak-thief could have gone in there, and, had he come face to face with her, merely apologised for entering the wrong room and quickly made his exit without arousing too much suspicion. But in Roper's experience sneak-thieves relied on speed and silence rather than muscle. They were quickly in and quickly out again. They didn't kill unless they were cornered, and rarely then. But this intruder had. Despite the sound of the shower, he had gone into the bathroom . . .

He felt the texture of the soil change abruptly under his brush, brushed some more and slowly revealed part of a terracotta sphere, which might easily have been a mere potsherd but might equally easily be part of an entire pot. Another ten minutes of patient work revealed that it was a decorated clay ewer, or, rather, it was most of a ewer, because you could never be certain that anything was whole until it was all out in the daylight. At which point he called Lange over, because the exact spot of its finding had to be photographed and logged, and the artefact's ultimate removal had to be carried out by experienced hands, which his were not.

And at the nine-thirty coffee break, on the dot, came the inevitable daily visit from the local constabulary, and today the sergeant attached to the Director of Antiquities' Office was accompanied by Major Spiridakis.

'Slumming, Major?' asked Roper, as the sergeant went over to Lange with his clipboard.

'I tried to ring you at the hotel, but they told me you had left early. And last night again also, but you had gone to bed.'

'And when you rang earlier last evening,' said Roper, 'I was at dinner with Miss Carmody.'

'I guessed that for myself,' said Spiridakis. 'I knew that whatever was detaining you had to be far more important than anything I had to tell you. How are you getting along, the two of you?'

Roper held up a pair of crossed fingers, and Spiridakis seemed cruelly disappointed that he wasn't prepared to say more on the matter. 'If you don't mind plastic cups, I can rustle you up a coffee. There's a quiet spot over there.'

When Roper returned with a brace of scalding hot plastic cups, Spiridakis was sitting down on a handkerchief draped over a grass tussock to protect the seat of his immaculate uniform.

'So what's new today?' said Roper, sitting beside him with his knees drawn up. Somewhere to the west thunder rumbled.

'She was struck with two blows,' said Spiridakis, blowing over his coffee. 'The weapon was probably cylindrical—or it might even have been two cylinders closely side by side. Sergeant Stepanikis has suggested that they might have been the legs of a small camera tripod.'

'Bully for Sergeant Stepanikis,' said Roper. 'He sounds a bright lad.'

'He is ambitious,' said Spiridakis. 'Also he is from the mainland so he has to prove himself to the rest of the squad. I looked at some camera tripods in the photographic shop in the town earlier on. Unfolded, they weigh next to nothing, but folded they would make an excellent weapon.'

'And something anybody could carry about without causing suspicion.'

'There is also that,' agreed Spiridakis. He took a tentative sip of his coffee, and grimaced. 'This tastes worse than the water my wife pours away after she has washed the dishes.'

'Probably recycled from yesterday's brew,' said Roper. 'By Friday it's even worse. How about Doctor Gribo, any news of him yet?'

'Nothing,' said Spiridakis. 'But later today, perhaps.'

'Did your pathologist get any closer with the time of death?'

'Sad to say, no. But from the condition of the postmortem lividity he agrees with the local doctor. Some time between ten o'clock on Monday night and four o'clock Tuesday morning. Although I tend to favour the earlier time—between the time she left Miss Carmody and, say, midnight. According to Miss Carmody, Mrs Gribo was a

woman of habit when it came to her bedtime. So...'
Spiridakis flourished a hand.

'How about the checking of aircraft passenger lists?'

'Being done. Here and on the mainland. I have been
promised photocopies as soon as possible. As I said, the
affair of poor Mrs Gribo is being taken very seriously by
everyone.'

Thunder rumbled again.

'Miss Carmody and I were going into Iráklion this afternoon,' said Roper, looking up anxiously at the sky, although overhead it was still cobalt blue.

'A summer storm, that is all,' said Spiridakis. 'And with
luck it will stay in the mountains. But an umbrella would
be wise, I think. A few hours and it will pass over.' He
tipped the dregs from his cup into the dry soil, where it was
soaked up like blotting-paper. 'Tell me, Douglas,' he said,
to the air in front of him, ' —at the risk of offending you—
have you ever considered Miss Carmody as a suspect?'

'Briefly,' said Roper. 'Didn't you?'

'Of course,' said Spiridakis. 'But I wondered if you had.
And what you would have done in that instance.'

'Put it this way,' said Roper. 'I certainly wouldn't have
been driving to Iráklion with her this afternoon.'

'Always the policeman,' said Spiridakis.

'So are you, I reckon,' said Roper. 'And if Miss Carmody had done it, I'd have worked that out for myself by
now.'

'Good,' said Spiridakis. 'Then I too am satisfied.' He
rose and shook out the handkerchief he had been sitting
on, folded it carefully and slipped it inside his tunic. 'Oh,
and there is one more thing. My wife is a woman of
abounding curiosity. She would very much like to meet
yourself and Miss Carmody. Perhaps dinner tomorrow
evening?'

'Be delighted to,' said Roper. 'And I'm sure Miss Carmody will be too. Thank you.'

Spiridakis took out his pocket-book and scribbled a few lines on the back page and tore it out. 'My address,' he said. 'Say nine o'clock?'

'Nine'll do fine,' said Roper. *'Efkaristo polli.'*

'My pleasure,' said Spiridakis. *'Andio,'* and with that he touched the visor of his cap and skidded down the dusty slope to join his sergeant.

IOÁNNIS SPIRIDAKIS poured another glass of wine for her, and across the table Douglas was head to head with the Spiridakises' oldest son, who was gravely explaining, in English that was almost as good as his father's, the secrets of the card trick he had just performed. The boy was ten, the oldest of three, and there was a daughter too, of not much more than twelve. And still Mrs Spiridakis, who in fact could not be many years past thirty, was able to look as if she had just stepped out of the pages of *Vogue*. Her name was Melina and she taught mathematics at a high school in Iráklion, to which she drove every morning, collecting another teacher on the way who shared the cost of the petrol.

'How on earth do you find the time?' asked Sheila.

'Oh, we manage,' said Melina Spiridakis, in her delightfully fractured English. 'And Ioánnis is one of the new sort of husbands. Not that he can always be here when he is most wanted, of course, because of his work. But when he is able, he cooks and vacuum cleans, and puts the children to bed and gets them up in the mornings. And believe me, there are not many wives on *Kriti* who can say that of their husbands. It is a man's place here, and many of them are still living in the middle of the nineteenth century.' She left a short pause hanging and leaned closer. 'But you should know that it is not always easy to be married to a policeman.'

'Oh, it isn't quite like *that*,' Sheila hastened to assure her, lest that idea gathered too much momentum. 'We've only known each other a few days. Since Susan Gribo died.'

'Oh, yes,' said Melina Spiridakis sadly. 'Poor woman. But you never know how these things progress. When I first met Ioánnis he had just come back from England, and I did not care much for him—I was a student then myself. But one thing led to another and before I quite knew where I was we were married and now I would not have it otherwise. So, you see, these things just happen.'

'I don't think it's going to happen to me like that,' said Sheila. Across the candlelit table—they had eaten out on the terrace with the fragrance of jasmine all about them— Spiridakis was performing a card trick of his own. It was quite late, gone twelve o'clock, and the children had been given ten minutes' notice of bed.

It had been a delightful evening. Greek food, Greek wine, Greek camaraderie, Greek sky strewn with stars—or perhaps it was all Cretan. In either event, it didn't matter. The Spiridakises' house was a handsome villa, high up at the edge of Agios Nikólaos, a few miles along the coast from Agios Mateos with a view overlooking the distant harbour and the lights of the town.

The talking had been almost non-stop. During the war, both Melina's and Ioánnis' grandfathers had fought with the *Andárte* up in the mountains, some uncles too, and an aunt who had been no more than a schoolgirl used to carry messages for them—and sometimes a map hidden in her knickers—to tell them where the Germans were going to be next. Many young Germans had died on Crete at the hands of the *Andarte*. And so had many of the *Andarte* at the hands of the Germans.

And then the children finally went to bed and Spiridakis poured more wine and lighters flared as cigarettes and cheroots were lit—Melina Spiridakis smoked her cigarette in a holder—and the talk started up again, and really it was all too pleasant to end. But it did, at a few minutes to one o'clock, when the doorbell was lightly rung and Spiridakis got up to answer. Melina Spiridakis sighed and said: 'It will be work. Always it is work.'

Which it was. When Spiridakis reappeared it was behind the smartly-dressed young man with whom he had been looking through the hotel register the other day, and whom Roper recognised as Sergeant Stepanikis, he who had advanced the theory of the camera tripod.

'Something has come up,' said Spiridakis.

'It always does,' said his wife dispiritedly.

'Good or bad?' said Roper.

'More interesting,' said Spiridakis. He held out his hand and Stepanikis passed him a manilla envelope. 'Mrs Gribo's passport has been found.'

'Where was it?' asked Roper.

'With a man we know here in Agios Nikólaos,' said Spiridakis. 'He deals in passports. Illicitly of course. Tonight his premises were raided and this was found, with many others, most of which have been reported stolen.'

'Did he say how he came by Mrs Gribo's?'

'He says he bought it off someone else we are familiar with. Part of a package. At the time, he opened none of them—the exchange took place in a *taverna*—and did not do so until he was safely back in his apartment. And naturally, when he saw that one of the passports was that of Mrs Gribo he was going to bring it in to us tomorrow and say that he had found it in the street. That, at least, is his story.'

'How about the other man, the one who sold it to him?'

'We have them both,' said Spiridakis. 'Stepanikis arrested the second man himself.'

'Good work, son,' said Roper, which Spiridakis translated into Greek together with what were clearly some congratulations of his own. 'And now,' said Spiridakis, turning back to his wife and his guests, 'I must go. I am so sorry. Perhaps we may do this again before you go home.'' He came around the table and squeezed his wife's shoulder as he kissed her good-night.

'*Pottai?*' she asked him. When?

'*Avrio,*' he said, which Roper's little Greek recognised as 'tomorrow', which it already was.

And after a brief handshake all round Spiridakis and his sergeant were gone, and there was the sound of a car starting out in the street.

THEY DID NOT see him again until late the following afternoon, Saturday, in the hotel. Shabby in frayed jeans, a faded checkered shirt and down-at-heel sneakers, he and Sergeant Stepanikis, similarly dressed, had spent the morning driving around in an unmarked car, thereby catching a great many local villains unawares as they crept up behind them then made themselves known.

It seemed that the man who had sold the passport to the main dealer had himself bought it from another man who had been only too glad to be rid of it when he had realised who its original owner had been. And that man, when Spiridakis and Stepanikis had finally tracked him down playing *tawli* in one of the town's seedier *kafenion*, had initially sworn, on the grave of his dead mother, that he had genuinely found the passport. No, he had not stolen it. No, he had never seen the *Kyria* Gribo in all his life, and no, he had never even wiped his shoes on the doormat of the hotel where that lady had been staying.

'Where did he say he found it?' asked Roper.

'Beside the road to Neápolis. On Wednesday morning. It was lying on the grass. Open, as if it had been thrown from a car.'

'Think he might be telling the truth?' asked Roper, recalling that the road from here to Neápolis was also the road to Iráklion airport, which might be a pointer to something . . .

'He could be. The cover of the passport is faded, as if it has been out in the sun for a while. But on the other hand, this man is someone else who is well known to us. And his only alibi for the night Mrs Gribo was murdered comes from his woman-friend in Elounda. She says he spent the night with her. But she also is not reliable. For a few more days we shall hold them, I think, and visit the woman again.'

'How about fingerprints on the passport?'

'Now that is particularly interesting,' said Spiridakis. 'From what we can see, inside the passport there are several prints of Mrs Gribo. But outside there are none—except of the men who later handled it, the ones we have in custody.'

'So it was wiped,' said Roper.

'I would say so,' agreed Spiridakis. 'But why did whoever stole it choose to throw it away?'

'Because he probably got to thinking it was too hot to handle,' suggested Roper. 'But it's interesting it was found on the road to the airport.'

'Someone not from the island, do you think?'

'Possibly,' said Roper. 'It could be he was on his way to the airport, decided it was too risky taking a stolen passport through Customs at the other end, and threw it away.'

'But the same would apply to the jewellery also.'

'Not if he had a woman accomplice.'

'Yes, perhaps,' Spiridakis agreed again, but more reluctantly now. Whatever he thought deep down inside, it was easier for him to discard an outsider as a suspect. And Roper knew the feeling. After days of banging your head against a brick wall, you suddenly latched on to a suspect—in Spiridakis' case it was three suspects—who knew something or had handled something or found some vital piece of evidence—or said he had, although you suspected he hadn't just found it. And regardless of the rights or wrongs of the matter he was all you'd got, that tiny glimmer of light at the end of your tunnel, and you had to squeeze him until you'd wrung every last pip out of him because somebody upstairs behind a desk was squeezing you. In Roper's case it had been Detective-Superintendent George Mower, but old George had retired yesterday and when Roper returned from this holiday he would be slipping into Mower's chair and the man squeezing him then would be the Assistant Chief Constable (Crime). In Spiridakis' case it was the local Mayor who wanted answers, and an arrest or two would probably keep him out of Spiridakis' hair for a week or more, or certainly buy Spiridakis enough time to keep away the detectives from Athens. And, of course, the news of the arrests would also be in all the papers and at least it would look as if the Cretan police were doing something, which was important because pretty soon the United Kingdom's Foreign Office would also be piling on the pressure to get some action regarding the untoward death of one of its citizens.

So it was self-evident why Spiridakis, honest copper though he probably was, was eager to point a finger as quickly as possible. And perhaps there was even a chance he was right, that one of the three arrested men had killed Mrs Gribo after all.

AND THE NEXT MORNING, Sunday, photographs of all three men stared sullenly out of the news-stands, but it was Monday before Roper and Sheila Carmody were temporarily drawn back into the investigation, this time by young Sergeant Stepanikis.

They were at lunch when he appeared in the arched entrance of the dining room with Mr Krasakis, then made his way on his own to their table.

'What can we do for you, Sergeant?' asked Roper.

'Apologies—and to you, *Despinida* Carmody,' said Stepanikis. He spoke his halting English with a mid-Atlantic accent, as if he had learned it by rote from gramophone records. 'But there has been a development—that is what Major Spiridakis has told me to tell you. This morning a goat boy found these.' Fishing in his pocket he brought out a small plastic bag of jewellery and laid it on the table. 'The Major wishes to know if *Despinida* Carmody has seen these before—or possibly some of them. It is possible they are from the *Kyria* Gribo.'

Sheila drew the bag closer. 'May I tip them out?' She made a pouring action over the table.

'If you wish,' said Stepanikis. 'But not to touch them once you have, please. I will put them back again.'

Roper passed his unused cheese-knife across the cloth to her. 'Poke 'em about with this,' he said.

She spilled out the contents of the bag and hooked several of the articles aside with the knife, but the only thing she could honestly say she recognised was a flexible gold bracelet set with blue gem-stones and probably late Victorian.

'Certain about that, are you?' asked Roper, and for a moment he sounded quite different, just like a policeman.

'Yes, I'm absolutely sure,' she said. 'She was wearing it on the flight over here. And this brooch, too, I think. I don't recognise anything else.' Most of the remaining gee-gaws proved to be simply fine-quality costume jewellery when examined closely enough.

'She,' said Stepanikis. 'That *is* the *Kyria* Gribo?'

'Yes,' she said.

'Thank you, *Despinida*,' he said, leaning over her shoulder and gathering all the bits and pieces together again with the end of a pencil before turning the bag into a temporary glove to pick them all up. 'Major Spiridakis will be most grateful. Thank you. And you, too, *Kyrios*.'

'Who found them, Stepanikis?' asked Roper.

'A boy,' said Stepanikis. 'He was bringing his goats for milk. The bag was in a bush near the road. The boy gave them to his father and he gave them to his policeman. Fortunately.'

'Today?'

'This morning, *Kyrios*. At six o'clock. But from the condition of the original bag, we think it had been out in the sun for two or three days.'

'Near a major road was it?'

'Yes, *Kyrios*. Four kilometres west of Mália.'

'And that's on the way to the airport too,' said Roper.

'Yes, *Kyrios*,' said Stepanikis. 'That is what Major Spiridakis has also said.'

'Have they located Doctor Gribo yet?'

'No, *Kyrios*,' said Stepanikis. 'We are still waiting. But also the office telex machine has broken since Saturday and we are waiting for an engineer from the mainland.' His expressive shrug made it clear that only on his native mainland could things be expected to go smoothly and telex machines be repaired at a moment's notice.

AND THAT EVENING they splashed out on a dinner in the elegant restaurant of the Hermés along at Agios Nikólaos, or rather Douglas did because he declined to let her pay even for the bottle of wine they shared. And since they could only have got a table at the Hermés by booking a day or two in advance, she was drawn to conclude that Something was Up, and she could only hope that things weren't to get too deedy, and that he wasn't going to ask her to marry him or anything foolhardy like that, because things were going along very nicely for her, thank you very much, and a week of a man's company, albeit a particularly pleasant week, was hardly the foundation for tying herself down to ironing his shirts for the rest of her life—although she had to admit that he was probably more than capable of ironing his own.

But by the time he had scanned the bill and handed over a couple of travellers' cheques to the waiter, and dropped a tip on the tray after them, she was able to loose her breath because Nothing, after all, was Up.

But what he had wanted to do, as she had, was to clear the air a little, which they began to do in the taxi on the way back to Agios Mateos. And finished while they stopped off for another coffee beside the harbour wall before finally returning to the hotel.

'What I'm saying is,' he said—he had assumed his air of gravitas again—'I'd like to keep in touch.'

'Yes,' she said frankly. She had never been one to beat about the bush either. 'So would I.'

'We could go out and about a bit. Back home, I mean.'

'That would be nice, too,' she agreed.

He took a sip of his coffee. The cheroot he had taken out of the packet, when the waitress had brought their coffees, was still unlit.

'What it all boils down to,' he said then, 'is that I'm a copper, and I've seen too many other coppers' relationships fall by the wayside. The hours are lousy, and even with the rank I've got, you still get phone calls in the middle of the night. Or you've arranged to meet somebody and you have to call it off at the last minute. Or you don't even get the chance to call it off until afterwards, by which time it's too late, and things start getting very uptight. You saw how it was the other night with Melina and Spiridakis. There aren't many women who want to put up with that for the next thirty years or more.'

'It's much the same with me,' she said. 'I like my job— but I have to leave home at seven o'clock in the morning and often don't get home until seven or eight in the evenings. There aren't many men who'd fancy putting up with that either. Besides which, I often go in at the weekends to help out if there's a big sale coming up.'

Which appeared to set the seal on the matter because at last he lit his cheroot and relaxed a little.

'I really have enjoyed this week,' she said. 'Despite all that other wretched business.'

'So have I,' he said. They exchanged addresses. He wrote his in a notebook, a copiously filled notebook she noticed, and tore it out, and she wrote hers on a page of her diary. And then they remembered telephone numbers—home and business—and exchanged those.

And back at the hotel, the two of them were saved from what might have been embarrassment at bidding each other good-night by Mr Krasakis bobbing up excitedly from behind his counter.

'There has been a telephone call for you, Meestair Ropair. From Major Spiridakis. He has left a telephone number for you. He is at home. He says it does not matter what is the time.'

'Thank you, Mr Krasakis,' said Roper, greatly relieved that Spiridakis had inadvertently provided him with an excuse not to escort Sheila upstairs on this night in particular. And she didn't look at all that displeased, either, so perhaps it was all for the best. 'I'll make the call from the booth.' Then he said to her, 'I'll see you at breakfast tomorrow. We'll take a drive out somewhere.'

'Yes,' she said. 'Goodnight. And thank you for another lovely day.'

'I enjoyed it too,' he said. 'See you tomorrow.'

And then he was in the booth and waiting for Krasakis to disentangle himself from the cables of his switchboard and dial Spiridakis' number.

'Spiridakis,' a tired voice said at his ear.

'Douglas Roper, Ioánnis. I'm sorry to ring so late, I've only just got back to the hotel. I take it you've got some news.'

'Yes, news,' said Spiridakis. 'Our telex machine has been repaired at last. I thought you might be interested to know that *Kyria* Gribo's husband has been traced.'

'Whereabouts?'

'Scotland,' said Spiridakis.

'Since when?'

There was a pause. 'Do I detect a note of suspicion in your voice?'

'No, not really,' said Roper. 'But when a married woman gets done in, I always like to know what the husband was doing at the time.'

'I do also,' said Spiridakis. 'But *Eyatros* Gribo is definitely out of the running on this occasion. He has been touring Scotland in a camping van since Monday, July 27th. And on the morning of the day his wife was killed he was fishing in Loch Tay, and for this he had a reliable witness, a policeman. A Sergeant Mackintosh—like the raincoat—spoke with *Eyatros* Gribo at nine o'clock in the morning. It seems that *Eyatros* Gribo went back to his camping van for his breakfast and found that it had been broken into. And in the evening of the same day he was in a village called Killin. A fact verified by another policeman who happened to see the camping van parked there that evening at eight o'clock and the next morning also at seven o'clock—and *Eyatros* Gribo standing near the window with soap all over his chin because he was shaving. And in the afternoon of the same second day *Eyatros* Gribo made a telephoned booking into a guest-house at a place called Lochearnhead because the weather was so bad. He arrived there in the late evening. Again there are witnesses.'

'The Scottish police seem to have been uncommonly thorough,' said Roper.

'Because I asked them to be,' said Spiridakis. 'Like you, I always suspect the husband first. But in this instance it was a geographical impossibility. So it is back to square one, sad to say.'

FIVE

THE AIRCRAFT took off with a sickening lurch and Iráklion was soon left behind. Next stop Athens. She had arrived in Crete by sea, because everybody had told her that was the best way to come to an island, especially Crete, and it had been nice, but the ferry trip had taken nearly all day. Which was all very well at the start of a holiday but a tedious way to finish it. And she had had the good fortune to be allotted a seat by the aircraft window and could see the Mediterranean sparkling beneath her in the midmorning sunlight.

The last few days of her holiday had been brief, bright and episodic. Douglas, who was flying home at lunchtime, had foregone his mornings at the dig, and they had spent one day in the Dikti mountains and taken lunch in a monastery, served by monks, where no bill had been presented but an offertory box had stood prominently in the doorway. And after that lunch they had visited the Spiridakis family again and not left on that occasion until nearly three o'clock in the morning.

And this morning, sharp at eight o'clock, Douglas had stacked her two suitcases and her flight-bag in the back of that awful little car—although she had grown quite fond of it in the end—and driven her around the coast-road to the airport. Here he spirited up a luggage trolley for her and stayed with her in the departure hall until her flight was called and it was time to say goodbye. At which juncture she felt bound to bob up a couple of inches on her toes, kiss him roundly and say, 'It's been absolutely lovely.

Thank you for everything.' And he'd said, 'And you too. Stay safe. I'll ring you.' And then she was swallowed up in the moving crowd.

At midday she was flying out of Athens and her holiday was all but over, and the man sitting beside her was reading a copy of this morning's issue of the London *Daily Mail*. Just below his thumb she glimpsed a headline: GRIEVING DOCTOR TO FLY TO CRETE TO BRING HOME WIFE'S BODY.

'I do beg your pardon,' she said, 'but may I borrow that when you've finished with it?'

ROPER STEPPED INTO the lift. It was eight o'clock. Monday morning. Not just the start of another week, but of another leave-year, and the only thing to look forward to was Christmas. And whoever was up there in charge of the weather this morning was chucking it down by the bucketful, and it looked like going on for days—or even for ever.

'Which floor, sir?' asked the blond and baby-faced youth who had held the lift doors open for him.

'Third,' said Roper. 'Thanks. Haven't seen you around here before.'

'Starting this morning, sir.'

'Copper or office staff?'

'Copper, sir. DC Makins. Serious Crime Squad.'

Ye bloody Gods, thought Roper. They got younger every day. Now they were sending him pink-cheeked boys who were scarcely out of school.

The lift stopped with a jerk, an inch too low. When Roper had gone off on holiday it had been stopping an inch too high. The doors ground open and the schoolboy stood aside for him. 'D'you mind pointing the way, sir? I'm reporting to a Sergeant Morgan.'

'That way, son,' said Roper. 'Second door on the right.'

The boy strode off. Decent haircut. Smart suit, and he wasn't wearing suede shoes, which, as far as Roper was concerned, were certain death. He himself stopped off at the coffee machine, pressed home his ten-pence piece before he spotted the OUT OF ORDER notice taped over the menu display, so got only an empty cup and a buzz of machinery. Nor was his ten-pence piece returned. Nothing had changed.

In his new office, a dark and smartly dressed young woman had moved George Mower's year-planner further along the cork notice-board and was tacking up his own old one from his ertswhile office. And the new chair he had indented for had arrived and there was a new visitor's chair too.

'Good-morning, sir,' the young woman said over her shoulder.

'Morning,' growled Roper irritably, dragging his arms out of his wet raincoat and hanging it up on a coatstand that had seen many years of brutal service and certainly hadn't been either his or ex-Superintendent Mower's. Which only added to his early morning choler. 'And who might you be?'

'WDC Weekes, sir.'

'With my mob, are you, Constable?'

'Yes, sir,' she said. 'I was posted here last week.'

'Right,' he said. 'Got a job for you.' He pointed at the offending coatstand. 'Somewhere in this building there's one of those, only it's a good 'un. Edwardian, with brass feet and a brass drip-tray for umbrellas. And I know for a fact Mr Mower didn't take it away with him because he'd bequeathed it to me. Find it, please. And tell Sergeant Morgan I'd like to see him.'

She pinned him with dark and gimlet eyes. But in the face of his expressionless stare, she could only say 'yes, sir', grit her teeth and go.

She headed straight for Sergeant Morgan's screened-off desk in the squad room, storming right up to it despite the man sitting in Morgan's visitor's chair.

'He's back,' she raged. 'The new Super—'

'Correction, Alison,' said Morgan. '*You're* new. He's been here forever.'

'Well, whatever. I thought you said he was a *good* bloke!'

'He is,' said Morgan. 'As a rule.'

She hoisted a belligerent eyebrow. 'The one I've just met's more like a Captain *bloody* Bligh. He really is *bloody* rude.'

'Probably suffering from post-holiday depression,' said Morgan. Thus far she had liked Sergeant Morgan; which was more than she could say for the Superintendent, *or* for the new inspector who had turned up last Friday and was already queening it about the place as if he owned it.

'He wants me to find his *bloody* coatstand! My God, I'm supposed to be a police officer not a *bloody* errand-girl.'

'The ACC's secretary nicked it,' said Morgan. 'I think I saw her sneaking into the lift with it on Friday morning. Find it, and he'll be your friend for ever.'

'You mean I've got to go up and bluster it out with the *ACC?*'

'Use your charm,' said Morgan. 'Believe me, Alison, Mr Roper's been drooling over that coatstand for years, and old George Mower promised it to him. Mind going with her, George?' he asked the man sitting opposite him.

'Sure,' said George, rising from his chair and smiling at her sympathetically, thereby dissolving her anger on the spot because he was about the most gorgeous thing she'd seen in years.

'DC George Makins,' said Sergeant Morgan, effecting the introductions. 'And this is DC Alison Weekes. Show him the ropes, will you, Alison?'

'Hi,' she said, as they shook hands and she saw that he had baby-blue eyes as well.

The two of them were all but out of the door when she belatedly remembered her second instruction from the superintendent.

'—Oh, and by the way, he wants to see you.'

'HOW ARE THINGS?' asked Roper.

'Fine, sir,' said Morgan, staring fixedly over Roper's head.

'Not much paperwork in the trays.'

'It's been quiet, sir,' said Morgan.

Roper eyed him quizzically. 'So what's up?'

'Nothing's up, sir.'

'Yes, there is,' countered Roper. 'You haven't given me three sirs in a row for years.' They had covered a lot of ground together, he and Dan Morgan. 'The new inspector been bugging you?'

Morgan stayed sullenly silent. And that wasn't at all like Morgan.

'I asked you a question, Dan,' said Roper.

'And I can't answer it, sir,' said Morgan, still not quite meeting Roper's eye.

Roper tried another tack. 'What's the new WDC like?'

'First class, sir. Looking for promotion.'

'And how about the lad, Makins?'

'Good record. Seems reliable.'

'And that's all you've got to say?'

'Yes, sir,' said Morgan.

'All right,' said Roper tiredly. 'You can tell the new inspector I'd like a word. Please.'

'Right, sir,' said Morgan. He paused briefly, as if he had something else to say, but then changed his mind and went out, closing the door none too quietly behind him.

'INSPECTOR DAVID PRICE, is it?' asked Roper, as they shook hands across the desk.

'Yes, sir,' said Price. He was Welsh, like Dan Morgan. He was somewhere in his late twenties, fair-haired and very sure of himself. According to his file he was a university entrant, with a degree in physics from Cardiff, which probably meant that he was in the fast lane for promotion. Not that Roper set great store by that. He preferred men like Morgan who had come up the hard way and for whom coppering was a way of life.

'Slotted in all right?'

'Yes, sir,' said Price, leaning back in his chair and negligently crossing his legs. 'I'm still feeling my way. It's mostly catching up on old paperwork.'

'If you need any advice—'

'No, sir, I can manage,' Price interrupted.

'Good,' said Roper icily. 'How are you getting on with the crew?'

'No problem,' said Price. 'We had a new DC started this morning. I haven't met him yet, so I can't speak for him.'

'Getting on all right with Sergeant Morgan?'

'Well, to be frank, sir, that is a particular black spot. He does seem to object to my arrival, but that's only to be expected, isn't it?'

'Is it?' said Roper.

'Well, he's not very bright, sir. But I expect you noticed that for yourself.'

'No, I didn't, as a matter of fact,' said Roper, smiling glassily. Those who knew him well would have recognised that smile as a danger signal, but Inspector Price knew him not at all and went on blithely: 'He's a bit slow on the uptake, isn't he?'

'He doesn't have a university degree, if that's what you mean,' said Roper, still smiling. 'And it depends how you treat him.'

'I shouldn't have to *treat* him, sir,' said Price loftily. 'He's just a sergeant and I'm his guv'nor. It's as simple as that, really, isn't it?'

'No, sir, it *bloody* isn't, sir,' said Roper. 'Sergeant Morgan was a copper when you were in infant school. He's reliable. He's honest. He might be a plodder, but then so am I. And he's only a sergeant because that's all he wants to be. He's happy that way.'

Price at last recognised the red light for what it was.

'And if ever you want a bit of wisdom, Inspector, you'll find Sergeant Morgan the man to give it to you. I speak from experience.'

Price by now had uncrossed his legs and was sitting upright. 'Yes, sir,' he said, looking suitably chastened.

'Right, sir,' said Roper. 'Tread softly, Inspector, and we'll get along all right together.' He nodded curtly towards the door.

Price got up and went, and no sooner had the door closed behind him than Weekes and Makins came in manoeuvring George Mower's Edwardian coatstand between them.

'Brilliant,' said Roper, glancing at his watch. Weekes had been gone scarcely fifteen minutes. 'Where'd you find it?'

'The ACC's secretary had it, sir,' said a surprised Weekes. 'She didn't think you'd notice it had gone missing. She says she's sorry. Do you want us to take the old one back?' She had never seen such a change in a man. He looked almost affable.

'No,' he said. 'I'll get somebody else to do that. Take a seat, the pair of you, and tell me something about yourselves.'

'GOOD LORD,' she exclaimed dazedly, when she and Makins were out in the corridor again.

'What's up?' asked Makins.

'Him,' she said. 'The Super.'

'Seems a decent sort of bloke to me,' said Makins.

'That's the weird bit,' said Weekes. 'He did to me, too.'

'A WORD, DOUGLAS, please,' said the ACC (Crime), as the Monday morning inter-departmental meeting broke up soon after eleven o'clock and everyone else returned to their various offices. 'Good holiday?'

'Yes, sir, thank you,' said Roper.

The two of them sat down again at opposite ends of the long oval table in the conference room. The ACC clasped his hands on its gleaming mahogany top and examined his thumbs at some length.

'Your name came up on a telex from Interpol while you were away,' he proposed eventually. 'Understand you found the body of that Mrs Gribo. You were putting up at the same hotel, apparently. Keep your ear to the ground, did you?'

'I didn't get involved, sir,' said Roper. 'If that's what you mean.'

'No, of course not,' said the ACC. A big, bluff, balding man, he would soon follow George Mower into retirement. 'I wouldn't expect you to. But Doctor Gribo's making noises about the police on Crete dragging their heels. Fair comment, d'you think?'

'No, sir, I don't,' said Roper. 'I got to know the man in charge of the investigation pretty well. I'd say he's very concerned.'

'The Gribos are local people, you know.' The ACC took out a packet of cigarettes, plucked one out and lit it. He offered up the packet to Roper, but Roper shook his head. The ACC's face disappeared for a moment behind a veil of smoke. 'They live—or rather he does and she did—over at Nuncton Zelston. He's got a shared practice a few miles away in Monksbridge. One of those medical centres where each of the doctors is a specialist in something or other. Gribo's a bit of a psychologist, apparently.' And then he finally got to the nub of his conversation. 'Thing is, Douglas, I don't want you deeply involved, because strictly speaking it's none of our business, but I'd like you to keep an eye on it from this end. Attend the funeral perhaps and chat the man up, let him know we're not uninterested. Don't want you to spend too much time on it, of course...'

LESS LIKE WORK was the phone call that was switched through to his office a few minutes before lunchtime.

'Roper,' he said.

'Sheila, Douglas. I rang you earlier, but the operator said you were in a meeting.'

'Get home all right?'

'Fine. I tried twice to ring you at home over the weekend too, but you must have been out. I really must thank you for those flowers. How on earth did you manage to get a bouquet like that delivered at five o'clock on a Friday evening? I'd only been home a few minutes.'

'We have ways,' he said. Then came clean. 'Actually, I got Spiridakis to organise it from Crete before I flew back. I figured you'd be home before they arrived.'

'Well, they're lovely,' she said. 'And I've got some of them here in the front office this morning. I won't keep you, but it really was very kind and thoughtful of you.'

'I'll phone you this evening.'

'Yes,' she said, 'do. And perhaps one evening this week you can drop in for dinner.'

'Yes,' he said. 'I'll look forward to that. Give you a bell later.'

And at lunchtime a depressed George Mower called in to ask him out for a drink.

'Once a copper, always a copper, eh, George? Just can't leave it alone, can we?'

'Already under the missus' feet,' said Mower, gloomily, over his pint. 'And I can't stand the sound of that bloody vacuum-cleaner she's just bought. And now she's talking about getting one of those new-fangled dishwashers.'

'Perhaps she wants to retire a bit, too,' said Roper.

'Yeah, I suppose,' Mower growled grudgingly. 'There's always that.'

IF THE EYE of the hurricane could be allowed to include an armed robbery in Dorchester—albeit the arm had only been a sawn-down walking-stick in a supermarket carrier-bag, and the youth who had perpetrated this mischief had then crashed his motor-cycle less than a hundred yards away from the building-society office in question—two aggravated burglaries and the hijacking of a lorry-load of whisky that had been foolishly left overnight in a public car park while the driver enjoyed the company of a lady-friend, then everything in Roper's domain could be said to be tranquil for the first few days.

On the Tuesday, he and Superintendent Curley, who was the officer in charge of all the uniformed foot-soldiers at this end of the county, took delivery of their shared secretary, a Miss Pringle, a brisk, bespectacled lady of middle years. And Miss Pringle not only filed documents in their correct slots but was able to work the newly arrived word processor to the manner born. And since she could spell, and was a punctuator and grammarian of no mean ability, she looked like being a gem.

On Wednesday Doctor Gribo reared his head again. His face was on the third page of the *Daily Mail* which was lying folded on Dan Morgan's desk. DOCTOR GRIBO FLIES TO CRETE TO BRING HOME WIFE'S BODY. That had been late yesterday afternoon.

'Didn't know you read the *Mail*,' said Roper.

'It's Alison Weekes',' said Morgan. 'She spotted that, and thought I might be interested. It must have happened while you were out there.'

'It did,' said Roper, picking up the paper. Gribo was a tall, lean, dark-haired man, forty-five-ish. He didn't look all that happy, which was justified in the circumstances. 'More or less under my nose. It was me who found the body.'

'Bloody Norah,' said Morgan, sitting back in his chair. 'You never said a word.'

'One of those things,' said Roper absently, reading. 'I tried not to get caught up in it.'

'Superintendent Curley got involved,' said Morgan. 'It was one of his lads who called at Doctor Gribo's home when the call came out to find him. But apparently Gribo was in Scotland.'

'Yes,' said Roper. 'So he was. The Cretan police have picked up three local villains who might be likely.' And according to the *Daily Mail* they were still holding them.

'Perhaps they're more than likely,' said Morgan. 'The authorities over there seem to have released the body pretty quickly.'

'They've got a bright copper working on it,' said Roper. 'Name of Spiridakis. No slouch. He's the boss man, but he still gets into a pair of jeans and does his own legwork.' So perhaps the three men Spiridakis had arrested were the villains after all. Or, alternatively, Spiridakis was being pushed hard from upstairs and had been told to release the body to cut down on all the publicity. As Morgan had commented, the body of Mrs Gribo had been released with a haste that was almost indecent. Apart from the short paragraph about the three suspects still in detention, the *Mail*'s report was mostly human interest stuff about Doctor Gribo, and there was nothing about the current doings on Crete, or even if there were any.

'I'd like you to do something for me, Miss Pringle,' Roper said in the early afternoon. 'Not official business exactly, but it'll be something you can do if ever you get a spare few minutes.'

'Of course, sir.'

'Mr Roper'll do, Miss Pringle.'

'And Gwen,' she said. 'I'd much rather you called me Gwen. What do you want me to do exactly?'

And the good Miss Pringle had clearly found her few spare minutes during the course of the afternoon, because there, on the cork board beside the doors to the lift, by the time Roper went home for the day, was the result of her work under the heading: *Unofficial Notices Only!*

It had been pinned between a notice offering a child's bicycle for sale and another that proclaimed the imminent organisation of a treasure-hunt and called upon any interested parties to write their names, legibly, and no humorists please, in the space beneath. MRS SUSAN GRIBO,

Miss Pringle had typed, and twice underlined. And beneath that, still in capital letters: WILL ALL OFFICERS AND CIVILIAN STAFF PLEASE KEEP ANY REFERENCES THEY FIND IN THEIR NEWSPAPERS ABOUT THE ABOVE LADY AND HER FAMILY, AND THE CASE IN GENERAL, CUT THEM OUT AND HAND THEM TO MISS GWEN PRINGLE, THIRD FLOOR. THANK YOU.

The whole had been bordered with a blood-red marker.

'What's that Miss Pringle of yours up to, Douglas?' asked a frowning ACC (Crime), as he and Roper went up in the lift together on Friday morning. 'Keeping some kind of Black Museum scrap-book, is she?'

'You asked me to keep an eye on things from this end, sir,' Roper reminded him. 'Without spending too much money.'

'Oh, yes,' said the ACC vaguely. 'So I did.'

It was that Friday too that Roper called on Sheila Carmody for dinner at her house on the western outskirts of Bournemouth.

'You've got some nice bits and pieces about,' he observed appreciatively, over his pre-prandial whisky. 'How did you manage to gather all that Royal Doulton together in one lifetime?'

'My grandmother's and my mother's,' she said. 'All I've done is to add to it.'

For the first half-hour they were strangers again, but the atmosphere improved after the steak and kidney pie and half the bottle of hock she had bought on the way home. Not until nearly eleven o'clock did the subject of Susan Gribo crop up again.

'I see the husband's come back with the body,' she said. That had been yesterday evening. It had merited only twenty or so lines shared between only two national newspapers. 'That seems awfully quick to me. When you read about a murder over here, it's usually a couple of months at least before the family get back the body.'

'It can be longer than that sometimes,' said Roper. 'Depends what kind of progress the forensic people make with the post-mortem samples.'

She grimaced. 'Wish I hadn't brought the subject up now. More coffee?'

IT WAS ON THAT same Friday too, and late on that evening, that a certain Alexandra Higgs went unsteadily and warily to her front door and put her eye to its squint-hole before she dared to open it.

'God,' she whispered. 'I thought you were a damned policeman.'

A look of alarm crossed her caller's face as he stepped past the door and then closed it quickly behind him. 'They haven't been here?'

'No,' she said. 'Not yet.' Her voice was slurred and her cropped black hair was awry. And when he turned into her front room, that was in a mess too. Prominent on the coffee table was a half-empty vodka bottle, and a glass with a fly crawling around the rim. Newspapers littered the carpet in front of the fireplace.

'Get you a drink?' she said.

'No,' he said. 'And it would be wiser if you didn't have any more either. Looks as if you've been at it all day. Have you?'

'I didn't go to work,' she said sullenly. 'Couldn't. The best I could do was another trip to the bloody off-licence.'

'Stupid,' he said. She was rapidly going to pieces. Dangerous. And he could smell the sour odour of alcohol that clung to her, which was even more dangerous.

'I was *stupid* to get involved with you in the first place,' she retorted. Glass clattered against glass as she stooped and tipped a double slug of vodka into her tumbler, and spilled some over the back of her hand and the top of the coffee table.

'If the police did come here,' he warned, watching the glass rise shakily to her mouth, 'and saw you like this, it wouldn't take 'em long to put two and two together. A smart woman like you, living like this.'

'Smart?' she scoffed thickly. 'Me? God, I've never felt less smart. All day, nobody to talk to. Except the bloody interfering woman next door and the man in the off-licence.'

'Look,' he urged. 'If you lose your nerve now, we're right up the bloody creek.'

'No ifs,' she said. She swept back an untidy sickle of hair that was stuck to her forehead. 'We're *already* up the bloody creek. I had a nightmare about it all, last night. Woke up bloody near screaming my head off. It's quite a mercy I live alone, isn't it?' She smiled lopsidedly, sniffing wetly, her eyes bloodshot and out of focus. And then her smile crumpled and she looked close to tears.

'You're getting maudlin,' he cautioned. 'Don't.'

'I'm scared,' she said. 'God, I really am bloody scared. Every knock at the door, the postman slipping something through the letter-box. Even the milkman pushing the front gate open—and next door's bloody dog barking.'

'You've just got the jitters,' he said, reaching out and taking the glass from her. 'Leave this stuff alone and they'll go away.'

She shook her head fiercely, and reached out for the glass—but he was quicker and snatched it out of her reach.

'No,' he said.

'Please,' she pleaded, and at last the tears sprang. 'I'm frightened. I really am bloody frightened. There was a policeman outside the off-licence this morning. He was on a motor-cycle. Talking into his radio. And I almost...' Her voice tailed away at the sudden look of menace that had darkened his eyes.

'But you didn't,' he said. 'And you won't.'

She shook her head again. 'No,' she said. 'I won't.' Her hand reached out for the glass, and this time he let her have it.

'Look,' he said, more kindly now. 'I've got a few odds and ends in the car. I'll sort out something to help you sleep.'

'I've been drinking,' she said. 'Will that be all right? To take tablets, I mean.'

'Oh,' he said cheerfully, 'that won't matter. Not with these. I'll make sure you get a good night's sleep. And when you wake up in the morning you'll find a whole new world outside.'

'God,' she murmured. 'God, I really do hope so. I don't think I can stand much more of this.'

'Don't worry,' he said softly, gently squeezing her arm. 'You won't have to.'

SIX

AT SIX FORTY-FIVE ON Monday morning Kevin Shotter roller-skated up the front path of Number Six, The Row, in the village of Chumpton. It was another filthy wet morning, so he was in a hurry to finish his round and get home to his breakfast, but as soon as he saw yesterday's newspaper still sticking out of the brass letter-box he knew that he was in for more aggravation. Number Six was one of those houses on his round that had a wire basket behind its letter box. Which was all very well for mail to drop into but was an absolute pig of a thing when you tried to stuff in eighteen inches of folded newspaper. Yesterday he hadn't been able to stuff it in all the way, and whoever lived there clearly hadn't seen fit to push in today's paper after it.

Then, as he gave the soggy end of yesterday's paper one last determined push, the object of his struggle suddenly gave way, and there was a terrible crash on the other side of the door, loud enough to rouse whoever was in there and send him or her hotfoot from their bed if they weren't already up and about.

Kevin could have shot off on his roller-skates and been well out of the way by the time the occupant reached the door. But he decided to brave it out, and stayed, this morning's paper still in hand, profuse apologies all ready, even though it wasn't entirely his fault.

But even after a minute or more, no one came and the door stayed shut.

So he plucked up enough courage to knock on the big old iron door-knocker, tentatively the first time, but very much louder the second. And then he knocked once more. At which point presumed that the customers had gone off on holiday and simply forgotten to cancel their newspapers, in which case no one was ever going to know that it was Kevin Shotter who had pushed the mail-box off the door.

But then he decided that they would, or might, and that it would be best to mention the matter to Mrs Croker when he got back to the newsagent's, just in case. And even offer to pay for the damage.

Then he decided it might be wise to assess the damage in case he couldn't afford it and had to tell his father too. So he raised the flap of the letter-box and peered in. He could only see one corner of the wire mail-box as it lay on the floor near the door, but there was a litter of newspapers and letters stretching half-way along the passage. And there was a light switched on at the top of the stairs, and another one clearly in his view through the open door of the kitchen. And Kevin was sure he could smell gas.

AT EIGHT-FIFTEEN the same morning, Roper pulled in behind the line of cars parked in The Row and tugged on his handbrake. One of the cars he recognised as Dave Price's, another George Makins' and right up front was a Panda car. As he stepped out on to the wet grass verge and locked his door, a white van from Forensic drove up and parked in front of the Panda.

Just inside the open front doorway of Number Six was a newly broached carton of elasticated, plastic overshoes. He paused briefly to slip a pair over his own shoes, then stepped carefully over and around the welter of newspapers and mail that lay scattered along the hallway between

the door and the stairs. There was a nose-clogging smell,
but it wasn't gas.

Inspector Price's head appeared around the door frame
of the back room.

'He's here, guv'nor,' he said. 'You just have to follow
your nose.'

'So I noticed,' said Roper.

In the stiflingly hot little sitting-room, the stench was
even worse. Someone had opened a window, but it hadn't
helped. The constant buzz was that of countless flies.

The balding middle-aged man lolled in a red-upholstered
armchair, his head, his upper trunk and one arm dangling
over its side. He was beginning to decompose in the heat
from an electric fire and the flies were crawling sicken-
ingly around his nostrils and in and out of his gaping
mouth. He had clearly been dead for some considerable
time. Weeks, probably. The top of his head had been laid
open, and the blood that had run down his trailing arm
and dripped on to the carpet had already turned crisp and
dark brown, the colour of rust where the carpet had
soaked it up.

Roper turned away before his heaving stomach got the
better of him. 'Who found him?'

'I did, sir,' said the uniformed young constable standing by the window. His face was drawn white and tight.
'Robson, sir. Area beat-officer,' he added, by way of in-
troduction. 'I got a phone call from the local newsagent,
sir, a Mrs Croker. One of her delivery lads shoved a paper
through the door this morning and took the mail-box off
its moorings. He went back to the shop to tell her what
he'd done, and she had her head screwed on enough to give
me a bell. The lad had noticed a couple of lights switched
on as well and thought he could smell gas. That's what got
her worried.'

'How many papers out there?' asked Roper.

'Eight, sir,' said Robson. 'The boy took today's back with him, so this must have happened some time between last Saturday week and yesterday week.'

'Know who he is, do we?'

'Haddowes, sir,' said PC Robson. 'The neighbours knew him as Albert and they think his middle name was Frederick. He's lived here for the last five years or so. Widower.'

'Any milk on the front step, was there?' asked Roper.

'No, sir,' said Robson. 'But there're several cartons of it well past their use-by dates in the fridge. So it looks as if he collected it once a week from a supermarket. And the fridge is pretty well stacked up with grub so it looks as if he bought all that in one go as well.'

'In work, was he?'

'Security guard, sir, according to a neighbour. Night work mostly.'

'Didn't any of the neighbours notice he'd gone missing?'

'We've only spoken to the lady in Number Eight, so far, sir. From what she says, he was a pretty quiet sort of bloke, but she didn't see him all that much anyway. And she hasn't lived here all that long herself.'

'Anybody organised the doctor yet?'

'I have,' said Price. 'Doctor Hall. He'll be here in twenty minutes.'

'I thought Doctor Clusky was the area-doctor in this neck of the woods?'

'He's on holiday, sir. Majorca. Doctor Hall's on the books as his locum.'

'Well, stay with him,' said Roper. When it came to murder investigations, he preferred to have familiar faces about him. 'And make sure he goes through all the procedures. And if he doesn't, tell him to.'

The two technicians who had driven up in the Forensic van had stepped into white paper boiler-suits and plastic overshoes. Both carried the tools of their trade in aluminium suitcases.

'Where d'you want us to start, Mr Roper?' asked the senior man.

'One of you upstairs,' said Roper, brushing another fly from his cheek.. 'The other one on the doors and windows. I don't want anybody in here till the photographer's done his stuff.'

A FEW MORE MINUTES had passed. The photographer had arrived and so had Frank Osborne, the Coroner's Officer. Roper stood in the doorway of Albert Haddowes' bedroom. You could learn a lot about a man from the state of his bedroom.

This one was sparse, almost Spartan. The only things on the dressing-table were a cheap china ashtray and a fading photograph of a group of young soldiers in a small silver frame. The photograph had been taken a long time ago. Whether or not Haddowes was in it was impossible to say. Each side of the fireplace stood a stained plywood wardrobe, circa the years immediately after the war, which would probably have been about the time the Haddoweses had married, and the floor was covered with equally old Wilton carpet, worn through to its backing here and there. The bed was a double, with only one pillow humped under a plain white duvet. There was no photograph of the late Mrs Haddowes.

But there was a strict sense of order here. Little dust, no clothes left lying about, no fly-specks on the fringed silk lampshade, clean windows and clean net curtains. So perhaps Haddowes had been an ex-soldier. There were a lot of ex-soldiers in the security business.

'Found his papers, sir,' said the Forensic technician who had been going through the chest of drawers at the foot of the bed. He had lifted out a scuffed and well-worn fibreboard attaché case and set it on the duvet. It was crammed full of manilla envelopes and old tin boxes, biscuit tins, toffee tins, an Oxo tin.

'Looks like army discharge papers in this one,' he said, passing over an envelope.

Roper took it from him. According to its contents, Haddowes had been a staff-sergeant in the Wessex Fusiliers. He had volunteered for the army in 1945, signed on again in 1950, had been wounded in Malaya, fighting the communist guerillas, and wounded again in Aden during the troubles there in the 'sixties. Having attained the rank of staff-sergeant, he had finally been discharged in 1970 with an exemplary character, a clutch of medals and a full pension.

Another envelope contained Haddowes' and his wife's birth-certificates, another their marriage certificate, another Mrs Haddowes' death certificate. She had died as recently as 1981. In a longer, fuller envelope were the deeds of the house. One tin contained mementoes of Haddowes' army days—medals, tunic buttons, cap badges, sets of fabric arm-stripes, a lance-corporal's, a corporal's, a sergeant's, and a staff-sergeant's gold sleeve-badge. The Oxo tin held items of cheap jewellery, all of them neatly wrapped in tissue paper, all of it doubtless Mrs Haddowes' that her husband hadn't been able to part with. All the milestones of a man's life in a few old tins. It was often the way, but Roper had never ceased to feel depressed when he came across such trivial treasures, usually in ordinary little houses like this one where the inhabitants hadn't had all that much to start with, and finished up with precious little more.

The sound of an unfamiliar voice talking to Price drew him back downstairs. The new arrival was Doctor Hall, a dark, balding man, heavily built and wearing horn-rimmed spectacles. The two of them were standing in the doorway of the back room and waiting for the photographer to finish with the body. Another uniformed constable had arrived and had taken up a post by the front gate. A few of Haddowes' neighbours had gathered out there too.

Roper and Hall exchanged the briefest of greetings.

'I'll leave you with Inspector Price, sir,' said Roper. 'And have a chat with you when you've finished.'

'Right,' said Hall. He was about forty. Mercifully, he looked competent.

'We need some more hands, George,' called Roper to DC Makins who was just turning into the front room. 'Uniforms and DCs. Door to door, both sides of the street. Find out if any of the neighbours saw anything unusual going on around here lately. And I want to know if he had any next of kin and where we'd be likely to find 'em. And find out who his employers were and tell them we'd like a word with them too. And any friends and associates he might have had. Do your best to find out who they were.'

'Will do,' said Makins, and about-heeled smartly to hurry out of the front door and down the garden path to his car and his radio. The pavement in front of the house was already being taped off and the constable who was out there was at least succeeding in shepherding away the neighbours, the only exception being a stalwart woman in a pink nylon overall with whom the constable came back to speak when all the others had moved away. He listened to her with his gaze tipped intently downward, then lifted the tape to let her duck underneath and walk beside him to the gate.

'Know something, does she?' asked Roper, as the constable came up the path while the woman waited at the gate.

'Mrs Moore, sir,' muttered the constable. 'She's the neighbour from Number Four. She says she wants a word with whoever's in charge. I think she'd like to give Mr Haddowes a character reference, sir,' he added, with a touch of irony.

'All's grist, Constable,' said Roper. 'And she might come up with something we ought to know about. If Mr Price wants me I'll be in Number Four.'

HE SIPPED AT a cup of tea in Mrs Moore's cramped but spotless kitchen, which was a mirror image of the one in Number Six.

'*She* was a lovely woman,' said Mrs Moore, sitting opposite him. 'I really can't think how she put up with him.'

'A nasty piece of work, was he?' enquired Roper encouragingly.

'Nasty?' she retorted. 'What! If my Eric had treated me the way Albert Haddowes treated her I'd have left him the first week. He was one of those sergeant-majors in the army. And even after he wasn't, he sergeant-majored her something awful. If ever she talked to me over the garden fence and he was home, he used to stand at the back door and stare at us. And she used to sort of shrivel up and scuttle back indoors. He was a real pig.'

'Knock her about, did he?'

It had only been a chance shot on Roper's part, but Mrs Moore's eyes fixed him beadily. 'Knock her about? What! We used to hear it through the wall, and they're good strong places these. She died of him. That's what all the neighbours think.'

'You mean he killed her?' asked Roper, his ears pricking more interestedly.

'By inches. He wore her out. One night there was a terrible commotion in there. We heard glass breaking, and when my hubby looked out of the window, there was this dinner plate and half a dinner lying on their front path. It was him. He threw it at her. Said it was cold. And one night, late, there was so much screaming and shouting in there that my Eric had to ring the police. And they came, and *they* had to call an ambulance. She was in hospital for two days.'

The sympathy that Roper had earlier felt for the late Albert Haddowes was fast disappearing, because this wasn't just neighbourhood gossip any more. If the police had in fact been called to Number Six, it would be on record. He drew his pocket-book closer on the table and scribbled a note to himself.

'Do you know if he had any friends, Mrs Moore?'

'I couldn't say. I never saw many people come to the house. I know *she* had a sister and a niece, but if they ever visited I never saw them. He drove them away, I expect, because they were *her* relations. But mornings I know he went along to the British Legion Club, so he might have had friends there, although I really couldn't see him being friendly with anybody.'

'But you did see some people come to the house?'

'Occasionally,' she admitted grudgingly. 'But mostly they stayed on the doorstep. The most regular caller was a man in a little black van. He used to bring Albert home from work sometimes. Early in the mornings, that was. And sometimes they used to unload cardboard boxes from the back of it and take them indoors. Must be full of cardboard boxes in there.'

Which wasn't true, from what Roper had seen of the house so far, but he let her go on.

'It was a van from their firm, the place where Albert worked, you know. He was in security.'

'Know the name of the security firm, do you, Mrs Moore?'

She did, and its telephone number. So she had obviously seen the little black van a great many times. The man who had driven the van was short and dark and wore glasses, looked permanently ill.

'What sort of boxes were they, Mrs Moore?'

'All sorts,' she said. 'The corrugated sort mostly, those big brown ones.'

'Did you ever see any of these boxes going out again?'

She shook her head. 'No, I didn't,' she said, then added meaningfully, 'but there was always a bonfire burning in his garden.'

'Always?' asked Roper, tying her down more tightly now because nobody took home cardboard boxes merely to put them on bonfires in their garden.

'Well, no,' she conceded, seeing how purposefully his ballpoint was poised over his notebook, and knowing vaguely what perjury meant. 'But once a week at least, and always when I'd got washing out, as if he was doing it deliberately, you know. Hard, he was, really hard. Mrs Gault, over at Number Seven, her Dennis is in the church choir and when they came round carol-singing last Christmas and knocked on Albert Haddowes' door, he just opened the window and told them to sod off. Mean, you see. I think if ever Jean, that was Mrs Haddowes, wanted a new pair of shoes she had to practically go on her knees and beg him for the money. Well, perhaps that's an exaggeration, but the poor woman never was able to look smart, really smart, you know. He did, though. A proper toff, he always looked.'

'If we can get back to Mr Haddowes' other visitors, Mrs Moore,' suggested Roper, to her obvious disappointment.

She frowned. 'Well, like I said, he didn't seem to have many. And it isn't as if I spend all my time lifting the net curtains, if you know what I mean.'

'I'm sure you don't, Mrs Moore,' Roper assured her, smiling winsomely.

She thought some more. 'No,' she said. 'I really can't remember anybody in particular.' But then she changed her mind. 'There *was* a man, looked like an insurance collector, that sort, you know. I saw him about three or four weeks ago. He called twice, two days running. But he only went in there once and didn't stay for more than five minutes. And there was a girl too, well a woman really, fair-haired, came in a smart car. She stayed the best part of an hour. But we all thought she was one of *those*...well, you know, him being a widower and all that. She was all tarted up, you know, and came with a little bag, like one of those weekend bags. Mrs Gault over the road, she saw her too, and she thought the same. That she was one of those...you know. Would you like another cup of tea, by the way?'

'No, thank you, Mrs Moore.' Roper steered her back to the nitty-gritty before she drifted off again into more of her wild conjectures. 'When did you last see Mr Haddowes? D'you remember?'

'Last Saturday week,' she said. 'The afternoon. About four o'clock. He was loaded up with carrier-bags. He'd been to do his shopping. Every Saturday afternoon. Regular as clockwork.'

'But you didn't see him at all this last week?'

She shook her head again. 'No,' she said. 'Last Saturday week with all his shopping, like I said. I never saw him after that.'

'Did you hear him in the house at all? Television, vacuum-cleaner, anything like that? After you saw him with his shopping.'

'No,' she said, frowning deeply. 'No, I can't say I did. But then he never was a noisy sort of man. Not after *she* died, anyway.'

'So you hadn't seen Mr Haddowes for a week.'

'No,' she said.

'You didn't think of knocking on the door, to see if he might have had an accident?'

'If he'd been a nicer sort of man, I might have,' she retorted scornfully. 'But he wasn't, so I didn't. And anyway,' she added more practically, 'it's the holiday time, isn't it? How was I to know he hadn't gone away for the week?'

BACK AT Number Six, Roper slipped on a clean pair of overshoes. Price was still in the back room with Doctor Hall who had reached the point of putting away his instruments. The flies still buzzed and were already settling back on Haddowes' face.

'He's been dead for the better part of a week, Superintendent,' said Hall, catching sight of Roper as he clicked shut the catches of his instrument case and stood upright. 'I doubt even the pathologist will be able to get much closer that that. The cause of death appears to be a single blow to the head, probably delivered from the back.'

'Why the back, sir?' asked Roper, because it was a rare doctor indeed who would dare to advance such a theory so assuredly.

'Because so far as I'm able to ascertain, he was a singularly robust man. Healthy skin, good muscle-tone. Had he thought someone was about to attack him from the front, I think he would have been able to put up a bloody good fight. But since there are no signs of a struggle, I suggest that whoever did it was standing behind him. He probably never knew what happened.'

'Hopefully,' said Roper, because whatever kind of roughneck Haddowes had been to his wife, no man deserved to finish up with a hole in his head and flies crawling all over him.

'Quite,' said Hall as he departed. 'Unless there's anything else, I'll write up my notes in the car. I'll try to get copies of my report to you early this afternoon.'

'Seems a smart bloke,' Roper observed to Frank Osborne, the Coroner's Officer, an ex-policeman himself and once a familiar face back at County. 'How about the postmortem examination?'

'The Coroner's arranging it now,' said Osborne. 'He's doing his best to fix it for either later today or first thing tomorrow. Doctor Weygood's the duty pathologist, by the way.'

'Lucky old us,' said Roper sourly.

'I thought you'd be pleased about that,' said Osborne, with a sniff.

'Ecstatic,' said Roper. 'How long before he gets here?'

'Almost an hour,' said Osborne.

Roper returned to the hallway. DC Makins was back. He had spoken with a Mrs Gault, over the street at Number Seven. She too had seen the many visits of the little black van that had dropped off Albert Haddowes in the early mornings, and she too had been able to give the telephone number written on the side of the van.

'—So I gave 'em a ring,' said Makins. 'The boss doesn't turn up until nine o'clock. Name of Wallis. But I spoke to one of the supervisors, and he said that Haddowes started a fortnight's leave on the first of August and was due back at work again on the seventeenth, which was last Monday. He simply didn't turn up.'

'Didn't the firm check up on him?'

'They kept ringing him, but nobody answered the phone. And one of the other supervisors called here personally last Friday morning but couldn't get an answer either. Haddowes was a supervisor too, by the way.'

'So why didn't the firm contact us?' asked Roper.

'I asked that,' said Makins. 'But the bloke I spoke to said we'd have to ask the boss. He sort of clammed up. I got the impression Haddowes wasn't all that popular there.'

Which was highly likely, given what Mrs Moore had told Roper.

'All right,' said Roper. 'Give this Mr Wallis a ring around nine-thirty. Meanwhile, I'd like you to ferret about for cardboard boxes.' Because, gossip though Mrs Moore might be, there was very rarely smoke without fire of some kind or another. And in Haddowes' case the fire had not been entirely metaphorical.

'I looked all over the place early on, sir,' said Makins. 'I didn't see any.'

'How about a ladder?'

'Garden shed. Saw it just now.'

'Good,' said Roper. 'Fetch it out and take a look in the loft.'

As Makins made his exit the forensic technician who had been working upstairs came down.

'Any joy?' asked Roper.

'Nothing significant yet. No signs of robbery, no signs of forced entry. I've lifted a few sets of fingerprints, but they're probably Mr Haddowes'.'

By eight forty-five Superintendent Curley had sent along a half-dozen uniformed officers to conduct the door-to-door enquiries under the aegis of Dan Morgan, who had also arrived by then. And it was shortly after that that a dust-covered DC Makins came down from his foray in the attic. Roper was nosing around the kitchen. Like a lot of men who lived alone, Haddowes seemed to have existed mostly out of cans.

'Anything up there?' asked Roper.

'Like an electrical warehouse,' said Makins. 'Toasters, irons, fans, fan-heaters, hair-dryers, the lot. You want it, he'd got it. And all the stuff's in its original manufacturers' cartons. It's all stacked under polythene sheets. And there's a bundle of flattened corrugated cardboard boxes tied up with string up there, too.'

Which Haddowes probably hadn't had the time to burn on one of his bonfires.

'How many cartons, d'you think?'

'Fifty or sixty,' said Makins, 'at a guess.'

Roper thought long and hard about that. It seemed that the late Albert Haddowes had been a villain in more than one direction.

'Get in touch with Records, George. We think his full name was Albert Frederick Haddowes. Age about fifty-five. See if he's got any form. And then get in touch with Superintendent Curley's duty-sergeant. See if he's got any record of any of his lads ever calling here about a domestic incident. Mrs Haddowes died in 1981, so he needn't check any further forward than that.'

Makins was soon back. Haddowes was on record, convicted in 1975 for an aggravated assault on the barman of a public house who had refused to serve him when Haddowes had appeared, already drunk, on the premises where the barman worked. Haddowes, on the grounds of his unblemished army service, had been given a year's probation.

'And I checked with Mr Curley's desk-sergeant. His lads were called here twice. Once in August '79, soon after the Haddoweses moved in here. The call was made by Mrs Haddowes herself, but when they got here, she decided not to press charges. And the second time was in November '80. The call that time was made by a Mr Moore. When they got here that time, Mrs Haddowes was nursing a broken arm and she'd lost a tooth. They tried to get her to press charges, but she told 'em she'd only fallen down the stairs. They're pretty certain it was down to friend Albert, though. But all they could do was call for an ambulance and leave it at that. Mr Curley sent along a WPC to have a chat with Mrs Haddowes while she was in hospital but she still wouldn't say a word against Haddowes. Frightened of him, probably.'

So the garrulous Mrs Moore had been right on the button. Albert Haddowes was a thug and a petty thief, either or both of which might be the reason he was presently sprawled in his sitting-room armchair with the top of his head caved in.

And since Mrs Moore had been right on two counts, she was probably right on yet another, namely that Haddowes had been driven home from work some mornings by a man who subsequently assisted Haddowes in carrying some of those cardboard boxes into the house. Because wittingly or unwittingly, that man had been Haddowes' accomplice, and if he had been the driver of the security firm's van then it was odds-on that he was a security guard too. And, whoever he was, that particular gentleman had to be the first suspect to fill the frame.

SEVEN

THE IRASCIBLE Doctor Weygood swept all before him at nine-thirty. A narrow, cadaverous man with hair that had been once ginger, he was quickly down to his shirt-sleeves and tugging on a pair of latex gloves.

'Those newspapers in the hallway, Mr Roper,' he enquired snappily, as his fingers lightly probed the wound in Haddowes' skull while his woman assistant flapped away the buzzing flies with her clipboard, 'what's the earliest date on those?'

'Sunday the sixteenth, sir.'

'And he was last seen . . . ?'

'The day before. Afternoon.'

Sounds about right,' said Weygood, still probing. 'Right parietal fragmented, Miss Glover.' His assistant paused in her flapping to make a note of that on her clipboard.

'Single blow, d'you reckon?' asked Roper.

'Can't say,' said Weygood. 'But very likely. Tell you more when I've had him on the table.'

'When can you look him over properly, sir?'

'In the state he's in,' said Weygood, rolling off his gloves preparatory to sweeping out again, 'the sooner the better. The Coroner suggested this afternoon, which is remarkably inconvenient so far as I'm concerned, but necessary. Perhaps you can arrange a venue for that, Mr Osborne?' he suggested to the Coroner's Officer. 'And if it's of any interest to you, Superintendent, I agree with Doctor Hall. The fellow was probably killed from the back and was sit-

ting down at the time. And if he was, then you're probably looking for a right-handed assailant.'

'A useful bit of information, that, sir,' Roper dared
drily. 'I'll send a couple of the lads out to bring him in.'

But Weygood, not a man famed abroad for his sense of
humour, only gazed at him blankly.

By ten o'clock, Haddowes' body had been taken to the
mortuary and Roper, with Makins at the wheel, was on his
way to Dorchester to interview Mr Wallis, for whom Albert Haddowes had worked as a security guard.

'Well, actually, he's a night-duty supervisor,' explained
the affable but anxious Mr Wallis. Smart haircut, smart
suit, hi-tech office, young Mr Wallis was clearly doing well
in his chosen profession.

'How long has he been working for you, sir?'

'Three years,' said Wallis, demonstrating his efficiency
by reaching out sideways for Haddowes' personal file and
opening it on his blotter. 'August '81. Three years almost
to the day, in fact. He spent six months as a guard, then we
promoted him to an area supervisor. He has an excellent
army record.' Wallis riffled through the file and slid a set
of photocopies across the desk. They were copies of the
army documents the forensic technician had found in
Haddowes' bedroom.

'Are these the only references you have for him, Mr
Wallis?'

'No,' said Wallis, dipping into the papers again. 'He
gave us the name and address of his last commanding-
officer as a personal referee—that's this one here.' Another sheet of paper came across the desk, a sheet of thick
blue notepaper, handwritten, its signatory a Lieutenant-
Colonel Angus Trehearne. Its tribute to ex-Staff-Sergeant
Haddowes was glowing. 'And this one's from his previous employers.'

Roper picked it up. Not glowing, more cautious. Before joining Mr Wallis' organisation, Haddowes had worked for Artos Chemicals Ltd, specialist suppliers of pigments and binders for the paint trade. Haddowes had been in charge of their security arrangements, and had been—to the best of their knowledge, they had been careful to write—industrious and honest. That reference, unlike Colonel Trehearne's, was encapsulated in a mere three lines.

'You didn't think to take up references with us, Mr Wallis?'

'Well, no, we don't generally do that,' said Wallis. 'In fact his army record more or less spoke for itself. Should we have?'

Roper didn't answer that, because Mr Wallis had plainly had doubts of his own about Albert Haddowes.

'Supposing *I* asked you for a reference for him, sir?' asked Roper.

Wallis' expression seemed to close up, almost as if a screen had dropped in front of it.

'That's a serious question, sir,' said Roper.

Wallis mulled that over, toying with a propelling pencil he had picked up from beside his tooled-leather blotter. 'Well,' he ventured cautiously. 'He isn't exactly a likeable man.'

Roper waited patiently for an explanation of that.

'Put it this way,' said Wallis. 'He's heavy-handed. With the staff. We've had several good people leave because of him.'

'How heavy-handed, sir?' prompted Roper, when Wallis again seemed reluctant to go on.

'Well,' said Wallis, revolving the pencil between the fingers of both hands and subjecting it to a lengthy, frowning scrutiny before looking up again. ' "Threatening" would be the word to describe his behaviour, I suppose. And he's started to pick on our very best men. The ones we really *know* are reliable. Old hands, you know? And staff come and go quickly enough in this line of work without some loud-mouthed supervisor threatening to report them for every real or imagined misdemeanour. For instance—' From a reluctance to talk, Mr Wallis had now rushed into full spate. '—one of our more valued clients reported some petty pilfering and asked us to put an extra man on duty each night. Which we did, an absolutely first-class guard, been with us for years. After his first night on duty there, he reported here the next morning and handed in his notice. When I asked him why, he told me that he'd had a lot of mouth from Haddowes the previous night. Fortunately, I persuaded him to stay on condition we took him out of Haddowes' area. The next night I put another good man on duty there. He lasted a week. He'd had two run-ins with Haddowes, apparently. The first time Haddowes had caught him smoking on the premises, and the second time he was using one of the lifts to do his tour of the upstairs floors. Both of which were forbidden, but we know it happens and usually turn a blind eye to it. Haddowes upbraided him in no uncertain terms and the man simply walked out on the job there and then. Mind you, to be fair to Haddowes, we write the rules and he's an absolute stickler for them and that's what we pay him for of course, but the last two months or so he has tended to overdo it. In fact, not to put too fine a point on it, we're looking for a way to get rid of him.'

'And that's why you haven't chased him too hard when he failed to report back for duty after his holiday?'

'Exactly,' said Wallis. 'To be frank, we *hoped* he wouldn't come back.'

'And this pilfering you mentioned, when was that reported to you exactly?'

'In early July,' said Wallis.

'Which was about the time Haddowes started pulling rank on the other staff you sent to that same place.'

'True,' said Wallis.

'Some kind of electrical firm, was it?'

'Well, yes, it was,' said Wallis, looking surprised. 'It's an electrical-goods warehouse in fact. But how would you know that?'

At which point Roper had DC Makins read out the list of boxed electrical artefacts he had found in Haddowes' loft.

'Good God,' the dismayed Wallis exclaimed. 'You're telling me that all that thieving was down to *Haddowes?* He's the very man I told to keep an extra eye on the place. Call in there every two hours, I said, keep everybody on the hop, I said. And all the time it was bloody Haddowes himself? Are you sure about this?'

'It gets worse, Mr Wallis,' said Roper. 'We don't think Haddowes was working alone. According to a witness, another one of your guards was seen on several occasions helping Haddowes into his house with all the gear he'd lifted. And they were using one of your marked vans, as well.'

'You're kidding.'

'No, sir,' said Roper. 'Wish I was.'

It took some time for Wallis to come to terms with that. Then he stared back grimly across the desk. 'I take it from all this that you've got Haddowes in custody?'

'Yes, sir. In a manner of speaking.'

'Well, you can tell him from me that that's he's bloody well fired,' retorted Wallis.

'More exactly, he's in the mortuary, Mr Wallis,' said Makins.

Wallis blanched, but only for a moment. 'Well, in the circumstances, I can't exactly say I'm sorry. That'll save me all the legal hassle of giving him the sack, won't it? I've got insurance cover, thank God, but that won't help the firm's reputation.'

'We think Mr Haddowes was murdered, Mr Wallis,' Roper broke in. 'And it's possible that his activities at this electrical warehouse might have something to do with it.'

'Murdered?' exclaimed Wallis as the real reason for their visit dawned on him. 'And you think whoever killed him works for *me!*'

'It's possible, sir,' said Roper.

Wallis fell back limply in his chair. 'My God, that's terrible. I can't say I liked the man, but Heaven forbid that he should finish up murdered.'

'We need names, Mr Wallis,' said Roper. 'According to Haddowes' neighbours, this other guard sometimes used to drive Haddowes home from work in the mornings.'

'It could be anybody,' said Wallis. 'We run four vans. The supervisors make their tours in them, and we also use them for taking cleaning supplies around. I run an office-cleaning operation as well. Or, rather, I do until news of all this business gets out. Have you got a description of this other man?'

'Short, thin, dark, wears glasses,' said Makins. 'Looks ill.'

'No...' he said, slowly shaking his head as a particular face obviously came to mind. 'It couldn't be... The only man I've got who fits that description is Derek Jewkes. He's just a driver and odd-job man. Been with us for ten years or more. Not very bright, but reliable. He certainly wouldn't *kill* anybody.'

'Is he on the premises now, sir?' asked Roper.

ACCORDING TO his file, his full name was Derek William Jewkes, a sad-sack little man with a stooped back and cheap spectacles. He looked as if he cut his own hair and there was dandruff on the shoulders of his crumpled black uniform.

Wallis had lent them his office. Roper gestured to a chair and Jewkes shuffled forward hesitantly and lowered himself into it.

'We're police officers, Mr Jewkes,' explained Roper, as he too sat down. 'I'm Superintendent Roper and this is Detective-Constable Makins.'

Jewkes blinked nervously behind his spectacles and took a tighter grip on the arms of his chair.

'Got any ideas what this might be about, Mr Jewkes?'

Jewkes shook his head, his eyes huge behind his spectacles. 'Look, I have *got* a driving licence,' he protested anxiously. 'It's just that I lost it a couple of weeks ago.'

'It's nothing to do with your driving licence, Mr Jewkes,' said Roper. 'I'm afraid we're going to have to caution you. You don't have to say anything, but anything you do say will be taken down in writing and may be used in evidence. D'you understand that, Mr Jewkes?'

Jewkes nodded, his Adam's apple rising and falling as he swallowed apprehensively. He could crack in a trice, if he hadn't already. His eyes behind the thick lenses were those of a man in mortal terror.

'You're absolutely sure you understand?'

Jewkes nodded again, cleared his throat and whispered croakily, 'Yeah, I think so.'

'Albert Haddowes, Mr Jewkes,' said Roper. 'Friend of yours, is he?'

Jewkes shook his head furiously.

'But you give him a lift home sometimes? In the mornings? After work?'

Jewkes cleared his throat again. 'Yeah, well, I do,' he admitted in a strangled whisper. 'But he's a supervisor, see, and I have to do what I'm told.'

'Including thieving?' asked Roper, then, before Jewkes could answer, quickly changed his approach to one of camaraderie. 'It's Derek, isn't it?'

'Yeah, that's right,' said Jewkes, immensely relieved that he could at least answer that without incriminating himself.

'Mr Wallis speaks well of you, Derek. Says you're reliable. Good worker.'

'I like Mr Wallis,' said Jewkes, pressing his hands together and clamping them tightly between his knees. 'He's the sort of bloke you do your best for.'

The phone rang again. Roper reached out to pick it up. He spoke only his name, listened briefly with his eyes fixed on Jewkes, then quietly put the receiver down again. Derek William Jewkes was not on file at the CRO.

'I've just heard some good news, Derek. You've got a nice clean sheet.'

'Did have,' said Jewkes gloomily. 'Until that bastard came along.'

'The bastard being Albert Haddowes?'

Jewkes nodded.

'Put the screws on, did he?'

'Said I couldn't afford to lose my job. Not with seven kids to look after. He saw me in the van one day, and I'd got the missus with me. Midday, it was. My lunch-hour. I'd picked her up from the hospital and was giving her a lift home. She'd been pretty bad, see, and what I earn on this job don't run to forking out for mini-cabs. And we're not supposed to give lifts, see. It's one of the rules, us being a security firm and all that. It's a sackin' offence, see. He said he'd report me. I don't suppose anybody's got a fag, have they?' he finished hopefully, rocking miserably backwards and forwards in his chair.

Makins shook his head. Roper brought out his cheroots and lighter. Jewkes' shaky and nicotine-stained fingers fumbled one out and Roper struck the lighter for him.

'Give Haddowes a lift often, do you, Derek?'

'Lately, I have,' said Jewkes, luxuriously exhaling smoke. 'But that was legal. We can give other staff lifts, like, when they're in uniform.'

Roper waited patiently. There was no point in putting pressure on men like Jewkes. All would come out in its own good time.

'What happens, see, is that Albert uses my van when he's on night-duty. And I use it in the daytime. And what usually happens is that he drives it to my house, I go to work in it and he goes the rest of the way home on the bus.'

'But sometimes lately . . . ?' Roper prompted.

'I took him all the way home,' said Jewkes, reaching out for the glass ashtray Roper slid across the desk to him.

'Because . . . ?'

'He'd got all this gear in the back.'

'Gear?'

'Stuff he'd nicked,' said Jewkes. 'But I didn't know that at first, honest. The first few times, it was on board in one of those black plastic rubbish-sacks. Later he was packing it in corrugated cardboard boxes. Doing it in a big way, he was, that's what I reckon. And when I cottoned on to what he was doing, I told him I didn't want to be involved. I was scared, see. And that's when he told me I'd better keep my trap shut or else, 'cause he'd seen the missus in the van with me. And I couldn't report him, could I? I mean, that stuff was in my van, wasn't it? I mean, I guessed where it was all coming from and I go to that particular place meself, don't I? Dropping off cleaning stuff. 'Cause the firm's got this office-cleaning operation going as well, and what I do mostly is delivering all the cleaning stuff. Detergents and floor polish and all that sort of thing.'

'And where did you guess all this gear was coming from, Derek?' asked Roper, when Jewkes finally had to pause for breath.

'Diamond Electrics,' said Jewkes. 'It's a big warehouse place. That's where he was nicking it from. Gawd knows what he did with it all, because he must have taken boxes and boxes of stuff. I'm surprised nobody there sussed him out.' Jewkes broke off then and glanced anxiously around the office. 'Here—he's not about here anywhere, is he? Albert?'

'He's safely away, Derek,' said Roper.

Jewkes exhaled a gratified breath laced with cheroot smoke. 'You've got him, then?'

'Yes,' said Roper, carefully watching Jewkes' every subtle change of expression. 'We've got him.'

'Only I'm scared of him, see. And when he finds out what I've said to you, he's going to bloody kill me. A big bloke he is, see. And physical. Dead physical. Know what I mean?'

'He's never going to know, Derek,' Roper assured him.

'How many times d'you reckon you made one of these deliveries for him, Mr Jewkes?' asked Makins.

'A bloody lot,' said Jewkes glumly. 'Once a week at least, lately.'

'When was the start?' asked Roper.

'Just after last Christmas,' said Jewkes. 'I s'pose,' he went on, 'I'll be finishing up in the nick after all this lot.'

'Could be, I'm afraid, Derek,' said Roper, although it would be a particularly hard judge who put Jewkes away. He was cutting a sad enough figure here. Amidst the full panoply of Crown Court proceedings, if it ever got that far, a jury would find him downright pathetic, besides which this was his first offence and he had done what he had out of fear. 'But we'll do our best to put in a word.'

'Thank you, sir,' said Jewkes.

Roper gave him a few seconds' breathing space to enjoy the cheroot.

'When did you last see Albert Haddowes, Derek?' he asked then.

Jewkes corrugated his forehead. 'The Saturday he started his holiday. The morning. I took him home.'

'Have any stolen gear with him, did he?'

Jewkes shook his head. 'Just a carrier-bag. He had his vacuum-flask in it.'

'Do you know how Mr Haddowes disposed of all this stolen property, Mr Jewkes?' asked Makins.

'No, sir,' said Jewkes, still shaking his head at Roper's earlier question. 'He never said and I never asked. Didn't want to know, did I?'

'A drinking man is he, Derek?' asked Roper.

'Not so's you'd notice,' said Jewkes.

'Know the pubs he uses?'

'Not specific,' said Jewkes. 'But I know he goes to the British Legion Club a lot. Full of ex-soldiers like himself, see. I know he uses that. That's the one over at Monksbridge.' He watched Makins commit that to his pocketbook, then glanced across at Roper. 'He told me he was going to Greece, you know. For his holiday.'

'And did he?'

Jewkes shook his head. 'No. Course he didn't. He couldn't afford it. But he talks like that. Always braggin' about where he's been and what he's done. A real big-mouth, he is.'

'How about friends? Does he ever talk about them?'

'I don't think he ever had any. Not the way he looks down on everybody.'

'Relatives? Does he ever mention those?'

Jewkes shook his head. 'Not that I heard.' Then another idea came to him and he looked worried again. 'Look,' he said. 'You said Albert was never going to know I've blown the gaff on him, didn't you? But he will, won't he? Because he'll be beside me in court, won't he? He'll be standing there, won't he? And he'll know then, won't he?'

It was Roper's turn to shake his head.

'Mr Haddowes is dead, Derek,' he said.

Jewkes paled. 'Bloody 'ell,' he exclaimed. 'You didn't tell me *that*.'

'At least a week ago,' said Roper. 'I'm surprised you didn't know about it.'

But Jewkes was still looking inward to his own troubles. 'So I'll be carrying the can for this all on my own, won't I?'

'Did you kill him, Derek?'

Jewkes all but fell out of his chair, and this time shook his head with such fervour that he had to rearrange his spectacles. 'Kill him? Little bloke like me? And a big bloke like him? Here—you saying somebody's done him in? I didn't even know he was dead. I swear.'

'Relax, Derek,' said Roper. 'I believe you.' Jewkes was scarcely even a villain, let alone a killer. The only folly men like Derek Jewkes committed was to turn the other cheek once too often when the world at large knocked them around.

ROPER WAS BACK in Chumpton well before midday, no
further forward in finding the killer of Albert Haddowes
than he had been when he had first arrived there earlier
that morning. Despite a painstaking quartering of all the
windows and doors, no signs of a forced entry had been
found. The French door that led out to the tiny apron of
back garden was sealed up with paint and looked as if it
had been for years. The only other door to the garden was
in the kitchen, and that had a Chubb lock and two bolts,
all three of which had been secured; and the key to the
Chubb had been found tucked well out of sight on a loop
of string behind the refrigerator.

So it looked as if the killer had come into the house
through the front door. And there were only two conclu-
sions that could be drawn from that. The first was that he
or she had had a key, two keys in fact, because there was a
Yale and another Chubb mortice-lock fitted on the front
door. But with all those goodies stuffed away upstairs,
Haddowes would hardly have chanced giving someone the
keys and thereby the opportunity to call at the house and
ferret around while he was out.

Which left only the second conclusion: that Haddowes
had admitted his killer into the house himself. From which
it had to follow that the two of them knew each other.
Which wasn't all that much help because the statistics
showed that killers and victims, more often than not, were
very well known to each other, and were frequently re-
lated to one another. And both Weygood and Hall had
ventured the idea that Haddowes had been struck from
behind, and, since Haddowes had more than likely been
seated in his armchair at the time, he must have not only
known but also trusted the person who had stood behind
him.

Thus far, nothing had been found in the house that might have been used as a weapon. Whatever it was would have been heavy, probably a chunk of metal of some kind. There was nothing like that lying around. There were some garden tools in the shed, but none of them looked as if they had been moved in a long time.

The killer must therefore have taken it away with him, or her of course, although surely it could only have been a man who would have the weight and strength to deliver a crushing blow like that. And not only taken the weapon away, but perhaps brought it with him. And if he had, then he must have come here with the intent to kill, or at least considered there was some likelihood that he would have to.

And then came the big why.

Why had Haddowes been so brutally struck down? What had he done to provoke his killer?

Cheated him?

Doubtful. Because that would have made the killer a known enemy before he had arrived here. In which case, Haddowes would hardly have been likely to turn his back on him.

Threatened him? With the loss of his job, perhaps? Was the killer one of the other security guards Haddowes had brushed with? Well, that was certainly a possibility worth looking into. But then, again, would Haddowes have been likely to turn his back on such a man, since that man would have arrived in anger and hence presented a threat?

Robbery certainly didn't seem a likely motive. There was little here worth stealing—except the boxes in the attic— and apart from the blood-stained armchair and carpet, everything was in apple-pie order. Furthermore, Haddowes' wallet, with nearly £200 in it, had been found in a jacket draped over the back of a chair in the front room.

Dan Morgan returned to the house on the dot of twelve o'clock with the result of the door-to-door enquiries. No one in the street recalled seeing anybody calling at Number Six during the weekend in question, but that was over a week ago now and memories had had plenty of time to fade.

'How about unfamiliar cars parked in the vicinity?'

'Nobody noticed any,' said Morgan.

But it was the general opinion of those called upon that Albert Haddowes was not an amenable neighbour. He passed the time of day only grudgingly, if at all, and everybody knew about the way he had treated his wife.

And one other lady in The Row, a Mrs Silk across at Number Fifteen, had, a few weeks ago, seen the young blonde woman calling at Haddowes' house. And as Mrs Moore had reported, that young woman had been carrying a weekend bag. She had looked, according to Mrs Silk, very smart and stylish and had been somewhere around the thirty mark. She had arrived in a car and stayed in the house for about an hour.

'Does she remember what colour the car was, whether it was old or new, anything that might give us a lead on it?'

'She thought it might have been a dark red, but she's not entirely sure about that.'

So much for witnesses, or uncommon lack thereof. And, given a few more days, any trails that did happen to be lying about would dry up altogether.

EIGHT

BY THREE O'CLOCK in the afternoon, Haddowes' terraced cottage was quiet again. The two technicians from the forensic laboratory were still nosing around, but there seemed little hope now that they would turn up anything useful. With the immediate neighbours canvassed, the door-to-door operation had been scaled down and only the uniformed officers that Superintendent Curley had sent along were still involved with that particular side of things. But they were working through the outlying streets now, so there was probably little hope in that direction either. Price and DC Makins had driven over to the British Legion Club in Monksbridge, where, according to Derek Jewkes, Albert Haddowes had done most of his serious drinking, and perhaps even sold off some of his illicit goods to an unaware ex-comrade or two.

The only other immediately obvious avenue of investigation was a chat with the other security guards over whom Haddowes had held sway, and especially the ones he had rubbed up the wrong way. Dan Morgan and WDC Weekes were looking after that.

The sun had shown its face at last, but the house still felt chill and depressing, as if Albert Haddowes' unquiet spirit still walked here. In the room where he had been killed, dead flies lay everywhere, and the entire house smelled of fly-killer. In the kitchen one of the technicians was lying on his back and unscrewing the U-bend from under the sink. There had been many a scrap of evidence found in a sink-trap, not least traces of blood where a weapon had been sluiced clean after a crime such as this one.

Roper waited for the technician to slide out, the trap held carefully upright until he had tipped the contents into a jar and then screwed on its cap.

'Much more you can do?' asked Roper.

'Not a lot, sir,' the man admitted frankly. 'I reckon a couple more hours and we might as well call it a day.'

'Fair enough,' said Roper. 'If anything else does crop up, give me a bell. I'll be along at the mortuary.'

The man grimaced. 'Rather you than me.'

'Likewise,' said Roper drily. He had never been enamoured of mortuaries—the ambience of disinfectants, antiseptics, formaldehyde, dead flesh. And there was an atavistic part of him that was still superstitious enough to wonder if the pale lifeless bodies on the table really did feel nothing when that knife went in and made that first long cut, or whether they loosed a long, silent scream that no one ever heard.

By the time he arrived at the mortuary the autopsy was well under way. Frank Osborne, the Coroner's Officer, was already in attendance, capped and gowned, and Weygood's woman assistant was taking photographs while the man himself was laying aside flaps of Haddowes' bald scalp to reveal the shattered bone beneath.

'Thought none of you people were coming,' snapped Weygood testily, barely looking up.

Roper didn't answer and Weygood was too busy to pursue the point.

'Another photograph here, Miss Glover. Quickly, please!'

The harassed Miss Glover dashed to her master's bidding, and Roper and Osborne exchanged understanding glances across the examination table. But tartar though

Weygood might be to the living, no one could ever say that he didn't do justice to the dead.

Haddowes had looked a big, powerful man when he had been lolling in his bloodstained chair. Stretched out on the stainless-steel table he seemed even larger. On his outer left thigh was a transverse scar that looked like an old bullet wound.

'Quickly, Miss Glover!'

Poor Miss Glover dashed in with her Polaroid camera again. There was a brief stroke of light from its flash.

'One blow,' said Weygood. 'Something damned heavy.'

'Monkey wrench?' suggested Roper.

Weygood glared along the table at him. 'Can't make assumptions like that. All I'm prepared to say is what I've already said. Incise, please, Miss Glover.'

AT NINE O'CLOCK in the evening Roper was back behind his desk at County, a desk that had been tidy when he left it last Friday evening but that was now a littered raft of paper, photocopied statements, scene-of-crime photographs in all their colourful and gory details, a few Polaroid photographs that Weygood had let him have, and photocopies of Weygood's preliminary post-mortem report. And his in-tray was brimming with the paperwork that had built up during the day and was part of the never-ending nitty-gritty that the job was heir to. On top of the heap in the in-tray was another photocopied newspaper-clipping located by the indefatigable Miss Pringle from last Saturday's *Daily Telegraph*. The funeral service for the late Mrs Susan Gribo was to take place in St Philip's church at Nuncton Zelston that coming Wednesday afternoon at three p.m. The subsequent cremation would be private...

He dropped the photocopy back in the tray. Mrs Gribo was now well and truly in the past tense. He had heard no more from the ACC about Doctor Gribo getting him to hustle the Cretan police, so presumably he wasn't, and so far as Roper was concerned that particular matter was ended. He would tell Miss Pringle tomorrow to take her notice off the board. There was too much mayhem here now for him to bother about a murder in far-off Crete, intimately connected with that murder though he had been. Life was simply too short.

According to a memo from Inspector Price, a visit with George Makins to the British Legion Club in Monksbridge had turned up nothing except that six members had unsuspectingly bought electrical goods off Haddowes. As with his neighbours, Haddowes had not been a popular man there and spent most of his time, when he could find a listener or two, bragging about the campaigns in which he had fought and generally talking everybody else down. It seemed to be the general feeling that Albert Haddowes would not be sadly missed. The only really promising news-item was that Haddowes had eaten a hot steak and kidney pie at the club shortly before he left, which was some time around three o'clock on the afternoon of the Saturday on which it was presumed he had died. Which would be useful information when Weygood got down to examining the contents of Haddowes' stomach tomorrow as it would help to determine more closely the time of Haddowes' death.

The two men from Forensic had signed off at six o'clock that evening. The list of articles they had taken away for further examination ranged from the sink-trap to a pair of reading-glasses found under Haddowes' chair. Their preliminary report, for all their hard work, was really so much waste-paper because they had found nothing that pointed anywhere in particular.

At nine-fifteen he heard the lift doors gasp open and the voices of Morgan and WDC Weekes pass by in the passage. When he followed them into the squad-office, Morgan was hanging his jacket on the coatrack and Weekes was lifting the cover off her typewriter. DC Makins was the only other occupant of the office, and he was pecking away at another typewriter, transcribing the notes from his pocket-book that he had jotted down during the day. All three looked close to the end of their tethers.

To Roper's surprise, Inspector Price's office door was shut and the lights switched off.

'Mr Price out working somewhere, is he?' he asked.

'He went home, sir,' said Makins.

'What time?'

'About seven o'clock, sir,' said Makins. 'He had an appointment.'

Roper left it at that. Inspector Price would have to be sorted out tomorrow. Nobody went home early when everybody else was knee-deep in a murder enquiry. Old George Mower had often been found in his office at one o'clock in the morning, still beavering away in the light of his desk lamp.

'And we're back so late because we stopped off for a bite to eat,' explained Dan Morgan.

He and Weekes had had to travel as far afield as Shaftesbury, to the north of the county, and Lyme Regis to the west of it, in order to track down a couple of ex-employees of Mr Wallis who were known to have had serious disputes with Albert Haddowes. Between the two of them, they had interviewed over thirty security guards who at some time or another had worked with Haddowes.

'And?' asked Roper, but he guessed the answer before Morgan even opened his mouth.

'Not a lot,' said Morgan. 'Except the ex-guard we spoke to up in Shaftesbury reckons he saw Haddowes a few weeks back in Dorchester. He had a blonde woman with him. The two of them were coming out of a pub, and they went off together in a maroon Citroën hatchback. He thinks it might have been a Club.'

'Any other description of her?'

'About thirty,' said Morgan. 'Five-seven to five-ten. Green suit. Very smart. Said she didn't look like Haddowes' girlfriend because she was too up-market.'

Which wasn't much, but it was marginally better than nothing at all. And Mrs Moore had told Roper that she had seen a fair-haired young woman call at Haddowes' cottage. And a Mrs Silk, who had been interviewed later during the door-to-door enquiries, had seen a similar woman. And, more importantly, Mrs Silk had told the interviewing constable that she thought the woman in question had arrived in The Row in a dark red car. And given that few people were able to describe colours with any accuracy, dark red wasn't too many shades of the spectrum away from maroon. So it seemed highly likely that Mrs Moore and Mrs Silk had described the same woman, and since a similar woman and Haddowes had been seen coming out of a Dorchester public house together by yet another witness, it could be presumed that the relationship between her and Haddowes was more than a casual one. And, hopefully, she might come forward tomorrow when news of Haddowes' murder broke in the papers and the local radio.

THE NEXT DAY, Tuesday, started badly.

'That was a quick disappearing-act you did last evening, Inspector,' said Roper.

'Yes, I'm sorry about that, sir,' said Price. 'I had to see an estate agent about a mortgage. We're still living in South Wales, you see, and the wife's getting a bit fed up with not seeing me except on my rest days. We've managed to find a house in Dorchester and it's just a question of finance now.'

'You couldn't have phoned this estate agent? Put him off until this morning? On your way into work, for instance?'

'Well, yes, I suppose I could—'

'Then you should have,' interrupted Roper. 'At ten o'clock last night you were the only member of the crew who'd shoved off and left everybody to it. You're supposed to be my second-in-command here. It's bad for morale to see your guv'nor going home when you've got two or three more hours to go flogging your guts out on a typewriter.'

'It won't happen again, sir,' said Price.

'It had better not,' said Roper. At which moment there came a knock on the office door, and Dan Morgan put his head around the edge of it.

'Sorry to interrupt, sir. Message for Mr Price from Superintendent Curley. One of his lads found a woman with her head in her gas-oven this morning. Mr Curley wants to know if he can borrow a DC. He's got four men giving evidence in court this morning, so he's a bit short-staffed.'

'Send Alison Weekes over there,' said Price.

'Right,' said Morgan.

'Think it's wise to send Weekes on her own?' asked Roper when the door had closed again behind Morgan. 'She's hardly had time to settle in yet.'

'She's got to stand on her own two feet sometime,' said Price.

But Weekes was apparently already standing on her own two feet because at ten-fifteen Morgan was back in Roper's office. Weekes had just rung in from Monksbridge.

'The woman's name's Alexandra Higgs,' said Morgan. 'She's dark-haired, but Weekes reckons she's got a couple of weeks' growth of blonde sprouting through underneath. And as well as that, she's wearing an expensive green skirt. And there's a matching jacket slung over one of the chairs in her sitting-room. She says it could be a long shot, but Higgs might be a match for the woman who was seen with Haddowes. She's about the right age, too.'

'Inspector Price know about all this?'

'Yes, sir, I told him, but he says he can't do much about it yet because he's due in court at eleven o'clock. The brainless blagger who tried to do the building society with half a walking-stick.'

'Got the address?'

Roper and Morgan were in Monksbridge at ten-forty, and for the first time in days they had been able to leave their raincoats in the office. Fourteen, Crispin Close, was one of half a dozen ultra-modern brick cottages that were eyesores, set as they were at the end of a row of picturesque old Purbeck-stone houses, one with a thatched roof, that looked as if they had been there for ever. There were several cars parked in the vicinity, one white with a blue lamp on top and the County police insignia on its doors, another he recognised as being from the County car-pool so that was probably what Weekes had driven here in. There was an undertaker's hearse too, but its crew were still opening the rear hatch, so that was obviously newly arrived.

Weekes was in the hallway exchanging notes with a uniformed sergeant who was probably the local beat-officer. There was still a strong smell of gas.

'Who found her?' asked Roper, producing his warrant-card for the sergeant.

'I did, sir,' said the sergeant, passing the card back. 'The neighbours called the gas company in to look for a leak and the engineer called us because he couldn't get in. Newspapers in the porch go back to last Saturday and so does the mail, and when I looked in at the front window, the television was going full blast and the room looked as if someone had chucked a bomb in it. So I went round the back. And there she was with her head in the oven. Looks like she definitely intended to make certain. Drink, pills *and* the gas-stove. She must have been in quite a state.'

'I'll take a look before they take her away,' said Roper, already bracing himself against the stench from the kitchen as he approached its open doorway. The door between the kitchen and the garden was open too, and so was the window beside it, but it was a windless sunny morning and the air was still thick. At the kitchen table the Divisional Doctor—it was Doctor Hall again—was making copious notes on his pad and the raincoated man smoking a cigarette on the back step and looking in was Frank Osborne.

Roper held his breath and went down on his heels beside the body. He carefully hooked a finger around one of the corpse's chill ones and lifted it. It was loose and rubbery, so rigor mortis must have occurred then gone again. Days ago, probably.

'She's been dead three or four days,' said Doctor Hall, watching him.

'Anybody got a torch?' asked Roper.

Weekes passed her Maglite over his shoulder and he shone it into the dark of the oven. Weekes was right, Ms Higgs had been about thirty, dark-haired though dyed from blonde, and wearing a green twill skirt. Good-looking, possibly, although at this stage it was difficult to be certain. The smell wasn't only of alcohol and gas and vomit. One of her cheeks lay on a vomit-stained, embroi-

dered silk cushion that had been arranged on the bottom
shelf. The other shelves had been taken out and were lying
on the floor near the sink unit.

'It looks like a classic,' said Hall.

Roper made no answer. Suicides, in his book, were never
classic.

'And there is one more thing, sir,' said Weekes.

'What's that?'

'The gas-tap, sir,' said Weekes. 'When Sergeant Crisp
came in and turned it off, it was barely turned on at all.
About a quarter of the way at most. He made a particular
note of that.'

'Odd,' agreed Roper.

'I doubt very much she knew what she was doing by
then,' ventured Hall from behind them.

Well, perhaps, but it was certainly odd all the same.

'Sergeant Crisp said something about tablets,' said
Roper.

'I've got one here,' said Hall. 'Your young lady found
it tucked down beside a cushion in the sitting-room.' He
paused in his writing to hand Roper a small plastic envelope with a solitary pink tablet lodged in its bottom corner.

'Know what it is, do we?' asked Roper, tipping the bag
towards the window and just able to make out the characters T232 moulded into one face of the tablet.

'Sorry, I don't,' said Hall. 'But I'll look it up in my book
when I get back to the surgery and give you a ring.'

'I'd be obliged, Doctor. Thank you.' He turned back to
Weekes. 'Show me this green jacket.'

It was draped over the back of an armchair in the sitting-room, the same chair in which Weekes had found the
pink tablet, and was clearly the matching top half of the
crumpled skirt Higgs' body was presently wearing. So

Higgs had been a blonde and owned a green suit. Which might not signify anything at all, but it had been smart of Weekes to spot it and make the possible connection.

There was an empty vodka bottle standing on the coffee table, its metal cap lying in an otherwise empty ashtray, and beside the ashtray stood a dirty glass tumbler, a dead fly lying in the bottom of it with its legs in the air.

'And there's another empty bottle in the kitchen wastebin,' said Weekes. 'With the same batch number on the cap as the one on the table.'

Roper looked askance at her, pleasantly surprised. WDC Weekes was clearly going to go far if she stayed in the Force.

'Found the handbag she might have been using last?'

'In the hall,' said Weekes. 'On the telephone seat. Looks as if she dumped it there the last time she came into the house. I'll get it.'

She came back with a black leather handbag, open as she had found it. Roper tipped the contents on to the coffee table.

Just the usual odds and ends. Keys, lipstick, a plastic palette of eye-shadows, a wad of paper handkerchiefs. A wallet that contained only a ten-pound note, two credit cards and two postage stamps.

'But no diary,' observed Weekes.

And that was true too. In the course of his work Roper had had cause to tip out many a handbag and had invariably found a diary of some sort or another. Here there was no such thing.

'Take a look upstairs,' he said. 'You might find one lying around up there.'

Weekes went away and Roper returned to the kitchen. Doctor Hall was capping his pen, a gold pen, Roper observed, that complemented his gold-rimmed glasses and his immaculately cut, chalk-striped suit. There was something just a touch ostentatious about Doctor Hall.

In the light of what Sergeant Crisp had told Weekes, Roper experimented with the gas-tap of the oven. It had been designed to be child-proof, a knob fitted with a central button which had to be depressed before the knob could be turned. And he wondered why Ms Higgs, seemingly so determined to commit suicide, had not turned the knob all the way. 'I didn't think suicides went in for the oven these days,' he said. 'Not since we're using North Sea gas. It isn't toxic, is it, strictly speaking?'

'Well, no, strictly speaking,' agreed Hall. 'But one can still choke on it if one inhales it for long enough. I'd say that with all the pills and alcohol she'd taken, she probably turned on the gas, put her head in the oven and then was incapable of getting up again once she found she couldn't breathe.'

'D'you reckon she could have reached up as far as the gas-tap, lying the way she is?'

'It's possible, I suppose,' said Hall, but he looked doubtful.

So perhaps that was it. Deciding she didn't want to choke to death, Higgs had reached up for the knob to turn off the gas but had finally collapsed before she quite managed it.

A rap of knuckles sounded on the kitchen door frame. It was Dan Morgan, back from a foray around the outside of the house.

'Got a minute, guv-nor?' he said.

Roper joined him in the tiny hallway. 'Found something?'

'Could well be Weekes was dead right about Higgs being the woman who was seen with Albert Haddowes', said Morgan. He gave a small jerk of his head in the direction of the back garden. 'There's a lock-up garage behind there. The mechanism of the door's jammed so the whole thing's standing wide open, and her car's in there.'

'Don't tell me,' said Roper. 'It's a maroon Citroën hatchback.'

'You've got it,' said Morgan.

AND SO IT WAS. A maroon Citroën hatchback, a Club, with last year's registration plates and a lot of mud splashed around the door-sills and wheel arches. The brick-built garage was one of a row of four with up-and-over doors, all painted a uniform pale blue.

Earlier on, Weekes' theory that Higgs had had some kind of connection with Albert Haddowes had seemed like the longest of long shots. It no longer was.

'Get Forensic to check it over, Dan,' said Roper.

The two of them walked briskly back to the house. In the last few minutes the death of Alexandra Higgs had taken on an entirely different perspective. Maroon Citroën Clubs were not the commonest vehicles on the road. Alexandra Higgs had been a natural blonde and a blonde woman driving a maroon Club had been seen with Haddowes. And now Higgs and Haddowes were dead, and, moreover, dead within a few days of each other.

The telephone was ringing as they turned in through the front door. Roper left Morgan to answer it while he went on through to the kitchen, where Doctor Hall was closing his bag preparatory to leaving and Frank Osborne was talking to the two undertaker's men who were complaining about the time they had spent hanging around.

'They want to know if they can take the body away now, Mr Roper,' said Osborne.

'No, they can't,' said Roper. 'Tell them to come back in a couple of hours. Sorry, gentlemen,' he said to the two black-clad men. 'Something important's just cropped up. I'll have somebody give you a ring when we've got things sorted out.'

'Something that might suggest the poor lady didn't commit suicide?' asked Doctor Hall, standing up now with his bag hanging beside him, an anxious frown on his face.

'No, sir, nothing like that,' said Roper. 'But it's just possible she might be concerned in another case we're investigating. I'd like to put everything on hold for a bit longer.'

'Well, I'll get out of your way, then, Mr Roper. When I manage to identify those tablets, I'll give you a ring.'

As Hall went out, Morgan stood aside for him in the doorway.

'The phone call was from the Eastern County General Hospital,' said Morgan. 'Apparently Higgs was the secretary of the hospital director. She phoned in last Friday to say she was sick but would probably be in for work again yesterday. She didn't turn up and didn't ring in. They were wondering where she'd got to.'

'Did you tell 'em what had happened?'

'Just that she was dead.'

'Good,' said Roper. 'Now go back to your car and radio for a couple of Scenes of Crime Officers and a photographer. Then have a wander around the neighbours, find out if she had any visitors lately and who her friends were. And who her doctor was and what prescriptions he'd given her for tablets.'

'Right,' said Morgan.

Weekes reappeared. Thus far, she had not been able to locate Higgs' diary, if indeed Higgs had kept one.

'Forget that for now, Alison,' said Roper. 'I've got another job for you. Higgs was working as a secretary at the Eastern County General. I'd like you to go across there and ferret around, talk to her boss and any of the staff who knew her. See if anybody reckons she might have been depressed enough to commit suicide—and anything else you can find out about her.'

'RECKON IT'S A BIT SUSS, do you, Mr Roper?' asked Frank Osborne, as he and Roper stood by the kitchen door and watched the photographer unscrew his camera from the tripod and start packing his equipment away.

'Not sure yet,' said Roper. 'But whether she committed suicide or not there's a fair chance she knew Albert Haddowes. How soon do you think you can arrange a post-mortem?'

'Tomorrow, probably,' said Osborne. 'Today, at a push, if you think there's something a bit dodgy going on.'

'Today would be better.'

'It's all yours, Mr Roper,' said the photographer, hefting up his bag of paraphernalia and swinging the tripod over his shoulder. 'I'll try to get prints to you early this afternoon.'

'Thanks,' said Roper, and as soon as Osborne and the photographer had gone out of the door, Morgan went out after them to phone the undertakers. With the kitchen to himself now Roper again dropped down on his heels beside the body and took a really good look at it. An instinctive reflex had him smooth down the crumpled green skirt to cover the bare, white knees. No tights or stockings then, but bare feet in a pair of practical fur-lined slippers, a black stain just inside the heel of one. It looked like dried blood. A closer look showed that it was. And removing the slipper revealed a small, ragged V-shaped tear in the flesh of the heel it had covered. The wound had bled only a little, but sufficiently to stain the furry inside of the slipper.

Still holding the slipper, Roper walked the few paces to the sitting-room, in the doorway of which he dropped to his heels again. Both the room and the hallway were carpeted and where the two carpets met in the doorway the join had been bridged with an aluminium strip which moved at his touch, because the screws that held it down were loose. And one screw in particular was proud of the strip by a sixteenth of an inch or more. And if a naked heel had been dragged over it...

'That post-mortem, Frank,' he said, looking up at Osborne who had just come back and was standing over him. 'You can make it as soon as you like.'

NINE

It was well after midday before Morgan returned from his reconnaissance of Higgs' neighbours. According to them, Higgs was sociable enough but a quiet sort who minded her own business and did not pry into that of others. She had lived in her house since it was built, some three years previously, and the last sighting of her had been by her immediate neighbour, a Mrs Odell, last Friday morning at some time around eleven o'clock.

Mrs Odell had told Morgan that she had returned from her weekly expedition to the supermarket and had been putting her car in her garage when she noticed that the adjacent garage door, Alex Higgs' garage, was wide open and that her car was inside it. And Mrs Odell, a keen member of her local Neighbourhood Watch Committee, had felt bound to apprise Alex Higgs of this foolish omission. She had taken her shopping indoors, then at once called next door. She had rung the bell several times, received no answer, turned away and started back down the front path.

At which point, turning to close the gate, she glimpsed the distant figure of Higgs approaching. Higgs had been wearing a green suit, carrying an opened umbrella—although, as Mrs Odell recalled, it had been raining earlier but was not at that time—and hugging a plastic carrier-bag close to her chest. From which Mrs Odell had concluded that Higgs had nipped out briefly to the local shops, of which there was a row just around the corner.

As Higgs drew closer, Mrs Odell saw that she looked unusually dishevelled. A snappy dresser as a rule, Higgs was wearing a pair of flat brown shoes, was bare-legged and wore no make-up. She was also in a hurry, because when Mrs Odell told her about the garage door all Higgs had replied was, 'I'll see to it later. Thanks.' She had then more or less jostled Mrs Odell aside and hurried indoors without another word.

Mrs Odell had then opened up a little more and ventured the opinion that Alexandra Higgs seemed not to have been her usual self just lately. For some peculiar reason, Higgs had had her wealth of long blond hair not only cropped short but dyed black into the bargain! And what she had been cuddling to herself in the plastic bag had looked like a bottle. And her eyes, as they had stared into Mrs Odell's, had looked wild and frightened, well, perhaps that was just imagination, but they had certainly looked strange. And despite Mrs Odell's warning, the garage door had remained open throughout the weekend.

'How about men friends?' asked Roper.

'If she had one she was pretty discreet about it,' said Morgan. 'And if she did, he was never seen calling here.'

Weekes returned from the Eastern County General Hospital soon after one o'clock. She had found out marginally more.

'Her boss says she'd definitely been acting strangely lately. She started work there three months ago, and he says she seemed like the answer to all his prayers. She'd got a degree in business management and he reckoned it wouldn't be long before she was his assistant rather than just his secretary. She really had her finger on the button—I quote.

'But then she started to go to pieces—again I quote—about three or four weeks ago. She came in one morning and asked if she could take three days' leave because an aunt had died and it was down to her to make the funeral arrangements because there were no other relatives. When she came back to work, she'd had her hair shorn and dyed—told everybody she was fed up with being blonde. She seemed brittle and nervous and started to make a lot of little mistakes, little misspellings and leaving a nought or two out of financial statements. Nobody complained seriously because they thought she was upset about the aunt and would soon get over it.

'But she only got worse. Going home in the afternoons, saying she'd got a headache, turning up late in the mornings. Her boss guessed she was heading for some kind of nervous breakdown and suggested she might have a chat with one of the hospital's own doctors. But she wouldn't go. And then, last Friday, she didn't turn up at work at all, rang in to say she felt groggy, and one of the other women there had to fill in for her. And this morning, when they rang here because she hadn't turned up yesterday or today, Sergeant Morgan told them she was dead.'

So suicide it might have been after all, despite the half-hearted way the gas-tap had been turned on and that suspicious-looking wound on Higgs' heel.

At three o'clock in the afternoon Roper was back behind his desk at County. Higgs' body was now lodged in the mortuary, and her house and her Citroën Club were being thoroughly examined in the hope that some fragment of evidence might be found to link her more positively with Albert Haddowes. Because if it could be proved that she did have some connection with Haddowes then her suicide would definitely merit a more thorough investigation.

There might even be a remote possibility that she had killed him, and that she had committed suicide out of remorse. Although that didn't seem likely somehow. Desperate women sometimes picked up a knife, but rarely a cosh. A wild stretch of the imagination presented a picture of her as Haddowes' lady-friend. Except that there had been at least twenty-five years between them, and, from what Roper had heard, Haddowes was a long way from being a ladies' man. A lesser leap of the imagination put her in the frame as a relative of Haddowes. Because Mrs Moore had told Roper, had she not, that Haddowes had had both a sister-in-law and a niece knocking around somewhere. Higgs seemed to have been a little too young to have been Mrs Haddowes' sister, so if she were either of the two then it was more probably the niece.

And if she had been Haddowes' niece it made it even more curious that he and she had died within days of each other. A coincidence? Or something more sinister?

According to her boss and several of her colleagues at the hospital, Higgs had been acting strangely during the last few weeks. Mrs Odell had seen Higgs last Friday with 'wild and frightened eyes', which was perhaps a little colourful but nevertheless painted a picture of a woman strained to breaking point. So what had happened during the last few weeks to cause that sudden change? The death of Haddowes? A love affair that had gone wrong?

He reached out for the intrusively chirruping telephone. It was Dan Morgan on the internal line from the squad office.

'I've managed to track down Higgs' doctor, guv'nor. A Doctor Barbara Tandy. She's one of the partners along at the Monksbridge Medical Centre. According to her record, Higgs registered with her three years ago, and she's only seen her twice since then. The last time was in February and all she prescribed was a course of antibiotics.'

'I see,' said Roper. 'Thanks, Dan.'

But then, as he reached out to drop the receiver back on its rest, he had a sudden flash of recall. Doctor Rex Gribo was also one of the partners at the Monksbridge Medical Centre, but before he had time to properly digest that co-incidence the telephone chirruped again and he snatched it up.

'You've got an overseas call, sir. A Major Spiridakis. Says he's calling from Crete. It's about the murder of that Mrs Gribo.'

Roper picked up his ballpoint again and drew his jotter closer. 'Put him on,' he said. 'Ioánnis, how are you? And Melina?'

'Well,' said Spiridakis, loudly and clearly enough for him to have been in the same building. 'You are also, I trust? And Miss Carmody?'

'Both,' said Roper. 'To what do we owe the pleasure?'

'News,' said Spiridakis. 'Stepanikis is telexing Interpol this very minute with instructions to pass the information on to you, but that could take hours so I thought I would use the excuse to speak to you personally. Something has come up. Since several belongings of *Kyria* Gribo were found on the road to the airport, so we are now thinking more seriously that she may have been murdered by someone not from the island. And I think we may have found the taxi-driver who drove her killer to Iráklion that night.'

'It's taken him long enough to come forward, hasn't it?' said Roper. 'Like a month? What's jogged his memory all of a sudden?'

'Money,' said Spiridakis. 'The mayor has put up a re-ward for information. At the time, I did not think it was a good idea, but now it seems that it has paid off.'

'How d'you know he's on the level?' Roper never had cared for the reward system. It brought too many jokers out of their closets and started too many wild goose chases.

'From the information he gave us, I am absolutely certain that he is telling the truth,' said Spiridakis. 'His name is Andros Venizelou and he works out of Agios Nikólaos. He is not sure of the day or the date, but about four weeks ago—he thinks it was some time after midnight—he dropped off two passengers on the sea-front at Agios Mateos. And before he could drive away, a man who had been walking quickly along the sea-front approached him and asked what he would charge to take him to Iráklion. The man was English, Venizelou is almost sure of that. He explained to the man that he was taking no more passengers but was going home for the night. The man then offered him twenty thousand *drachmae,* which is roughly one hundred of your English pounds, an offer which Venizelou was unable to refuse, despite the lateness of the hour. Venizelou also remembers that the man was very out of breath.'

'Mr Venizelou would, wouldn't he,' said Roper, still doubtful. 'Perhaps he's adding a little colour to make sure you're getting value for money. Breathless killer flees scene of crime. It doesn't need a lot of imagination, does it?'

'Patience, Douglas,' said Spiridakis. 'It now becomes more precise. Venizelou also remembers that the man wound down his window as soon as he had sat down, and at one point threw something out of that window. Venizelou thought at the time it might have been an empty cigarette packet. To the best of his memory, that happened somewhere around the vicinity of Neápolis.'

'Which was where Mrs Gribo's passport was found,' said Roper.

'Exactly,' said Spiridakis. 'And then a few kilometres further on, the man tapped Venizelou on the shoulder and asked him to stop for a moment. The man left the car and went into some bushes beside the road. Venizelou had the impression that he had gone to relieve himself. Again, he cannot remember the exact locality, but he thinks it was a little beyond Mália—which is where the goat-boy found Mrs Gribo's jewellery in a plastic bag, if you remember.'

'I remember,' said Roper. 'It certainly sounds like your man, doesn't it. Does the taxi-driver have a description?'

'Not a good one. It was dark and where he picked him up was between street-lamps. But the man was bald and wore spectacles. He was darkly dressed. Venizelou is also fairly certain that he was carrying a bag, perhaps a flight bag.'

'Height?'

'He is not sure. He was sitting in his taxi and the man was standing on the footway.'

'How about build?'

'Again, he does not remember. All he is sure about are the bald head, the spectacles and the flight bag.'

'Does he remember where he dropped this man off in Iráklion?'

'Yes, he does. The bus station near Kountoryoton Square. Again, he tapped Venizelou on the shoulder and told him to stop.'

'Did he go into the bus station?'

'Venizelou did not stay to watch, regrettably.'

'Not much to go on, is it, Ioánnis?'

'Agreed,' said Spiridakis. 'But it is just remotely possible that we might now have a name for this man. We have been collating aircraft passenger lists and checking out passengers' names with all the hotels on the island. A Mr M R Robinson flew out of London Gatwick at twelve fifty-five on Monday, August the third. That is London time, by the way. It was a non-stop Olympic Airways scheduled flight which landed at Iráklion at nineteen-hundred, Athens time. And the next morning an M R Robinson also appeared on the passenger list for the ten twenty-five Olympic Airways flight from Iráklion to Gatwick, which landed there at twelve-thirty, London time. And now the curious part: despite the fact that Mr Robinson was booked into the Hotel Ionia in Iráklion for the night of August the third he did not arrive there and the room was given to someone else. So we checked all the other hotels and rooming-houses in Iráklion and it seems that he slept in none of them, or certainly not as M R Robinson. From which we can only assume that he spent the night with friends, or walked the streets or slept in the lounge at the airport.'

'Do you have an address for this Mr Robinson?'

'Yes, we do,' said Spiridakis. There came a faint rustle of paper. 'Twenty-four Masons Avenue, Dorchester. Is that far from you, Dorchester?'

'I could chuck a feather at it,' said Roper as he scribbled Mr Robinson's address. 'Know where he got the tickets from?'

'A record of that would be best available at your end. Perhaps you will phone the airline office at Gatwick?'

'I'll do better,' said Roper. 'I'll ask Mr Robinson himself. But I can tell you who Robinson isn't, and that's Rex Gribo. Firstly, Gribo's got a good head of hair, and secondly he couldn't possibly have done it in the time-scale you've just been talking about and been seen in Scotland at the same time by a couple of police-officers.'

'I agree totally,' said Spiridakis. 'I met the *Eyatros* Gribo when he came to Iráklion to collect the body. He gave me the impression of a man holding back very much anger. He made it plain that he was disappointed that we appeared to have done so little towards catching the murderer. And I cannot blame him for that, of course.'

'I shall probably be meeting him myself tomorrow,' said Roper. 'If I can find the time, my guv'nor's asked me to show my face at the funeral service. I presume this telex that's coming is going to be a formal request to us to track down this Robinson and interview him.'

'It is a last resort, of course, Douglas,' said Spiridakis. 'We realise that the chances of his being our man are slim. In short, we really expect the English police to do nothing but go through the motions as we would ourselves if the positions were reversed. You are not too busy, I trust?'

'Up to our necks at the moment, old lad. A murder and a suicide that seem to be connected and hardly a scrap of evidence in sight. But interestingly, the suicide victim was the patient of a doctor who's in partnership with Rex Gribo. And that's not a coincidence, by the way. She just happened to live in the same neighbourhood as the practice, like a couple of thousand other people.'

Spiridakis laughed. 'I have converted you, then. You now agree that coincidences are only the result of other pre-ordained circumstances which meet at a single point.'

'I always did, Ioánnis,' said Roper. 'But not in so many words.'

'TAKE THE NEXT ONE on the left, Dan,' said Roper, running a forefinger across the street-map on his knees. 'Then the second on the left.'

It was four-thirty of the same Tuesday afternoon. Morgan was driving.

'Now right,' said Roper, as he spotted the street-sign for Masons Avenue. It was a tree-lined cul-de-sac of well-kept, thirties-style bungalows on the northern edge of Dorchester.

'What number was it?' asked Morgan, slowing the car to a crawl.

'Twenty-four,' said Roper. 'It's on your side.'

They reached the end of the street, across which were the green, spiked railings of a school playing field.

'They seem to finish at number twenty,' said Morgan.

Roper leaned forward to peer past him out of the side window. They were stopped outside number twenty. The number on Roper's side was nineteen.

They both got out of the car. Roper went up the side entrance of number twenty and Morgan to the side entrance of number nineteen. Both saw only back gardens of those properties, and the spiked iron railings looked as if they had been there for forty years or more. They called at several other bungalows. There never had been a number twenty-four, and Mr M R Robinson had never been heard of.

'Perhaps your Greek major made a mistake in translation, guv'nor,' ventured Morgan.

'He's not that sort,' said Roper. 'But we'll check with the airline when we get back to the office, just in case.'

'Or the bloke gave a false address,' suggested Morgan.

'Aye,' said Roper. 'I'd say that was a lot more likely.'

'I QUITE AGREE,' said the ACC. 'It's all beginning to look decidedly fishy.' It was five-thirty in the evening and Spiridakis' telex had at last arrived via Interpol in Paris and the Yard in London. There was no doubt about the address Mr Robinson had given to the airline. It was the non-existent house at twenty-four Masons Avenue.

'If it's okay with you, sir, I'll run a few checks myself.'

'Frankly, I think you ought to,' said the ACC. 'It will at least look as if we're doing something constructive. And I think we ought to be putting up some kind of show in case Gribo beards you at the funeral tomorrow. Then you'll be able to look him in the eye without flinching. I know you're busy, but needs must when the Devil drives, hmm?'

'Got a job for you, George,' said Roper, dropping the telex on to Makins' desk on his way back to his office. Makins and Inspector Price had just returned from the Court, where they had wasted most of a day to see the would-be raider of the building society bound over subject to a psychiatric report. 'Olympic Airways. Give 'em a ring and ask them if they can tell us where the Mr Robinson mentioned there might have got his tickets. Try their office at Gatwick first.'

Once told why the question had been asked of it, the airline was quick to respond and within ten minutes Makins and Roper were face to face again in Roper's office.

'The Goldfinch Travel Agency, sir. Budbury Road, Dorchester. They were sent to the agency by registered post on Thursday, July thirtieth.'

'Have you rung the agency?'

'I just did, sir,' said Makins. 'They're shut for the day. All I got was their answering machine.'

Which was a very great pity. Because now that it was known that Mr Robinson had given a false address he was definitely in the frame for murder.

Alison Weekes, who had spent the last few hours in attendance at the mortuary, returned wearily to the office soon after seven o'clock.

'How did it go?' asked Roper.

'Not particularly helpful from our point of view, sir,' said Weekes, fishing in her briefcase and bringing out a thin swatch of photocopies stapled together, which she passed across the desk. 'That's Doctor Weygood's preliminary report. He says his first thought is that Higgs was a particularly determined suicide, and he certainly has no way of proving otherwise. She'd taken in a lot of alcohol and probably some kind of sedative, but from the state of the blood vessels in her eyes, he's recorded the death as asphyxia. He's sent some blood samples off for testing, which'll give him some idea of the levels of alcohol, drugs and inhaled gas. He says that could take two or three days and might cause him to revise his initial findings. And he's got the results back on Haddowes' samples. Says if it's any help to us, Haddowes had eaten some kind of meat, probably in pastry, some time between four to seven hours before he was killed.'

Which was probably the hot steak and kidney pie that Haddowes had eaten in the British Legion Club in the afternoon. He had eaten it at around three o'clock, so he must have been killed some time between seven o'clock and ten o'clock that same evening.

'How about the tablets? Was he able to identify them?'

'Not for the time being, sir, no,' said Weekes. 'I told him the number-code that was on them. He looked through a couple of books he carries about, but they weren't listed in either of them, so he thinks they're probably something new on the market. But as soon as he finds out what they are, he'll let you know. He says if there is any suspicion that Higgs was helped on her way the origin of the tablets could be important.'

'What did he say about that tear on her heel?'

'Not much, sir,' said Weekes. 'He says it could have happened any time during her last twelve hours or so. But if the blood on the screw the SOCO took away matches Higgs', and it was recently deposited, then it might hint that she was dragged into the kitchen while she was semiconscious and that obviously someone else was concerned in her death. It's all in the report, sir.'

'Fair enough,' said Roper. It seemed that Weygood too was up against his own brick wall, and that any further

avenues of investigation hinged upon the provenance of
the tablets Higgs had taken. And the quicker that was established the better.

As soon as Weekes had gone, Roper picked up his phone
and asked the operator to put him in touch with Doctor
Hall. Hall had had several hours now to identify the tablet he had taken away and it was about time he came up
with an answer, even a negative one.

'Ringing for you, sir.'

'Thanks,' said Roper around the cheroot he was lighting, then drew his jotter closer. The phone at the other end
rang for so long that Roper was about to hang up when
suddenly there was a click, and a brusque male voice said,
'I'm sorry, the surgery's closed for this evening. I suggest
you ring the night-emergency number.'

'Is that Doctor Hall?' asked Roper, before his respon-
dent could ring off.

'No,' the voice replied. 'Doctor Hall's along at the hospital. I'm Doctor Gribo.'

An ice-cold finger trailed slowly up Roper's spine. 'I'm
Superintendent Roper, sir, County police. I've been expecting a call from Doctor Hall. He was going to identify
a tablet we found at the scene of a suicide this morning.'

'Oh, yes,' replied Gribo, less curt now. 'He did, or rather
I was able to identify it for him. I'm surprised he hasn't
been in touch. Too busy, probably. The tablet's a new
tranquilliser, just in from Germany.'

'When you say new, sir, does that mean there's something special about it?'

'Well, yes, it's purportedly faster-acting than anything
on the market at the present time, and purportedly less
addictive. It's currently undergoing clinical trials. I know
about it because I'm prescribing it myself for a select few

patients at the hospital. It certainly seems to be effica-
cious thus far.'

'So it isn't generally available, sir?' said Roper, hud-
dling the receiver closer. 'I mean, I couldn't get it even on
prescription at my local dispensing chemist?'

'No, you couldn't,' said Gribo. 'Not until the trials have
been assessed. From what I know, only a dozen or so hos-
pitals in the country have been issued with samples for
testing purposes. Which makes me wonder how the lady in
question managed to get hold of some.'

Roper declined to rise to that. There were a few other
strings he wanted to draw together first. 'This hospital you
refer to, Doctor Gribo, would that be the Eastern County
General?'

'Yes, it would,' said Gribo.

'And is that where Doctor Hall is this evening, if I need
to speak to him personally?'

'Yes, it is,' said Gribo, helpfully. 'Shall I give you the
telephone number?'

'No, it's all right, sir,' said Roper. 'We keep numbers like
that on the switchboard. Thanks for your help—'

'Before you go,' Gribo broke in quickly, 'did you say
your name was Roper?'

'I did, sir,' said Roper, guessing what was coming next
and getting it almost word-perfect.

'There was an Englishman called Roper in Crete at the
time my wife was murdered. I understand from the Cretan authorities that it was in fact a man of that name who
found Susan's body.'

'Yes, that was me, sir, unfortunately,' said Roper.

'I see,' said Gribo. There was a long, long pause. 'Is it
possible that we can meet somewhere and have a 'chat?
Over a drink perhaps?'

'I shall be attending Mrs Gribo's funeral service tomorrow, sir,' said Roper. 'Perhaps we could arrange something then.'

'Yes,' said Gribo. 'Indeed. I look forward to meeting you, Mr Roper. Thank you. Good-night.'

'Good-night, sir,' said Roper, and laid his receiver back in its cradle a lot more thoughtfully than when he had picked it up.

Whether he called it a coincidence or a train of predestined events meeting at a single point, much had come together in the last few minutes.

Doctor Hall, who had examined Higgs' body that morning, was in partnership with Doctor Gribo whose wife had been bludgeoned to death in Crete. Both saw patients at the Eastern County General Hospital where Alexandra Higgs had been the secretary to the director. The Eastern County General was one of only a few centres in the United Kingdom where those tranquillisers were presently available. Doctor Gribo had access to those tablets and had just admitted dispensing them to some of his patients, and a patient of Doctor Tandy, another of Gribo's partners, had come into possession of some and taken an overdose of them.

It was possible, even probable, that Higgs had stolen the tablets herself. She was, after all, a fairly senior member of the hospital staff and probably had access to every department, including the pharmacy. But how had she known which tablets to take? Had someone given her advice? Surely even the most determined suicide would need to know how lethal his or her overdose was going to be before they took it.

But supposing that, given the inadequately turned-on gas-tap and the peculiar wound on her heel, Higgs' life had been taken by someone else? Like someone else who could have taken those tablets from the hospital store, like Doctor Gribo?

All of which was piling wild hypothesis upon wild hypothesis. Or was it really so far-fetched?

Gribo and Higgs worked in the same hospital—and so did Doctor Hall, come to that—so it was highly likely that they had known each other. Gribo's wife had been bludgeoned to death and so had Albert Haddowes. It was also highly likely that Haddowes had known Higgs, now also dead.

And was it also possible that all or any of them might also have known Mr M R Robinson, of no known address except a false one, who had flown to Crete and back either side of the time Mrs Gribo had been murdered and not arrived at the hotel he had booked a bed in? And again, was it also possible that M R Robinson was the breathless man who had hired Mr Venizelou's taxi to take him to Iráklion that night, and on the way got rid of several artefacts that had been the property of Susan Gribo?

And was M R Robinson also the killer of Haddowes, given that the method employed in both instances was the same?

The answer was a tentative 'yes'. In this line of work nothing was ever impossible and sometimes a leap of the imagination from the factual into the apparently bizarre often found a landing place on good solid ground.

He rose to stretch his legs. There was presently only one red flag pinned into the county map on his office wall, and that was stabbed into the village of Chumpton and signified the site of the murder of Albert Haddowes. The yellow paper flag that flew over the town of Monksbridge—which was also where Doctors Gribo, Hall and Tandy had established their practice—signified the site of Alexandra Higgs' suicide.

After a couple of contemplative draws on his cheroot he plucked out a spare red flag from the edge of the map and stuck it in firmly beside the yellow one. He did not take the yellow flag out—it was too soon for that and there were too many questions still to be answered—but the two flags thus, side by side, went some way to express the doubts that had been simmering inside him all day.

Like Spiridakis, Roper simply could not believe that all those coincidences could come together in the one place at the one time. In some way they had been predestined, he was almost sure of it now.

And was the epicentre of the untimely deaths of Higgs and Haddowes not here in Dorset at all, in fact, but in the more exotic clime of far-off Crete?

TEN

THE GIRL'S NAME was Janice Wilkenshaw. Snub-nosed and punk-haircutted, she was the general dogsbody at the Goldfinch Travel Agency, at the door of which Roper and DC Makins had met sharp at nine o'clock on Wednesday morning.

'It was early,' she said. She was seated behind her desk, her hands pressed together between her plump knees. 'Mr Drew had asked me to come in early that Monday as a special favour.'

'Janice lives locally,' explained the youthful Mr Drew, who was standing behind her. 'Almost round the corner, in fact.'

'Me and my boyfriend have got this flat above Jelke's the bakers, in High West Street,' explained Janice helpfully but unnecessarily. 'So it wasn't any bother.'

'And I live up in Yeovil,' said Drew, 'and I didn't fancy getting up an hour and a half earlier for the sake of one customer who wasn't likely to be in the shop for more than a few minutes.'

'So what time did he arrive, Janice?' asked Roper, for the second time.

'He was on the doorstep when I got here,' said Janice.

'Which was when?' asked Roper patiently and for the third time.

'About twenty to eight,' said Janice at last. 'Like a cat on hot bricks, he was. A bit cross actually, because Mr Drew had told him over the phone that someone'd be here at half-past seven. But we've got one of those clock-radio-alarm things and we didn't have the instructions with it so we never have been able to set it properly and—'

'I think you're going on a bit, Janice,' cautioned Mr Drew.

'Sorry,' said Janice, looking chastened and pressing her knees even tighter together.

'So you gave him the ticket personally,' said Roper. 'Do you usually do that?'

'It depends if we really know who we're dealing with,' said Drew. 'If we recognise them, then yes.'

'And you recognised Mr Robinson?'

'Oh, yes,' said Janice. 'I was the one who arranged his air tickets. And I remember him specially because when he first came in he knew exactly what he wanted, routes and take-off times and all that sort of thing. Most of the people who come in are a bit vague, you know. Some of them aren't even sure where they want to go. I had a couple in yesterday who thought the Algarve was in Spain, for instance. And he paid spot cash. I mean money-cash, ten-pound notes and things.'

'We got the impression he was a seasoned traveller,' said Drew.

'Do you remember what this Mr Robinson looked like, Janice?' asked Roper.

'Oh, yes,' she said. 'Big. *Really* big, you know. And he wore glasses.'

'How tall?'

'Very,' said Janice, who without her stiletto heels would scarcely top five feet and was therefore perhaps not the best of judges.

'Mr Drew?'

'Sorry,' said Drew. 'The only time I saw him was when he first came in here, and that was several months ago.'

'Anything else you remember about him, Janice?'

'Well,' said Janice, frowning into space. 'He wasn't bald like Yul Brynner was bald because he had hair at the sides and back, but the top of his head was sort of shiny like.'

From his document case, Roper took out Miss Pringle's newspaper cutting showing Dr Gribo on his way to Crete. Carefully folding it so that Janice and Drew couldn't see the caption he held it out to each of them.

'This couldn't possibly be him?'

Drew shook his head.

'No,' said Janice. 'Sorry. Too much hair.'

'But you still have his address on your computer?' said Roper.

'Oh, yes,' said Drew. 'We keep names and addresses for six months in case somebody makes a complaint or an insurance claim. Although I'm not sure I can let you have access without a warrant or something of that sort. I'm not being obstructive, of course, but it's something we make a practice of. Personal privacy and all that sort of thing. I'm sure you understand.'

'Yes, I do understand, Mr Drew,' said Roper. 'And I could get a warrant by this afternoon, but time's a bit pressing, you see, sir. So perhaps I ought to tell you that Constable Makins and I are here in pursuance of a murder enquiry.'

Janice's eyes popped huge and round.

'And you think this Mr Robinson might be involved?' asked Drew, also somewhat taken aback.

'Let's say he might be a witness we'd like to talk to, sir,' said Makins.

'Well, that certainly puts a different aspect on the matter,' admitted Drew reluctantly. 'But I'm still not certain how the law stands on that sort of thing.'

'Let me suggest another way then, Mr Drew,' said Roper, who having come this far refused to be baulked.

'We'll tell you what *we* know about Mr Robinson and all you've got to do is say yea or nay. How does that suit you?'

Drew lifted his hands in instant agreement. 'Fine,' he said. 'Seems the best way out all round. Mind finding Mr Robinson's info on the computer, Janice?'

Janice teetered on her spikes to another desk where the agency's computer held pride of place. She switched it on and expertly dabbed out a sequence of keys. Drew by this time had gone to stand behind her and was watching the screen.

'Right,' he said. 'We've got him up.'

'Mr M R Robinson,' said Roper, over the top of the computer screen, 'Twenty-four, Masons Avenue, Dorchester.'

'Right,' said Drew.

'Wrong,' said Roper. 'There *is* a Masons Avenue, but there is no number twenty-four and there never has been. I know. I've been there.'

'But why on earth would he have given us a false address?' asked a puzzled Drew.

'That's precisely what we're trying to find out, Mr Drew,' said Roper. 'The hinge-pin of our enquiries, you might say. D'you mind telling us exactly when Mr Robinson came in here and booked those tickets?'

More forthcoming now that he might have been duped, Drew peered closer at the screen. 'April the fifth, this year.'

'Well in advance then,' said Roper.

'Seemingly,' said Drew. 'But then a lot of people do. And it's always the best way if you want to fly to somewhere like Crete at the height of the holiday season.'

'But he booked to fly back the day after he flew out,' said Roper.

'Correct,' said Drew.

'A bit strange that, sir,' commented Roper. 'Someone forking out several hundred quid on a scheduled flight to spend just the one night on Crete. That didn't strike you as odd at the time?'

'Well, no, it didn't, in fact,' said Drew. 'I thought he might have been an executive of some sort flying out for a business meeting.'

'He looked the executive sort, did he?'

Drew deferred to Janice, whose last sighting of Robinson had been the more recent.

'Well,' she said, wrinkling her snub nose thoughtfully. 'It's hard to say, really. But he was certainly dolled up smart. Not exactly trendy, you know, he was a bit past that, but he was certainly very smart. Suit and tie and everything.'

'Can you put an age to him, Janice?' asked Makins.

'Hard to say,' she said. 'He was wearing glasses, and glasses make people look older, don't they? And I never have been very good at guessing people's ages. 'Bout forty or fifty, I suppose. Could've been even older than that, of course.'

Something else struck Roper then, born of an earlier fragment of their conversation. 'This Mr Robinson booked his flight last April, you say?'

Drew checked the computer screen. 'Correct.'

'And he was booked to fly out of Gatwick around lunchtime on Monday the third of August?'

'Correct,' said Drew.

'And yet he didn't pick up his tickets until the morning of the third. And he'd got to get from here to Gatwick. Cutting it a bit fine, wasn't he?'

'Yes, well,' said Drew, 'I told him that when he rang here on the previous Saturday lunchtime.'

'So you've got a telephone number for him?' said Roper, brightening considerably. That was one thing that couldn't be faked.

'No,' said Drew. 'He said there was no point in leaving one, because his job took him around the country a lot. But he phoned here once a fortnight or so to keep in touch and on the week before he flew out he rang every morning to see if the tickets had arrived. He rang on the Saturday prior to his flight. I told him the tickets were here and he said he'd collect them early on the Monday morning. Which is why I made the arrangement with Janice to come in early. I did warn him that he might be pushed for time between here and Gatwick but he told me it would be no problem.'

'He came to collect his tickets in a car,' piped up Janice, as she suddenly recalled that. 'I remember, because he parked it half on the pavement and when he went out there was a policeman waiting for him. The law's got very hot on parking on pavements round here.'

'Can you remember what sort of car it was, Janice?' Makins asked, more in hope than expectation.

'No,' she said. 'Sorry. I sort of remember it was a cream one, but I'm not even really sure about that.'

'Did he buy any travellers' cheques from here, Mr Drew?' asked Roper.

'No,' said Drew. 'But we did organise some Greek currency for him.' He leaned over Janice's shoulder towards the computer screen again. 'Twenty-five thousand *drachmae,* according to our records, which is the limit a tourist is allowed to take into Greece. I seem to remember his telling me that if he needed any more he'd be using his credit cards.'

'That's right,' agreed Janice. 'He told me that, too.'

'And you made a booking for him at the Hotel Ionia?'

'That's right,' said Janice.

So Mr M R Robinson, if he existed anywhere but on a computer screen, was a big, bald man who dressed smartly and wore spectacles. He had gone to Crete with a handful of untraceable Greek banknotes, and maybe even a stolen or faked set of credit cards, and drove a car that might have been cream.

As ends went, this one could not have been deader.

AFTER LUNCH, Roper changed his striped necktie for a black one, and Dan Morgan, who usually affected the worn and crumpled look, appeared in Roper's office soon afterwards in a similar tie and a newly pressed dark grey suit. He brought with him the Cellophane-wrapped sheaf of flowers that had just arrived downstairs at the reception desk, the black-bordered card on the flowers bearing the legend 'from Sheila Carmody and Douglas Roper'. The funeral service for Susan Gribo was to take place that afternoon in Nuncton Zelston. And that afternoon too, Roper would have his first meeting with Doctor Rex Gribo, something he was looking forward to with more than casual interest.

With Morgan at the wheel, they set off for Nuncton Zelston soon after two-thirty. For the second day running the weather was fine, and according to the weather-guessers the whole of southern England was imminently due for a belated heat wave.

Nuncton Zelston looked as if it had not stirred in fifty years: tree-shaded and hedge-lined lanes, Purbeck stone cottages, some thatched, some stone-tiled, and not a flower or shrub out of place. And as Morgan observed pithily, he could almost hear the ten-pound notes crackling under the tyres.

They arrived early and Morgan reversed the car and parked it in a lay-by from which they could just see the entrance to the church. The cortège appeared a few minutes after three o'clock, the flower-decked hearse first and a dozen or more smart cars pulling in behind it. Thirty or so mourners climbed out to stand around in silent groups as the clergyman came to the lychgate and the coffin was slid from the hearse. The man talking to the clergyman in the shade of the gate was probably Doctor Gribo, but he was too far away for Roper to recognise him on the strength of a fuzzy picture in a newspaper cutting.

As the coffin was lifted on to the bearers' shoulders and the mourners sorted themselves out into a file behind it, Roper and Morgan climbed out of their car, closed its doors quietly, and went briskly after them.

THE LITTLE CHURCH was very cool, very quiet, every pot and niche brimming with flowers. Roper and Morgan turned silently into the right-hand pew nearest the door, with the sunlight through the doorway spilling on to the worn stone flags beside them.

The four black-suited bearers, having set the coffin on to its trestles in front of the altar, glided away towards the vestry. Hymn books rustled and throats were cleared.

Silence. The clergyman lifted his head solemnly to commence the service.

Then footsteps on the gravelled path outside, a shadow darkening the worn and laminating flagstones, then louder footsteps ringing on the floor of the aisle as the new arrival entered the body of the church. Several heads in the front pews turned to see who it was.

He was an extremely tall, elegant and silver-haired man in a dark grey suit and grey silk tie. His stride was purposeful. He looked neither to left or right and seemed unperturbed at being the momentary centre of attention. He chose an empty pew on the left-hand side of the aisle, with two rows of empty pews in front of him and more behind him so that he was completely isolated. The person who watched him the longest and closest was Doctor Gribo.

And just as he had been the last to arrive, the moment the service and eulogies were over, and even before the bearers had reappeared from the vestry, so the silver-haired man left his pew and strode ringingly back towards the door with his narrow face grimly set and with not a single glance behind him. His chill gaze met Roper's briefly, his shadow moved out of the doorway and he was gone in a receding crackle of gravel.

'Follow him,' Roper whispered to Morgan. 'See if he came by car, and clock its registration number.'

Morgan went out quickly. Roper waited for the coffin and mourners to file by, then tagged on to the back of the line. Gribo and the clergyman were standing in the doorway and shaking hands with everyone as they passed out into the sunshine, a courtesy Roper was able to avoid in Gribo's case by appearing to have trouble with the flowers he was carrying. It was his practice never to shake hands with anyone who might, even remotely, belong to the other side. Mrs Gribo's mortal remains might be well on their way to their last resting place, but who had sent them there had still to be tracked down.

'I'm sorry,' said Gribo, looking quizzically at Roper as if he were trying to remember him from a previous occasion. He was an inch or two shorter than Roper, dark-haired, and so sallow-skinned that his dark and penetrating eyes looked even darker than they were. His hand had fallen back by his side. 'Do we know each other?'

'Douglas Roper, Doctor Gribo. We spoke on the phone yesterday evening.'

'Oh, yes,' murmured Gribo. Since the newspaper photograph had been taken, he had grown a small moustache. 'Yes, so we did. The chap who found poor Susan.' He moved away out of the porch, taking a hold on Roper's sleeve and steering him out on to the gravelled path where most of the mourners were milling about. Still holding Roper's sleeve he guided him across the grass of the graveyard until he was sure they were out of everyone's earshot.

'I wasn't aware until yesterday that you were a police officer, Mr Roper. Is that a coincidence, or does it mean that you're working on this dreadful business of my wife?'

'A little of both, sir,' said Roper, to Gribo's disappointment, or what certainly looked like disappointment. 'I happened to be staying in the hotel where Mrs Gribo died, and I've been asked to keep an eye on any developments in the investigation at the Cretan end. There's not much else we can do from this distance.'

'Investigations at the Cretan end,' Gribo muttered scornfully. 'My God, I don't think they've moved an inch since Susan was found. I spoke to some fellow—Spiridakis, I think his name was—very sympathetic of course, but utterly helpless when it came to catching whoever it was. And Crete's only a bloody little island, isn't it? Sorry—' he added, closing his eyes and bridging his nose with a thumb and a forefinger and briefly touching the inner corners of his eyes as if to staunch unseen tears. Then he was calm again. '—this is neither the time nor the place to hold this conversation, is it?' He drew himself upright and squared his shoulders. From the tail of his eye, Roper glimpsed Morgan coming back along the path from the lychgate.

'You kindly agreed to have a chat, Mr Roper,' said Gribo. 'Does that mean officially or unofficially? Only that Spiridakis fellow was very cagey. Really wasn't prepared to tell me very much at all. Asked more questions than I got answers.'

'I doubt I can tell you much more, sir,' said Roper. The coffin was back in the hearse and the door was being closed on it. 'In fact there are a few questions I'd like to ask you myself. Just loose ends, sir. A tidying-up job, that's all,' he added reassuringly.

'Yes, of course,' said Gribo. 'Anything I can do to help. I usually manage to take Thursday evenings off. How about tomorrow, eight o'clock, say? I'm easy to find.' He reached into the pocket of his dark suit, produced a wallet, from the wallet a business card. 'My home address is on the back.'

'I'll be there,' said Roper. 'Eight sharp.'

'Thank you,' said Gribo, and hurried across the grass to the waiting mourners around the lychgate.

'Any joy?' asked Roper, as Morgan joined him.

'Daimler Sovereign. Current registration plates and sprayed British racing-green. I'd say it was a special order. So he's probably loaded.'

'Check the car out with Swansea as soon as we get back,' said Roper. Because whoever the owner of the Daimler Sovereign had been, he had come to Susan Gribo's funeral service like an angry man who had been determined to make as much of a scene as he decently could. He had arrived and left in a rage and spoken to no one and that had to signify that he had been an unwilling party to the proceedings. And if that was so, why had he turned up at all?

WDC Weekes was at the coffee machine when Roper and Morgan stepped out of the lift.

'Any luck at the hospital, Alison?' asked Roper. Weekes' afternoon job had been a visit to the Eastern County General Hospital and specifically the hospital pharmacy.

'Yes, sir. A fair bit,' said Weekes, then took a sip of her coffee.

'Go and get your pocket-book and join me,' said Roper. 'You can bring your coffee.'

He was changing his necktie when Weekes came into his office with her coffee in one hand and her pocket-book in the other.

'Take a seat,' he said, 'and tell me all.'

'Well, sir, I phoned them first and asked if they'd noticed if any of those particular tranks had gone missing. They phoned me back about ten minutes afterwards, said they'd checked and found that there were thirteen tablets they couldn't account for. So I fixed up an appointment and went across to see the head pharmacist, a Mrs Mortley. I got the impression she runs a pretty tight ship and everything that comes into or goes out of the pharmacy is logged on a computer. Some of the really expensive drugs are kept in a steel cupboard with a combination lock.

'The tranks were brought into the pharmacy by the manufacturer's sales rep on Thursday, August thirteen. Apparently, he'd visited the hospital a couple of weeks before and talked about the product with Mrs Mortley and several of the doctors who were in the hospital at the time. They agreed to help out with the trials and the rep said he'd send them some samples. Two hundred and fifty arrived, sixty have been dispensed, according to the computer, so there ought to be a hundred and ninety left, but there's only a hundred and seventy-seven. Which leaves a shortfall of thirteen.'

'Perhaps somebody miscounted on a prescription,' said Roper.

'Everything's double-checked,' said Weekes. 'And according to Mrs Mortley, mistakes like that just don't happen.'

'So they were nicked.'

'It looks that way,' said Weekes. 'Except that the pharmacy's hardly an open house, even to the hospital staff.'

'What about Alexandra Higgs?'

'She used to go into the pharmacy at least once a week,' said Weekes. 'But so did a lot of other people. And since the pills are on a trial, there are only a few staff at the hospital who are in the know about them. But on the other hand anybody could have read the bumf about them that Mrs Mortley keeps on her computer.'

'How about the doctors who've prescribed them?'

'A Doctor MacWhinny—and Doctor Gribo. Both treat hospital out-patients for nervous disorders. Gribo's a consultant there, by the way. Highly regarded.'

'And do they actually go *into* the pharmacy?'

'Yes, sir,' said Weekes. 'Frequently. But so do all the other doctors. It's the only place in the hospital where they can press a button and get all the information on particular drugs. Side-effects and all that sort of thing.'

'And are drugs like tranquillisers kept locked up?'

'Nominally, yes, sir,' said Weekes. 'But the cupboard's open most of the time because there's usually one of the pharmacy staff taking something apart or putting something back. Mind you, you'd be pretty hard put to steal from it if you didn't work in the pharmacy.'

'But it's a long way from being impossible,' said Roper.

'Yes, sir,' agreed Weekes.

'Did you ask this Mrs Mortley how many tablets constituted a fatal overdose?'

'Yes, sir. She said it depended on individual metabolisms and general state of health, but she reckons that half a dozen taken all at the one time would lay out the average person for at least twenty-four hours. And a dozen might be fatal if the person were left long enough without treatment of some kind. And the one thing that mustn't be taken with them is alcohol, even with the standard dose. And when I asked what would happen if someone mixed a dozen tablets with a pint of vodka, she said she wouldn't rate their chances of survival very highly at all.

'And then we got talking about Higgs. She didn't strike Mrs Mortley as being suicidal. She always seemed to exude self-confidence and was extremely good at her job. Hyper-efficient, according to Mrs Mortley. Oh, and something else, Mrs Mortley saw her with a man in the hospital car park a few weeks back. Her description was a bit vague, but she remembers that he was bald and fairly tall. She only saw his top half, but she thinks he was wearing some kind of black uniform with brass buttons.'

'Haddowes,' said Roper.

'That's what I thought,' said Weekes. 'Anyway, I went up to the hospital personnel department and asked if I could look at Higgs' records, but they wouldn't let me without a warrant. But the personnel officer was prepared to talk in general. According to her, Higgs went on the skids after her aunt's funeral—'

'Which we already knew.'

'Yes, I know,' said Weekes. 'But I persuaded her to at least let me have the dates when that happened.' She turned over another page of her pocket-book. 'The third to the fifth of August. And when she came back to work on the sixth, she didn't turn up until nearly lunchtime. With her hair cropped and dyed black, and looking like death—I quote.'

And death for Higgs it had eventually been. And coincidentally—or was it?—it had been on the third of August, when Higgs had first been absent from work, that Mrs Gribo was murdered in Agios Mateos.

'And I asked for information on Higgs' next-of-kin,' continued Weekes, 'but there was only the aunt and she was struck off when she died and they don't even have her address any more.'

'Pity,' said Roper. 'But well done anyway.'

Morgan came in as Weekes went out.

The registered keeper of the Daimler Sovereign was one Donald Arthur West of 14 Alwick Drive, Preston Park, in the county of Sussex. Not that that necessarily meant that he was the silver-haired driver of the vehicle that afternoon, but whoever Mr West was he would not have lent a car like that to someone he did not know uncommonly well.

'Tried Directory Enquiries for his phone number?'

'And tried the number,' said Morgan. 'I couldn't even raise an answering machine.'

'Try again tomorrow,' said Roper. 'And let me know when you come up with something.'

THE FORENSIC LABORATORY made contact soon after five o'clock that same evening. Preliminary tests on the loose screw taken from Higgs' carpet-edging had shown that there had been a minute fragment of flesh caught up on it and that it had been fairly recently deposited, certainly within the last week or so. Had the wound been on the underside of Higgs' heel then it could reasonably be supposed that she had walked barefooted over the screw at some recent time and snagged her skin on it. But the wound was at the back of her heel and the only way for that to have happened was for her to have been dragged over it, drunk, drugged, and probably inert.

ELEVEN

'WHAT WAS Doctor Gribo like?' asked Sheila Carmody, deftly trapping a pork-ball between the tips of her chopsticks. It was ten o'clock on that same Wednesday evening, their venue a pinkly lit Chinese restaurant near Bournemouth pier.

'Average sort of bloke,' said Roper, plying his knife and fork. He never had developed the knack of wielding chopsticks. 'He didn't think much of Ioánnis Spiridakis. Reckons he's a bit of a slouch. He wants me to go along to his house tomorrow evening and have a chat about it.'

'Should be interesting. Will you go?'

'Definitely.'

'Officially or unofficially?'

'Officially,' said Roper. 'Only I won't be telling him that unless I catch him out on something.'

'You've got doubts about him then?'

'Not sure,' said Roper. 'He couldn't have killed her personally because he wasn't there, but he might have made an arrangement with somebody else to have done it for him. Tell me,' he said then, changing the subject as he topped up her wine glass, 'why does a woman dye her hair?'

'Lots of reasons,' she said. 'Changing an image she's got fed up with, mostly, I suppose. Or to look young—or if they're very young, to look older. Or just to see what they look like some other way. What brought that strange question on?'

'An investigation we're handling. She was about thirty, good-looking, very bright, holding down a pretty responsible job and well on the way to get an even better one. The way we hear it, she had long blonde hair—natural, apparently—then one day she turns up at work after a few days' absence with her locks shorn down to boy-style and dyed jet black.'

'If she was a natural blonde, I'd say she was daft,' said Sheila. 'Blondes and redheads mostly leave well alone. Unless it was something to do with a man, of course, but it sounds a pretty drastic step even then. Or,' she added, more jokingly, as she helped herself to another pork-ball in batter, 'if she thought you were investigating her, she might have decided to disguise herself in order to slip away to furrin' parts.'

Yes, that was certainly an idea. It was something Roper hadn't thought of so far, that Higgs might have had some reason for disguising herself.

'Why are you investigating her?'

'Well, it looks as if she committed suicide, but on the other hand she might not have. It's also likely that she was in cahoots with somebody else, who was a bit of a villain; and her doctor's a partner of Doctor Gribo's; and she used to work in the same hospital where Gribo's some kind of consultant in nervous disorders.'

'Sounds a bit of a muddle to me.'

'Worse,' grumbled Roper. 'The whole thing's a mess from start to finish.'

'A strange coincidence that Doctor Gribo's cropped up again,' observed Sheila. 'Think there's anything in that?'

'That's what I keep wondering,' said Roper. 'He keeps turning up all over the place. The police doctor who examined the body is another partner of Gribo's, although

I didn't know it at the time. If I had, I'd have called in someone else to cast an eye over her.'

'That sounds like an awful lot of Gribos to me,' said Sheila.

'Aye,' he said. 'That's what I keep thinking. But it's not what I think, it's what I know, and I can prove beyond reasonable doubt, as the legal-eagles say. And I really can't prove a damned thing.'

'Perhaps Gribo'll slip up tomorrow and fill in some of the gaps.'

'I doubt it,' said Roper. 'If he's involved in any of it, he's been pretty smart so far.'

THURSDAY BEGAN with a phone call from Doctor Weygood, and that was to verify the nature of the tablets Higgs had taken and to confirm the quantity of alcohol and gas that had been found in her bloodstream. The percentage of absolute alcohol in Higgs' blood samples had been found to be 0.6 per cent, which was equivalent to fifteen single whiskies—half a bottle—which, especially in a woman, was enough to induce unconsciousness if taken over a short enough period of time, which it obviously had been.

'Which raises another point,' said Weygood.

'I know,' said Roper. 'If she was unconscious, how did she get from where the glass and bottle were to the kitchen.'

'Precisely,' said Weygood irritably, irked at being forestalled. 'It wouldn't have been *entirely* impossible, of course, but it has to raise certain doubts, especially considering that wound on her heel. And the tranquillisers, have you been able to ascertain whence they came?'

'Yes, sir,' said Roper. 'The pharmacy of the Eastern County General Hospital where Higgs worked.'

'Splendid,' said Weygood, with a rare magnanimity. 'But did she steal them for herself or did someone else?'

'Can't say,' said Roper. 'Wish I could. How about the gas she'd inhaled?'

'Only a very small concentration,' said Weygood. 'Barely perceptible in the blood sample. She might have choked on that but in my opinion it was more than likely that she gagged on her own vomit. All very sad and unnecessary,' he added, with an equally rare humanity.

'So what do you think: she was helped, or did she do it all on her own?'

'You know full well I'm far too prudent to answer that officially, Mr Roper,' said Weygood. 'That's your job. But if you had been a fly on my office wall yesterday evening, you might have heard Miss Glover say something like: "I honestly can't believe that this was a straightforward suicide". To which I replied something like: "No. No more can I, Miss Glover." But you won't be getting that in writing, you understand.'

'Understood, Doctor Weygood,' said Roper, with a small smile. It sounded as if Weygood was beginning to mellow with age. He would be retiring soon, too. 'And one more thing before you go: do you think Higgs would have had the physical strength to deliver the blow that killed Albert Haddowes? Or, put it this way, supposing Miss Glover had asked you that same question in the quiet of your office over a cup of tea?'

'I think a cautious yes, Mr Roper,' said Weygood. 'Assuming that she had good reason. Did she have a good reason?'

'I wish I knew, sir,' said Roper. 'Thanks for your help, anyway.'

Motive. That was the essence of everything at the moment, and there was a monumental lack of it. As yet there was no apparent motive for the killing of Albert Haddowes, no apparent motive for Higgs' suicide except an overwhelming guilt because she had killed Haddowes—an assumption which was riddled with doubts—and there was still no motive for the murder of Mrs Gribo on Crete.

There were only connections. A woman with a car similar to Higgs' had been seen with Haddowes. Higgs worked in the same hospital as Doctor Gribo. Mrs Gribo had been murdered, and a man called Robinson, or so he wished everyone to believe, had flown swiftly to Crete and back again at the time Mrs Gribo had met her end. And over that same period, Higgs had taken leave to attend her aunt's funeral and returned to work with an altered persona and her blonde hair shorn and dyed black. And it was more than possible that those apparent connections were nothing of the kind, that they were pure and disconnected coincidences, so that however often Roper tried to squeeze some sort of coherent order out of them and juggled with all their possible permutations, he was never going to make them a whole. According to the gossip, Haddowes had had a sister-in-law and a niece, and it was just possible that Higgs was the niece, and the sister-in-law was the aunt whom Higgs had buried. And assuming that was so—albeit another rash assumption—then all three were now dead and beyond the investigation's ken. And anyway, was their possible connection relevant to the investigation, was it worth looking into, did it matter, or would it provide yet another cul-de-sac, like that visit to Masons Avenue and finding the barrier of the spiked railings rendering further advance impossible?

Morgan called into Roper's office at lunchtime. He had made several attempts to contact the silver-haired Mr West during the course of the morning, but without success. He had left a message with the switchboard downstairs to ring

West's number every couple of hours and let him know if and when they managed to get an answer.

'I'm just sitting around, guv'nor,' complained a frustrated Morgan. 'I'm just not earning my crust.'

'Join the club, old son,' said Roper. 'There's not much going on in here either.'

IN THE AFTERNOON, however, there came a hint of gathering momentum, although it began with only a small stuttering lurch.

A Mr Woodley had just rung in. He had spoken to WDC Weekes.

'He and his wife want to speak to the senior officer on the Haddowes investigation, so he says. But he doesn't want to talk on the phone and doesn't want the neighbours to see police cars and uniforms outside his house. He says they're both prepared to come here, but only on the understanding there's absolutely no way their names get into the newspapers. I think he's a bit weird actually, sir,' added Weekes. 'It took me about five minutes to persuade him to give me his name. And he won't give me his address even now. Will you see him?'

'Is he still on the phone?'

'Yes, sir,' said Weekes. 'He says they can be here in half an hour.'

'Tell him I'll be waiting for him,' said Roper.

'I'm not even sure he's on the up and up, sir,' cautioned Weekes. 'He was very insistent on knowing if we had a car park, how big the spaces are, and if we charged for them.'

'Perhaps he's got a sense of humour.'

'No, sir, not this one. He's definitely an oddball.'

'Well, get back to him before we lose 'im,' said Roper. 'And tell him I await his pleasure. And join us when they arrive, please.'

They turned up soon after three o'clock. Roper's first glimpse of them was a squat, fat Austin A35 of early 'sixties vintage, its lovingly polished pale blue paintwork and chrome fittings twinkling in the sunshine. It quartered the half-acre of car park twice, tentatively nosed its snub bonnet into several wide and vacant spaces, thought better of it and finally settled itself between two white pursuit cars where it managed to look like a pekingese flanked by a pair of whippets.

Its passengers climbed out. Both were tall and plank-thin, both wore spectacles. Despite the heat of the afternoon, both wore dark and heavy outer coats, he a trilby hat pulled well down over his forehead, she a brown headscarf tightly knotted under her chin. Both ducked their heads furtively and hurried across the tarmac to the back entrance.

Weekes showed them into Roper's office, Miss Pringle close behind to do the honours with the tea or coffee.

'Tea, if you please,' said Mr Woodley, deeply and sonorously as he took off his trilby and held it across his chest like a mourner. 'Without milk and without sugar.'

'Not for me, thank you,' said Mrs Woodley disapprovingly, and examined the seat of Roper's new visitor's chair with great care before she lowered herself to the edge of it and took a tighter grip of the handbag standing on her lap.

Her husband sat beside her, his overcoat still buttoned and his trilby hat still held against his chest. He glanced pointedly at Weekes, who had brought in another chair and was sitting at the end of the desk. 'We were led to believe that we would be speaking with you alone, Superintendent.'

'WDC Weekes is a police officer, Mr Woodley,' said Roper. 'I can promise you our strictest confidence.'

The Woodleys looked at each other hesitantly. They were both in their early sixties. Roper had read somewhere that married couples eventually grew to look alike, as the Woodleys did, sitting there like a couple of stiff, prim cadavers waiting for a train. Both wore their sombre clothes like a clumsily assumed disguise.

'We read about it in the newspaper,' Mr Woodley began.

'The weekly *free* newspaper,' Mrs Woodley explained quickly. 'The advertising one. We don't *buy* newspapers.'

'And we usually throw the free newspaper *straight* into the dustbin,' said Mr Woodley. He had lowered his trilby hat to his lap and was clutching the brim with both hands as if he were hiding a rabbit inside it and didn't want it to escape. It was difficult to connect either of them with the big, blustering and thieving Albert Haddowes.

'But this morning Mr Woodley happened to notice Albert's name on the front page, under the headline. If it had been on the back page he wouldn't have seen it,' Mrs Woodley further explained.

Mr Woodley adjusted his spectacles and cleared his throat delicately. 'We have not seen him for years, of course. Not since Jean died.'

'The funeral,' said Mrs Woodley.

'Yes, quite,' agreed her husband. 'Jean's funeral. That was the last time.'

'Jean being . . . ?' asked Roper, recalling that Jean had been the name of Haddowes' wife.

'My sister,' said Mrs Woodley. Weekes' ballpoint stilled momentarily over her jotter and Roper sat more upright in his chair. 'She married Albert Haddowes. The Beast, we called him. A dreadful man.'

Mr Woodley cleared his throat warningly before his wife got too carried away on the subject of Albert Haddowes' shortcomings. 'It was not a happy marriage,' he explained. 'Not happy at all.'

'So you're Mr Haddowes' sister-in-law, Mrs Woodley?' asked Roper.

'Yes,' she agreed, with a disparaging twitch of her mouth. 'Regrettably.'

'Albert was not the pleasantest of men,' explained Mr Woodley.

'Yes, so we've heard, sir,' said Roper. It seemed at last that he was close to resolving at least one of the possible links that had been nagging at him for days. 'Do either of you happen to know a young woman named Alexandra Higgs?'

'My niece,' said Mrs Woodley, with tight-lipped disdain, and to Roper's further gratification. 'When her mother, my other sister, died, Mr Woodley and I took her in. Fed her, clothed her, saw that she went to a good school. *And* sent her money when she went away to university. Like a mother and father to her, we were; better in some ways. And when she left the university, we hardly ever saw her again.'

'A most ungrateful child,' said Mr Woodley.

'When did you last see her?' Roper asked.

'Christmas,' said Mr Woodley.

'Easter,' countered Mrs Woodley. 'She dropped by in her car. She was very adept at "dropping by". Always on her way somewhere, she was. Never stayed more than a few minutes, couldn't wait to be off again.'

'So you didn't see her at the funeral of her other aunt?' said Roper. 'Four or five weeks back?'

The Woodleys looked at each other blankly.

'She had no other aunts,' said Mrs Woodley sternly. 'Except my sister Jean. That's the Jean that married Albert Haddowes.'

'Do either of you know if Haddowes had any other living relatives, by any chance?' asked Roper.

'None,' said Mr Woodley. 'So far as we are aware.'

Roper considered that at some length, then said, 'Will you both excuse Constable Weekes and me for a moment?' And rose and went outside with Weekes close behind him. He waited until she had drawn the door to.

'Phone the Eastern County General Hospital's personnel manager again, Alison. I want to know the name of the aunt who was supposed to be Higgs' next of kin, the one she buried.'

'It's like I told you, sir,' said Weekes. 'The name was scrubbed off the computer when the aunt died.'

'She'll be on a file of some sort as well, bet your life. Get 'em to look it out. And if they want to see a warrant for a piddling thing like that, tell 'em we think we know how those tablets went missing from the pharmacy. You can mention Higgs' name as a suspect if you like.'

'Right,' said Weekes, and went off towards the squad office, while Roper held the door open for Miss Pringle who was coming along the passage with a laden tea-tray.

'I thought you might like some biscuits,' said Miss Pringle brightly as she set the tray on the corner of Roper's desk.

'No, thank you,' said Mrs Woodley.

'One hesitates because one can no longer trust the ingredients they put into them these days,' Mr Woodley explained gravely. 'But thank you for the thought.'

Miss Pringle distributed the three cups and saucers around the desk and stood the sugar bowl beside Roper's blotter. Mrs Woodley picked up her husband's cup of tea and scrutinised it closely before she passed it to him. Weekes had been dead right. The Woodleys certainly were an odd pair.

Woodley took a prim sip of his tea and Mrs Woodley watched with disapproval as Roper tipped two heaped spoonfuls of sugar into his.

'I am somewhat curious, Superintendent,' said Woodley, carefully setting his cup back on its saucer. 'We came here to talk of Albert Haddowes, and now you have raised the subject of my wife's niece for some reason. We wondered why that was.'

Roper braced himself to break the news to them. There never was a right time and never quite the right words, or if there were he had never managed to find them.

'I'm afraid I have some bad news for you both,' he said, and paused for a moment while they digested that and readied themselves. 'It's about Alexandra. I'm afraid your niece is dead, Mrs Woodley. I'm deeply sorry.'

They stared at him in surprise from behind their spectacles, Mr Woodley's cup poised in mid-air on its way to his mouth.

'We think it happened some time during last weekend,' said Roper.

Woodley's cup went quietly back on its saucer. Given the circumstances, both of them looked surprisingly calm.

'I have no doubt it was God's will,' said Mr Woodley solemnly. 'We had no idea that she was ill.'

'She wasn't ill, sir,' said Roper. 'Not according to the post-mortem examination. It's a little more complicated than that. All the evidence we've managed to gather so far points to Miss Higgs having taken her own life.' Or not, as the case might yet prove to be, but he deemed it wiser to withhold what was only guess-work for the time being. 'As I said, I'm deeply sorry to have to break the news to you both like this.'

'We are all in the midst of death all the time, Superintendent,' said Mr Woodley, his cup rising again as if this was something he had expected all along.

'She was *Mrs* Higgs, in fact,' said Mrs Woodley, showing as little emotion as her husband. 'There is a husband and a child.'

Which was a further complication Roper could well have done without.

'They are . . .' Woodley shrank from the word, but then forced it out of himself as if he were uttering an obscenity, ' . . . divorced. We believe the husband and child are presently living in New Zealand. The husband was . . . ah . . . given custody of the child. There is much we could tell you of Alexandra, Superintendent,' he added meaningfully as he dipped his nose into his cup again.

'Such as, sir?'

Woodley peered over the top of his spectacles at his wife.

'She was a hussy,' said Mrs Woodley.

Roper waited for more.

'Men,' explained Mr Woodley. 'Even as an adolescent girl.'

'Several times we were forced to lock her in her bedroom,' said Mrs Woodley. 'And at sixteen, she had started to wear make-up. Boys were *always* lurking around the house. She was a great trial to both of us.'

'And we were always perfectly reasonable,' went on Mr Woodley. 'We allowed her out at least two nights a week, and provided she told us exactly where she was going and with whom and was home by nine o'clock we *never* questioned her.'

'And then she met this young man at the university,' continued Mrs Woodley. 'We quite liked him, his parents were practising Christians, you see, like ourselves, and they married—'

'For which we paid *all* the expenses,' Mr Woodley broke in self-righteously. 'We begrudged her nothing.'

'—and we hoped she would lose her wildness and settle down,' continued Mrs Woodley, blinking behind her spectacles. 'But no sooner had the baby arrived than she left her husband and took up with someone else.'

'So she hadn't changed,' observed Mr Woodley. 'But she came from bad stock, you see. Her father was a most disreputable man. He drank.'

'Her mother was not all she should have been, either,' Mrs Woodley added darkly. 'One should not speak ill of one's own sister, but she wasn't.'

'But we never did understand Alexandra's pursuit of men because in every other respect she was such a *remarkably* intelligent young woman,' said Mr Woodley, as if this dichotomy still pained him and he was still seeking the answer to it.

'How about recent men-friends?' asked Roper.

'We have no idea,' said Mr Woodley. 'It would be true to say that we have not had her confidence for many a long year.'

'Did you know that she was working as a secretary at the local hospital?' asked Roper.

'No,' said Mrs Woodley, shaking her head. 'The last thing I heard from her was that she was thinking of leaving the agency she was managing and going on to something that paid better. That was at Easter.'

Weekes came back in after a courtesy rap on the door. As she resumed her chair she leaned across the desk and laid a folded sheet of paper ripped from a shorthand pad beside the cup and saucer on Roper's blotter.

He plucked it up and unfolded it.

The lady designated at the hospital as having been Alexandra Higgs' next of kin, and who was now supposedly deceased, was a Mrs Doris May Woodley. And since there were allegedly no other aunts of Higgs presently alive, that same lady was obviously the one sitting at the other side of his desk. He folded the paper and passed it back to Weekes.

'Do you know how well your niece got on with Albert Haddowes, Mrs Woodley?' he asked then.

'Oh, they were *very* thick together,' replied Mrs Woodley.

'Birds of a feather, one might say,' added Mr Woodley.

And, naturally enough, what they had really come here for was to put the boot in on Albert Haddowes the wife-beater, which they then proceeded to do in great detail and great and sanctimonious length, all but salivating over the drunken escapade in the public house which had nearly put him in prison.

'Not that we are vindictive people, you must under-stand,' explained Mr Woodley, when they had finally ex-hausted their accusations against the late Albert. 'But we felt bound to tell you everything we knew of him. We thought it possible that his depravity may have ordered his end. He would have kept bad company, you see, and it may not have occurred to you to enquire among his asso-ciates.'

'That's certainly an angle worth thinking about, Mr Woodley,' said Roper, straight-faced and to the Wood-leys' immense satisfaction, forbearing for the time being to tell them that a possible suspect was their late and un-lamented niece. 'You mentioned just now that your niece worked for an agency before she went to work at the hos-pital; it might be useful if we had a chat with the people there. Can you tell us anything about it?'

But neither of the Woodleys had even the faintest idea of the firm's name.

'But we know that she worked there for several years,' said Mr Woodley, 'and that she was what I believe is called an area manager.'

'And they gave her a car,' said Mrs Woodley.

'*And* free travel,' said Mr Woodley. 'Including abroad.'

'It was a travel agency, you see,' explained Mrs Woodley.

At which Roper lifted his head like a gun-dog.

'Does the Goldfinch Travel Agency in Dorchester ring any bells?' he asked.

But the Woodleys were too scrupulously honest to commit themselves to any name.

'But it was a *chain* of offices,' said Mrs Woodley. 'I know that because when Alexandra dropped in one day, she told me that she was on her way to the firm's branch in Torquay.'

'That was her area, you see,' said Mr Woodley. 'The south-west.'

'And the head office was in Dorchester,' added Mrs Woodley, as she suddenly remembered that too. 'Because she asked me once if she could use our telephone to ring them because she was going to be late for an appointment.'

Weekes saw the Woodleys back downstairs and Roper watched from his window as Woodley drove as cautiously out of the car park as he had driven into it. To the very end they had declined to give Roper either their address or telephone number, although he had managed to persuade them to sign Weekes' record of their joint responses and Mrs Woodley had signed herself as Doris M Woodley (Mrs), so she was definitely the lady lately deceased according to Higgs' hospital records. They had begged yet again that no connection be made publicly with their name and that of Albert Haddowes. At the office door, Woodley had put out his hand and assured Roper earnestly that he would pray for his every success in the investigation.

Perhaps they had not been able to tell him anything new, except to clear up the familial relationship between Higgs and Haddowes—which might turn out in the end to be totally irrelevant to the matters at hand—but the casual mention that Higgs had worked for a travel agency had interested him greatly. And the germ of an idea was sprouting at last.

TWELVE

A COMBINED CAMPAIGN with telephones and the Yellow Pages soon located the Wesco Travel Agency, the former employers of Alexandra Higgs, at their head office in Dorchester. It was a phone call from Dan Morgan that finally tracked them down.

'—and if we can get there before five-thirty, the boss man says he's willing to talk to us and help us all he can. He's sorry about the five-thirty deadline, but he's got a Chamber of Commerce dinner tonight and he's the main speaker, so he can't afford to be late. I'll nip along there now, if you like, and take Alison Weekes with me.'

'I'll come with you,' said Roper. 'No disrespect, Dan, but I've got a few questions I want to ask them on my own account.'

They were in Dorchester well before five o'clock. The Wesco Travel Agency's head office was situated on two floors above its own double-fronted shop front, and was one of eight branches according to a poster standing in the window.

One of the assistants led the way upstairs and handed them over to the managing director's secretary, who in her turn showed them into that man's palatial office overlooking the high street.

'Jack Gentry,' he said, rising from his chair and extending a hand across his desk.

'Superintendent Roper, Mr Gentry. And this is Sergeant Morgan.'

Gentry offered them both tea, or coffee, and seemed relieved when they declined. But then he did appear to be a busy man. He was about forty, thickly set, and with the bull-neck of a man who had played a lot of rugby in his time. The top of his desk was a colourful mosaic of printers' proof-sheets, presumably for next year's holiday brochures. He was briskly down to business.

'We're all pretty devastated,' he said. 'We had no idea that this had happened until I heard it from Sergeant Morgan earlier on. Some kind of accident, obviously.'

'No, sir,' said Roper. 'All the evidence so far indicates that Mrs Higgs took her own life, sad to say.'

Gentry looked the sort who was rarely dumbfounded by anything; but he certainly was now.

'But how . . . I mean, for God's sake, *why?* The Alex we all knew here just *wasn't* the suicidal type. She was a real go-getter, one of the world's greatest optimists. I just can't imagine her doing *anything* like that.'

'Well, to be strictly honest with you, Mr Gentry,' Roper conceded, 'we are looking into other possibilities, but we don't have any real evidence. We hoped you might be able to fill us in with a bit of background material on Mrs Higgs.'

'If I can,' said Gentry. 'But she never discussed her private life to any great extent, and I have to confess my surprise that she was a married woman. According to our records—' he paused briefly to grope beneath his sheets of proofs and finally produced Higgs' personal file '—she listed herself as single. Here, you see?' He had abstracted a sheet of computer print-out paper from the file and passed it across the desk. 'That's all the information she gave us when we took her on a few years back. And, so far as I'm aware, the only thing that changed was her address. She moved house about three years ago. Bought

herself a little two up and two down over at Monksbridge.
A new development. Only a small place, but it seemed to
suit her. You can keep that, by the way. I had it run off just
before you arrived.'

'Obliged to you, sir,' said Roper. 'Thank you.' Here at
Wesco too, Higgs had given her immediate next of kin as
Mrs Doris May Woodley. 'I hear she had a pretty good job
with your organisation.'

'Yes, she did,' agreed Gentry. 'She was my right arm,
you might say. A trouble-shooter *extraordinaire*. If a
problem came up in any of the branches, I'd fire Alexandra in their direction and she'd almost always sort it out in
a brace of shakes. Staff problems, customer problems, financial problems, Alex could sort them all out. When she
left my own workload doubled, that's how valuable she
was to us.'

'Did she give a reason for leaving?'

'She told me she wanted a change. I offered her another three thousand a year to stay, but she wouldn't. I
even offered her a junior partnership.'

According to the print-out, Higgs' salary upon depart-
ing Wesco Travel had been fifteen thousand a year, together with a company car valued at a further two
thousand a year. It seemed strange that she had been prepared to leave Wesco for a job that Roper doubted paid
much more than two-thirds of that and certainly wouldn't
have a car to go with it, simply for the sake of making a
change.

'Do you know if she had any men-friends, Mr Gentry?'

'Yes, I think so,' said Gentry. 'Latterly, anyway. I eat
across the road at the Red Lion. A couple of times I saw
her in there with a man. A dark-corner job. They looked
pretty close, if you know what I mean.'

'Any chance you could describe him, sir?' asked Morgan.

'No, not really,' said Gentry. 'Except I recall that he seemed a lot older than Alex, and I thought he might have been a policeman. He was wearing some sort of dark uniform.'

Albert Haddowes again, surely. For a niece and an uncle-in-law, Higgs and Haddowes seemed to have done a lot of drinking together.

'Any idea when that was, Mr Gentry?' asked Roper.

'Not long before she left us, I think,' said Gentry, frowning. 'A few weeks, perhaps.' Still frowning, he glanced down at his colourful sheets of proofs and fiddled absently with the bottom edge of one. 'Look,' he said awkwardly then, still fiddling, 'there is something else that perhaps I ought to tell you.'

And Roper, with an instinct honed by twenty-odd years of rubbing shoulders with other people's consciences, guessed that Jack Gentry was about to bare his soul before someone else bared it before him.

'You'll obviously be asking around,' said Gentry, 'so I might just as well tell you myself.' He looked up at last, and fixed Roper steadily in the eye. 'I had a big thing about Alex. I made a bit of a fool of myself, in fact. I'd never met anyone quite like her before, you see. She was gorgeous, smart, and so incredibly bloody bright. She could talk about anything, and when it came to wheeler-dealing, she could run rings around me. And of course, I fell. Jumped in with both feet, and generally made a right prat of myself.'

But, fortunately for Mr Gentry, whose desk sported a photograph of a good-looking, hazel-eyed woman with her arms about the shoulders of two husky and pink-cheeked teenaged boys—and Mr Gentry himself was also wearing a well-worn gold signet ring on his wedding finger—Alexandra Higgs had not reciprocated his flaming passion.

'Too bloody sensible, you see, thank God,' said Gentry, with wry admiration.

'And she stayed working for you, obviously,' said Roper.

'Mercifully, yes,' said Gentry. 'And we stayed good friends.'

'No grudges, then?'

'Definitely not,' said Gentry. 'And over the years, I cooled off and counted myself lucky that I hadn't made a bigger idiot of myself than I already had.'

'Fair enough, sir,' said Roper. 'I appreciate your telling me that.' Then, switching tracks, he asked: 'Does the name of Gribo mean anything to you, Mr Gentry? Mrs Susan Gribo?'

'Nothing,' said Gentry, shaking his head. 'Should it?'

'She might have been a client, sir,' said Roper. 'Might have booked a holiday in Crete. Flew out in July the twenty-fifth last. She presumably took a flight to Athens, coach to Piraeus, then definitely the ferry to Iráklion.'

'Gribo,' muttered Gentry, gazing up into space. 'Gribo. You know I've heard that name before, now you come to mention it. Wasn't it a Mrs Gribo who was murdered in Crete a while back?'

'That's exactly the lady, sir,' said Roper. 'Is there any way you can find out if she booked her holiday through Wesco?'

'Since you've been able to give me a date, then yes,' said Gentry. 'Certainly.'

THEY FOLLOWED HIM into the adjacent office, clearly the nerve-centre of the entire Wesco organisation, where one young woman was attending a clattering telex machine, another was speaking into two telephones at once, while another was transcribing information from a pile of forms into a computer keyboard.

'Got a job for you, Harriet,' said Gentry to the young woman manning the computer. 'The clients' history file for last July. What was the date, Superintendent?'

'Saturday the twenty-fifth of July,' said Roper. 'And the name's Gribo.'

They waited while Harriet unshipped the magnetic disc she was using and replaced it with another. After a humming pause her video screen produced a menu and her fingers dabbed nimbly over her keyboard.

Gribo, Mrs S, Roper read, when the legends on the screen stopped scrolling. *Oaktree Cottage, Mays Lane, Nuncton Zelston, Dorset.*

'All there, you see,' said Gentry enthusiastically. 'Flight times, hotel booking, absolutely everything. We pride ourselves on organising every last detail. We even manage most of the time to tell our clients their hotel room numbers.'

Mrs Gribo had been booked into Room Twenty of the Ariadni, the room she had changed on her arrival to be nearer Sheila Carmody, and the holiday had been booked late last March.

'Booked at this branch, was it, Mr Gentry?'

'Yes, it was,' said Gentry, leaning forward and pointing at the video screen. 'This bracketed ''D'' beside the date is the code which signifies the Dorchester office.'

'And would you know who came in and made the arrangements?'

'Sorry, no,' said Gentry. 'I can only presume it would have been Mrs Gribo herself. She would have needed to sign a contract, of course, and that'll still be on file. I can have that looked out for you, if you like.'

'Yes, sir, if you would,' said Roper. 'One last thing here though. Is there a record on your computer of which member of your staff took the booking in the first place?'

'Yes,' said Gentry, extending his forefinger towards the screen again. 'Here. These initials, "ADH". That would have been Alexandra. She didn't usually deal with the public, so we must have been short-staffed at the time, or it was a lunch-hour or something and she decided to fill in. She was very good at helping out like that.'

No, not just helping out, there was lot more to it than that, Roper was sure of it now. It was no coincidence that Higgs had been the organiser of Mrs Gribo's Cretan holiday, no coincidence that Mrs Gribo and Alexandra Higgs and Albert Haddowes had been toppled one after the other like a row of skittles, no coincidence that M R Robinson had flown to Crete on the day Susan Gribo had been murdered, while at the same time Higgs had attended the funeral of an aunt who was still very much alive. It had all been preordained, a crude and clumsy conspiracy. And slowly, but very surely now, it was beginning to come apart at the seams.

'What are the four stars beside the hotel name?' he asked in passing. Good a hotel as the Ariadni had been, it certainly hadn't merited a four-star rating, which was what it had on the computer screen.

'That means that one of our staff has actually been there,' said Gentry. 'And that we can personally recommend it.'

'Alexandra Higgs go there, did she?' asked Roper, the hairs at the back of his neck bristling with renewed anticipation.

'Is that important?'

'Yes, sir, it is,' said Roper. 'Very.'

The disc was changed for yet another. And there she was again, Alexandra Higgs. She had visited the Ariadni Hotel at Agios Mateos in July '83, and found the food, accommodation and site excellent value for money. Highly recommended for peace and quiet.

But the nearest thing to Higgs' name on Mrs Gribo's holiday application form were the initials 'AH', in pencil and ringed, at the top of the sheet. Ostensibly, Mrs Gribo had signed the form herself, and the counter-signatory for Wesco Travel was one Tracy Holder.

'This young lady still with you, sir?' asked Roper, circling Ms Holder's schoolgirlishly neat signature.

Ms Holder was quickly summoned, a pretty little blonde teenager, as neat and trim as her handwriting, but just a touch goggle-eyed with apprehension at being called suddenly to her boss's office and finding herself confronted by two police officers.

'It's all right, Tracy,' Gentry was quick to assure her, gesturing her into his visitor's chair. 'These gentlemen would just like a quick word.'

'We need your help, in fact, Miss Holder,' said Roper, proffering Mrs Gribo's holiday contract. 'Can you confirm that's your signature?'

Tracy nodded anxiously.

'Do you remember the lady who booked this holiday?'

Tracy shook her head.

'These ringed initials up here, "AH", know who put those there?'

Tracy cleared her throat and at last found her voice. 'Yes, sir,' she said. 'I did.'

Roper pulled up the other visitor's chair and sat down opposite her, doing his best to make himself as small and unthreatening as possible.

'Now this is important, Tracy. Can you remember anything at all, it doesn't matter how small, about countersigning that particular piece of paper, and why you wrote those initials on it?'

'Yes, sir,' said Tracy. 'Miss Higgs gave it to me. She said the customer had filled in all her details, but she—Miss Higgs, that is—had forgotten to countersign it. She said I could sign it if I liked.' She glanced guiltily over at Gentry. 'And have the commission.'

'All the counter staff get a five-pound bonus on all completed transactions,' explained Gentry. 'It helps oil the wheels. I hope you claimed it, Tracy?'

'No, I didn't, Mr Gentry,' replied Tracy. 'It didn't seem honest. And it wasn't right, because you've always said that we must always sign those in the presence of the customer. And I hadn't even seen the customer and I didn't want to get into trouble.'

'So what did you do, Tracy?' asked Roper.

'I took it up to Harriet in the Admin room and told her that it wasn't really my sale and not to book me down for the commission. I told her Mrs Higgs had seen to it all, and put her initials on it to remind Harriet. She said I was daft, it was like throwing money away, but I told her I definitely didn't want anything to do with it.'

'Did you tell Miss Higgs you'd done that?' asked Roper.

Tracy shook her head. 'Didn't dare,' she said. 'I was frightened of upsetting her. I mean, I know she was only being kind, but like I said, it didn't seem honest.'

'Thank you, Tracy,' said Roper, taking the form from her and extending a hand as he stood up. Her limper, colder hand came tentatively into his. 'People like us don't often come across honest folk like you. You've been an enormous help, and I mean that. We're greatly obliged to you.'

Caught between coyness and surprise, she blushed profusely as she retrieved her hand. 'That's all you wanted me for, was it?'

'Yes, that's all, Tracy,' said Roper, to what was obviously her immense relief. 'And thank you very much indeed.'

'And *was* it that much help?' asked Gentry, when Tracy had closed the door behind her and scuttled back downstairs.

'Indeed it was, sir,' said Roper. 'There's just one more thing I'd like to know,' he added, catching Gentry's surreptitious glance at his wristwatch. 'Did Alexandra Higgs have access to that computer we were looking at just now?'

'No, she had one of her own in her office,' said Gentry. 'If ever she wanted any information out of the main computer she used to ask for a print-out.'

'So it would be reasonable to say that Mrs Higgs might never have known that her name was attached to Mrs Gribo's holiday booking. That right?'

'Yes, I suppose it is,' agreed Gentry, 'and since she was management staff she wouldn't have claimed the counter-staff bonus for the deal in question, so it's likely she never knew her initials were keyed into the computer for that particular booking.'

But Roper thought that it was a lot more than likely. If his private theory was right, and most of it had proved to be right so far, never for a moment could Higgs have afforded to have her name linked with Mrs Gribo's on that computer. Nor would it have been if Higgs had chosen someone less honest as the recipient of her apparent largesse.

HE WAS BACK at County soon after six o'clock in the evening.

Two memos on his desk from Inspector Price. The switchboard downstairs had been ringing Mr West's number at two-hourly intervals during the day, and as of five o'clock had still received no response. Price had told them to continue until midnight, and start again from eight o'clock the next morning.

The other memo was of far greater moment. Doctor Weygood had rung in at five-fifteen. Concerned after his last telephone conversation with Roper, and even more concerned after hearing about the fragment of cutaneous tissue that the forensic laboratory had found on the screw that had held down Higgs' carpet-trim, he had returned to the mortuary that afternoon and taken another look at the body.

And specifically, what he had examined on that occasion had been the areas around the corpse's armpits. And what he had found, in the soft skin high up beneath the body's right arm, was a minute area of abraded flesh which might have been caused by the seam of a garment scoring across it under a lot of pressure. It had needed a magnifying glass to find it, but it was definitely there. As a consequence Doctor Weygood was now proposing that Higgs' body had probably been subjected to some rough handling either shortly before or shortly after her death.

So it was odds-on now that Higgs had been dragged into her kitchen while she was semi-conscious. Ergo: only a second party could have done that and therefore Higgs had been murdered, as Roper had suspected almost from the start. And that being so, it was probable that whoever had killed Higgs had administered those tranquillisers to her, and that that same whoever had stolen them from the hospital pharmacy. And the most obvious hospital functionary who had access to that pharmacy was yet again the dubious Doctor Gribo.

Roper took his electric shaver along to the senior officers' washroom and tidied himself up for his eight o'clock appointment in Nuncton Zelston.

'Gribo been complaining to the ACC again?' asked Superintendent Curley, who had come in to sluice his face preparatory to going off duty for the day, when Roper told him of his plans for the evening.

'Not that I've heard,' said Roper, knotting his tie in the mirror and folding down his shirt collar. 'He wants a chat about what happened in Crete. I thought I'd humour him.'

'Not your usual style, that, Douglas,' observed Curley shrewdly, meeting Roper's eye in the mirror. 'Got something on him, have we?'

'Not yet,' said Roper. 'But let's say I'm working on it.'

Curley smiled into the mirror. 'You're a cagey old sod, Douglas, d'you know that?'

'That's right,' agreed Roper. 'Who told you?'

THE EVENINGS WERE beginning to draw in and Roper arrived in Nuncton Zelston in the gathering dusk and a few minutes too early. He passed St Philip's church, where the funeral service had taken place last Tuesday, then turned into the lime-tree-lined avenue that led into Mays Lane.

Gribo's cottage was a sprawling, thatched affair, beautifully kept and newly whitewashed, with diamond-latticed windows, and a quarter of an acre of lavishly planted front garden. The two cars in the driveway were both grey Mercedes.

Roper was taking out his ignition-key when the cottage door was opened and two men came out to talk briefly under the porch—Gribo in his shirt-sleeves, and Doctor Hall in another of his hand-tailored suits. Hall raised a cheerful hand to bid Gribo goodnight, and headed for the foremost Mercedes. Roper climbed out of his car and slammed the door. A big man, Doctor Hall, bald and be-spectacled and smartly dressed, and with a pale grey car which might easily be mistaken for a cream one with the early morning sun shining on it; which was, come to think about it, a remarkably close match with the description of Mr M R Robinson as given by young Janice Wilkenshaw of the Goldfinch Travel Agency...

'Good evening, Superintendent,' called Hall, lifting a salutatory hand as he lowered himself into his driving-seat. 'Everything going all right?'

...yes, Doctor Hall really was *very* like. 'Yes, sir, fine,' replied Roper. And stood aside from the gateway while Hall drove out, looked left and right with unusually com-mendable caution—or perhaps because the law was watching him—and drove off in the direction whence Roper had come.

Gribo was waiting for him under the thatched porch.

'Thank you for being so prompt, Superintendent,' he said, extending a welcoming hand; and, short of appear-ing downright discourteous, Roper was forced to break one of his rules and shake it. And wondered whether he was in fact shaking hands with a cold-blooded killer or whether he might just have watched one drive away.

THIRTEEN

ROPER DUCKED his head to miss the top of the door-frame as Gribo ushered him into his sitting-room. The cottage was the genuine article, late eighteenth century probably, still with its original flagstone floors downstairs, what an estate agent would with justification have called a highly desirable residence.

There were some nice antiques sitting around too, rural craftwork mostly. The oak sideboard, black with age, was hand-hewn, the carpet on the floor a faded but fine-quality Bokhara, deep red once but now dimmed to a restful pink. The only anachronisms were the television set and the stack of hi-fi equipment in the corner by the window.

'Can I get you something?' asked Gribo, a hand poised over an array of bottles on the sideboard as he looked at Roper along his shoulder.

'Rather not, sir, thank you. I've still got some driving to do.'

'Yes, of course. You don't mind if I do?'

'No, sir, not at all.' Roper continued to look around, weighing, tagging. There was a fair bit of dust on the wooden mantelshelf over the fireplace, a glimpse of a used dinner-plate with a knife and fork on it, half-hidden under the chintz-covered armchair at the right-hand side of the chimney-piece.

'Charming old place you've got here, sir,' he observed, as Gribo turned away from the sideboard with a tumbler of whisky. It looked to be only a single.

'Yes, we—' Gribo corrected himself quickly. 'I rather like it. We came across it about six years ago, and fell for it. Do sit down, won't you.'

Roper loosened his jacket and sat down in the armchair nearest the window. The room had once been two, the wall between knocked down and a massive wooden beam put in to support the upstairs floor. From this lower viewpoint it was plain that Gribo had dined on spaghetti on toast this evening, the meal interrupted perhaps when Hall had called.

'I'm not really sure how to start this conversation, Mr Roper,' said Gribo, clasping his cut-crystal tumbler between both hands and gazing down into it. He was perched uncomfortably on the very edge of the other armchair.

'Well, if you've got any particular questions, sir, I'll do my best to give you an answer. Perhaps we can start that way?'

'Yes,' said Gribo. 'Yes, thank you.' He took a small sip of his whisky. 'The man I spoke to in Crete—God, I've forgotten his bloody name...'

'Major Spiridakis, I think you told me,' proposed Roper, helpfully filling Gribo's hiatus.

'Yes, that's it,' said Gribo. 'Him. I could hardly get anything out of him. I asked to see the post-mortem report, but he told me it was in Greek and that I wouldn't understand it. Her head was bandaged you know, Susan's, when I went in to identify her. I asked if the bandages could come off so that I could see what had happened for myself. I mean, the bloody man knew I was a doctor, I wasn't going to keel over and faint, for God's sake...'

'He was probably trying to be kind, sir,' said Roper.

'But you found her, you saw her. How bad was it, exactly?'

'I think Mrs Gribo's death would have been almost instantaneous,' said Roper. 'I wouldn't really care to expand on that, for the same reason as Major Spiridakis, except to say that it must have been a brutal attack. She probably knew very little about it.'

'They found her jewellery, you know, and her passport. Miles away from where it happened. I've got the jewellery upstairs. At least they let me have that. I had to bring her in through Customs, you know. The seals on the coffin had to be checked. She had to travel as cargo. How bloody *bloody* awful.' His disjointed outpourings momentarily done with, Gribo took another sip of his Scotch.

Roper had to admit that the man was certainly credible, as had Spiridakis when he had met him. If he was a killer, he was certainly a cool customer. But what he wasn't was a big, bald man with spectacles. Were he a villain on the run, and only identifiable by a verbal description—medium height, medium build, dark hair greying at the edges, particularly prominent eyes and lower jaw—he would be a hard man to find. He could, of course, have padded out his clothes, affected a pair of spectacles and shaved his head, but he could not possibly have grown back the head of hair he had now in so short a time. So he certainly wasn't the M R Robinson who had called at Mr Drew's travel agency to pick up those airline tickets that Monday morning.

'Did you get to know Susan at all?' asked Gribo. 'Meet her about the hotel?'

'No, sir, I didn't,' said Roper. 'I saw her, of course, but we only ever passed the time of day.'

'She met another woman out there, apparently. They went about a lot together. Unfortunately Major Spiridakis didn't know her name. I don't suppose you do, by any chance?' Gribo asked hopefully. 'I thought I'd like to write to her, meet her perhaps.'

'No, sir,' lied Roper, as Spiridakis too had obviously lied. 'I did see the lady with your wife, but I never knew her name. Sorry.' With the possibility of three people already dead at Gribo's behest, or even his hands, Roper had no intention of letting him make contact with Sheila Carmody in any way. Just in case.

'And, of course, the Scottish police couldn't find me for several days,' Gribo went on. 'It made me feel very shabby, that. Knowing that I'd been touring Scotland with my rods, without a care in the world, while she was lying in a bloody foreign mortuary.'

'You go fishing a lot, do you, sir?' asked Roper companionably.

'No,' said Gribo, looking up with his big dark eyes. 'That's the point. I hadn't done it since I was a boy. I decided to take it up again. The work I do, you see, it can get very depressing at times. One needs to get away from it. I mean right away, bury one's self somewhere and do something entirely different.'

'My work's much the same, sir,' agreed Roper sympathetically. 'We get to see the seamy side of life as well.'

Gribo nodded understandingly. 'Yes, I'm sure you do, Mr Roper. Anyway, I treated myself to a new set of rods and hired a camping van. Susan was going to come with me when I first mooted the idea, but then she backed out. She wasn't the camping kind, really. So I told her that I'd treat her to a holiday in the sun. All she had to do was pick somewhere and I'd foot the bill. She chose Crete. It was the first time we'd ever taken our holidays separately.'

Roper made a mental note of that: Mrs Gribo *herself* had chosen to go to Crete. Allegedly. Or had she been coerced? According to Sheila, Mrs Gribo did not like being out and about on her own. So would she have chosen to stay at such an isolated spot as Agios Mateos of her own volition? Or had Alexandra Higgs persuaded her to go there, to the very hotel that Higgs herself had visited and appraised the previous year? From which question sprang yet another possibility...

'And my own holiday was doomed from the start,' continued Gribo, still fiddling morosely with his tumbler. 'A divine sign, probably, but I didn't recognise it.'

'Understand your camper was broken into,' prompted Roper encouragingly.

Gribo took another sip of his Scotch. Or perhaps he only pretended to because the level in the glass seemed to be the same as when he had first poured it. 'The second Monday I was up there,' he said, 'I'd spent the weekend fishing around Loch Tay. I'd got up at first light, taken my gear out and sat on the bank till about eight-thirty. And when I went back to the camper for a bit of breakfast, I found the passenger-door swinging open. It looked as if it had been forced with a crow-bar or something, so I walked into Ardeonaig, which was the nearest village to where I'd parked, got there about ten to nine and a chap with a pony-trekking stables let me use his telephone to contact the police. And I've got to hand it to them, they were waiting at the camper before I got back. Sergeant Mackintosh, I think his name was. He couldn't do anything, of course, because whoever had done it was probably miles away by then, but he told me he'd report it so that I could put in a claim to the insurance company. He also suggested that I was a bit of a mug for parking where I had—amongst trees, you see, where the thief could have worked relatively unobserved—and to leave it in future where I could keep half an eye on it. And he was perfectly right, of course.'

'And did you claim on your insurance?' asked Roper.

'No, I didn't in the end,' said Gribo. 'It was hardly worth it. The camera that was stolen was about ten years old and scarcely worth more than a few pounds, so I didn't think it was worth the hassle.'

As soon as Sergeant Mackintosh had gone, Gribo had knocked together a breakfast for himself then driven a few miles further north to Acharn, where he had spent the rest of the day fishing in the pouring rain.

'I presume you'd managed to get the camper door fixed?' asked Roper, because if he had that might provide yet another witness as to what Gribo had been up to later that day.

'No, not exactly. I managed to wire it up. I couldn't find a garage that was prepared to fix it.'

'But you stopped off somewhere to buy some wire, sir, presumably?'

'I had wire in my gear,' explained Gribo. 'You'll find most anglers carry a coil of wire in their box. Useful for the occasional on-the-spot repair. We're pretty good at make do and mend.'

After an unsuccessful day in the rain—not a single catch, so he admitted—Gribo had decided to call it a day and return to civilisation, namely the village of Killin at the southernmost end of the loch. Which, as Roper recalled, was where a patrolling constable had spotted a camper much like Gribo's parked in the late evening, and where, in that same place, the van had been the following morning with Gribo inside it having a shave.

'And the next morning I moved down to Loch Earn,' continued Gribo. 'And the weather was terrible again. Didn't even catch a tiddler. Got thoroughly brassed off, and in the afternoon decided I'd book myself into a bed-

and-breakfast place for the night and generally dry myself out.'

Gribo took another modest sip of his whisky—or was it a cautious sip? Was he worried about alcohol making his tongue loose or taking the sharp edge off his wits?

Because it really was very pat, this saga of his Scottish holiday—times, days, places, names, right down to last detail. So much so in fact that Roper wondered if the account actually was an extempore one or if it had been minutely prepared for this particular occasion. And, he had not failed to observe, Susan Gribo, about whom, ostensibly, he had come here to talk, had ceased to be the subject of conversation at least ten minutes ago in favour of a blow-by-blow account of Gribo's fishing expedition.

So was this an unscripted conversation, or was what Roper was patiently listening to an elaborate and painstakingly embroidered alibi and the sole purpose for his invitation here tonight? And if it was an alibi it meant that Gribo needed one, and that the man was a fool because he was witlessly wandering into a quagmire from which he might never be able to extricate himself.

He was telling Roper now about his brief stay at the guest-house at Lochearnhead—

'—run by Mr and Mrs Murray. Nice people. I rang them in the early afternoon and promised to be there at seven o'clock in the evening, but I had to change a wheel on the camper and didn't arrive until nine o'clock, but they still managed to put a decent meal together for me. Most kind, I thought that was.'

'Stay long there, sir?' asked Roper disarmingly. 'In this guest-house?'

'No, I left after breakfast the next morning. Took myself further north. Loch Mullardoch. Up Inverness way. I found myself a nice slot to park in and spent the next few days there. Which is where they eventually found me and told me what had happened to Susan. I was devastated, of course, handed the camper back to the firm I'd hired it from in Glasgow and caught the first train back down here. I made arrangements to fly out to Crete; and the rest you know.'

His gaze lifted and met Roper's again, a searching glance that lasted a fraction too long. Was he wondering perhaps how convincing his performance had been?

'There's no more news from Crete, I suppose?' he asked then.

'Just a scrap or two, sir,' said Roper, deeming it time to put just the hint of a squib under Gribo's tail. 'They've come up with the name of a man who made the round trip to Crete from the UK about the time your wife was murdered. He flew out on the Monday afternoon and flew back again on the Tuesday morning. It might not be significant, of course, and so far he's only a name.'

'An Englishman?' said Gribo. 'That's hardly likely, is it? I got the impression from Spiridakis that he was looking around more locally.'

'Nobody's definitely said he's an Englishman yet,' said Roper. Then, doing some embroidery on his own account, he added, 'It's one of those names that could have come from anywhere. A bit like yours, sir, if you see what I mean.'

'Oh, I see,' said Gribo. For a moment or two then he had tensed. Now he was relaxed again, except for his eyes. They had become narrowed and watchful, not quite sure if he had been tricked just now or not. 'But I suppose you'll be looking for this man?'

'I don't really think it's worth the trouble, sir. Too little to go on, you see. And I tend to agree with Spiridakis. I think he's looking for a local man.'

Gribo lifted his glass and tipped back his head. When the glass went back to his lap it was empty. And Roper could see the relief writ large in his eyes. There was little subtlety about Doctor Gribo, and if and when the time came to get down to questioning him officially Roper doubted he would last the course.

'I want him found,' said Gribo abruptly.

'Well, to be frank, sir,' said Roper, with a plausible show of ineptitude, 'everybody's doing their best, but I wouldn't set our hopes too high. Only I'd rather you didn't quote me on that.'

Gribo glowered darkly, still prepared to fence if he had to but fairly sure now, or so it appeared to Roper, that he was safely behind the sandbags.

'Did your wife correspond with you at all while she was on holiday, sir?' asked Roper chummily.

Gribo shook his head. 'No,' he said. 'Since I was roving around Scotland there was little point. Why do you ask?'

'There might have been a faint chance that she felt threatened, and told you about it,' said Roper. 'It might have provided a lead of some sort.'

'Yes, of course.' Gribo nodded understandingly. 'I had something like that in mind myself. Which is why I wanted to speak to the woman that Susan had palled up with. I thought if I could persuade her to talk to you she might let slip something important that she hadn't realised she knew. I understand that happens sometimes.'

'Well yes, sir, it does,' agreed Roper, discouragingly. 'But not all that often, and first we'd have to find her. Could take months, and even then it might be a waste of time.'

Gribo sighed. 'Yes,' he said. 'I suppose it would.' He rose from his armchair, and something about the way he stood there told Roper that, for Gribo at least, their meeting was finished. He had found out all that he wanted to know. Or believed that he had. 'Are you sure I can't get you something before you go?'

'No, sir, thanks all the same,' said Roper, pushing himself to his feet and buttoning his jacket—just as a soft click sounded from its inside pocket, which he hoped Gribo, who was depositing his empty glass on the sideboard by then, was too far away to hear. 'I'd best be on my way.'

Gribo ushered Roper ahead of him into the hallway, and was about to overtake him to open the front door when Roper suddenly stopped and turned so that they all but collided.

'Alexandra Higgs, Doctor,' he said, as if the idea had only just occurred to him. 'I don't suppose that name's familiar to you, sir?'

'Yes, I think it is,' said Gribo, frowning too deedily down at his shoes before looking up again. 'If it's the same woman, she worked along at the Eastern County General. She committed suicide, so Doctor Hall told me.'

'And she was a patient of Doctor Tandy's, so I hear.'

'Really?' said Gribo, now looking too surprised. 'I didn't know that.'

'How about Albert Haddowes, sir? Is that a name that rings any bells?'

It did. The two of them stood no more than a foot apart, eye to eye, so close that Roper could almost smell the lie before Gribo opened his mouth under that silly little moustache.

'No, I can't say it does,' he said. 'It's certainly not a name that comes immediately to mind.'

'No, sir, I didn't think it would,' said Roper affably.

A FORLORN FIGURE rose from the slatted oak bench in the reception lobby. It was ex-Superintendent Mower, self-consciously sporting a visitor's identity tag clipped to his lapel.

'Let you out again, has she, George?' asked Roper.

'She's got me cooking,' grumbled Mower. 'I've just enrolled for evening classes. Bloody cooking lessons. Me!'

'You're kidding,' said Roper.

'I'm bloody not,' retorted Mower, miserably. 'She's even bought me a bloody pinny to wear. And then I call in here and they give me a bloody badge to ponce about in. I said to the bloke: "Son, I was a guv'nor in this place when you were wearing plastic underpants". He said it was all down to new security arrangements. Things aren't what they were, Douglas. Don't suppose you fancy a bevvy, by any chance?'

'Too busy, George, sorry,' said Roper, at which the ever cheerless Mower looked even more crestfallen. 'But I've got a private jar upstairs, if you don't mind watching me work.'

'Mind?' said Mower gloomily. 'Practically anything's better than going home.'

WHILE MOWER SMACKED his lips appreciatively over a glass of Glenfiddich, Roper made a brief phone call to the Dorchester office of the Wesco Travel Agency. He dialled the number on the off-chance, expecting to hear only an answering machine at this time of night, but instead was answered, if a little belatedly, by a breathless human voice, that of Harriet, the computer operator of the afternoon, who tonight was working some overtime to clear her paperwork.

'It's about Mrs Higgs again, Harriet,' said Roper. 'I need to know the number of the room that she stayed in last July at the Ariadni Hotel. It's fairly urgent.'

'Oh, I'm so sorry,' replied Harriet. 'That wouldn't be on the computer any more. Too long ago. All that's stored is Alexandra's recommendation.'

'You absolutely sure about that?'

'Oh, yes,' she said. 'Dead certain. Sorry.'

So with that avenue cut off, Roper tried another and hastily drafted a telex to Spiridakis on Crete:

PLEASE CHECK REGISTER OF ARIADNI HOTEL, AGIO MATEOS, FOR PERIOD JULY 1983. GUEST'S NAME: ALEXANDRA HIGGS, UK SUBJECT. NEED TO KNOW HER ROOM NUMBER. AND WAS ROOM-KEY MISSING AFTER HER DEPARTURE? REPLY MOST URGENTLY. REGARDS TO YOU BOTH. ROPER.

'Back in a jiff,' he said, and took the draft downstairs to the CAD room for overnight despatch.

'Never seen you move that fast before,' observed Mower when Roper returned. 'Got something big on?'

'I think I'm on to somebody,' said Roper. From the inside pocket of his jacket he took the pocket tape recorder which was officially employed as a dictation machine between himself and Miss Pringle, but which, that evening, had been used less officially, and even illegally. He rewound the tape, pressed the play switch and laid it on his blotter near Mower's elbow. 'Bend your ear to that while I make another phone call, George,' he said. 'I'd like to know what you think about it.''

He picked up his telephone and asked for an outside line this time, then dialled Sheila's number in Bournemouth.

'Any chance of your getting the afternoon off tomorrow?'

'Yes,' she said. 'Probably. Why?'

'Wondered if you fancied spending the weekend in Scotland.'

There was a stunned silence. 'That's awfully short notice.'

'I know,' he said. 'I'm trying to sweep you off your feet.'

She laughed, thought for a moment. 'Yes,' she said enthusiastically. 'Why not. I haven't been to Scotland for years.'

'Good,' he said. 'Pack your bag and I'll meet you at King's Cross around lunchtime. I'll give you a closer time in the morning when Miss Pringle's made all the arrangements.'

'You mean you haven't *actually* fixed it all up yet?'

'No,' he said. 'I'm trying to give myself a surprise as well. I'll give a ring tomorrow morning. About eleven?'

'Yes,' she said. 'Eleven's fine.'

'Can't say more,' he said. 'I've got a visitor.'

'Oh, I see,' she said. 'Take it as read from my end too, then.'

'I will,' he said. 'See you tomorrow.'

'Sounds a very understanding lady,' commented Mower, his whisky put aside, one hand curled round his ear as he bent closely to the muffled voices coming from the tape recorder.

'I got lucky,' said Roper, laying the receiver back on its cradle.

For a few more seconds the only sound in the room came from the tape recorder.

Then Mower said, 'He's got a good memory, this bloke. Who is he?'

'The somebody I think I'm on to,' said Roper.

'...and she chose Crete,' came Gribo's muffled and hollow voice. 'It was the first time we'd ever taken our holidays separately.'

'Can I take a guess?' said Mower. 'That's Doctor Gribo. The one whose missus got herself done in on Crete.'

'Close,' said Roper. He was very sharp, old George, always had been.

The voices talked on. An occasional rasping sound had been the recorder shifting about in Roper's pocket whenever he had moved.

'Some of these places don't come trippingly off the tongue, do they?' observed Mower. 'Ardeonaig, for a start.'

'Like you said, George,' said Roper. 'He's got a very good memory.'

'Or he's learned it all off by heart,' proposed Mower, his head still tipped intently over the recorder.

'More likely,' agreed Roper. While Mower continued to listen he went out to the passage and drew himself a coffee from the now repaired machine.

Five minutes later, the recorder clicked to a stop. Mower passed it back across the desk and Roper switched it off.

'Well?' he said.

'He's certainly got it all pat, hasn't he?' said Mower. 'I couldn't remember the details of my holidays as well as that. Can't be all invention, though, can it? Shouldn't think it'd take long to track down that Sergeant Mackintosh, for instance. Nor the couple who kept the guesthouse at Loch whatever-it-was. What are you after him for, anyway? He couldn't have killed his missus, could he?'

'Not personally, no,' agreed Roper. 'But he might have put out a contract on her. In which case he'd still need an unbreakable alibi, like the one you've just been listening to.'

'Not easy to get to Crete and back without being noticed,' cautioned Mower. 'You need a passport, and the airlines keep records.'

'The only lead we've got is an airline passenger called Robinson, M R, of an address that doesn't exist somewhere in Dorchester. So he was probably travelling under an assumed name as well, which probably means that his passport was as big a fake as he was.'

'Not easy to fiddle a passport, Douglas,' Mower further cautioned.

'George, if you need a passport desperately enough and you're prepared to bend the rules, it's a doddle. Given your full name, your date and place of birth, and a copy of your birth certificate, which I can get through the post without showing my face anywhere, I could have a passport in the name of George Mower in a couple of weeks.'

'True,' agreed Mower. 'But you need a photograph. And somebody with a bit of clout's got to sign it to certify that the photograph's a fair resemblance to whoever's photograph it is. And then the Passport Office phones the signatory to verify that everything's on the up and up. It's not easy to buck a system like that.'

'And who's the usual person folk to get to sign the back of their photograph and verify their application form?' asked Roper.

'Their doctor, as a rule,' said Mower.

'And that's just what Gribo is,' said Roper. 'A doctor.'

Mower savoured that over a sip of Scotch. 'So you ask the Passport Office to wade through all their application forms in the name of Robinson until they turn one up with Gribo's signature as a referee.'

'Doesn't work like that,' said Roper. 'They get those forms in by the hundreds every day. I know. I tried to get access to some passport information a few years back. At best, they need to know the passport number in question, or, failing that, the date when it was applied for. All we've got's a name. And that's only a probable. And it could have been applied for anytime over the last few years.'

'Looks like you're going to be a busy lad, then,' said Mower.

ROPER STOOD LOOKING down from his office window at the silent, floodlit and nearly empty car park. It was coming up for eleven o'clock. Mower had left half-an-hour ago, and since his departure Roper had put through a call to the Tayside Constabulary to make a tentative appointment with Sergeant Mackintosh on Saturday morning, played over the illicitly obtained tape recording once again, written a memo to Miss Pringle regarding rail tickets and hotel bookings, drunk another coffee and lit two more cheroots. And between times done a lot of thinking.

Theories were all very well. Everything seemed to point towards Doctor Gribo. But to finger his collar, and to keep the finger well and truly there, required proof. And proof, old chum, Roper told his reflection in the dark glass of the window, is what you have not got. Nor a motive. Husbands and wives still killed each other on the spur of the moment. But rarely planned to do so in the long term because in this day and age, when obtaining a divorce requires little more than a couple of signatures on a few scraps of paper, it is easy for each to off-load the other legally.

It was fairly certain now that Higgs had figured prominently in the death of Mrs Gribo. That Mrs Gribo's holiday had been planned by Higgs, that at least was a certainty, and surely more than mere coincidence, as was the fact that Higgs had spent a holiday in the same hotel, albeit a year before.

And Albert Haddowes had done more than stand on the sidelines. Was it possible that Haddowes had been M R Robinson? Given a pair of spectacles, he certainly fitted the description of Robinson given by young Janice at the Goldfinch Travel Agency—and a pair of spectacles, Roper recalled, had been found under the armchair in which Haddowes had died. But Haddowes hadn't owned a car, and, according to Janice, Robinson had arrived at the agency in a car the morning he had called into the shop for those airline tickets. All right, so he could have borrowed a car, or rented one—except that to rent one he would have to have produced his driving licence. But would he have chanced showing a driving licence with his own name on it?

But then, from one of the darker recesses of his memory, there sprang an image of Derek Jewkes, hunched, bespectacled and terrified, with dandruff powdering the shoulders of his security guard's black uniform.

'Got any idea what this might be about, Mr Jewkes?' had been Roper's first question of him.

And Jewkes' first blurted words had been: 'Look, I have *got* a driving licence. It's just that I lost it . . .'

At the time, Jewkes' immediate protestation had seemed totally irrelevant—George Makins wouldn't even have bothered to record it in his pocket-book. A knee-jerk reaction on Jewkes' part, that was all. But now, suddenly, it was a pin upon which other and more important matters might hinge . . .

Supposing Haddowes had in fact rented a car, in Jewkes' name, using Jewkes' stolen driving licence, Jewkes' licence having not been lost at all, but stolen by Haddowes for that very purpose?

And then something else that Jewkes had said in passing: 'He'—meaning Haddowes—'told me he was going to Greece, you know. For his holiday.'

At the time that had seemed irrelevant too. But at that time Roper had still to connect Haddowes with Higgs and Higgs with Gribo. *Had* Haddowes *actually* gone to Greece—or, rather, Crete?

And then further suppose, given Haddowes had hired that car, that he had rented it for a short term, like a couple of days, say the days over which M R Robinson had flown to Crete and back. Left it perhaps in the airport car park and collected it again on his return journey.

Or alternatively, had that car been hired for an even shorter time? Like a single day?

Because if it had, then Haddowes was unlikely to be M R Robinson, and somebody else was.

And then another thought: obtaining a passport in someone else's name was not difficult, but it might prove tricky if that someone else, by a remote chance, applied for a legitimate passport at the same time. But it was less risky if the someone else were dead, had died perhaps fairly recently, perhaps at the Eastern Country General, and had perhaps been a patient of Doctor Gribo's who would thus have access to that patient's records.

It would all have been so easy.

FOURTEEN

SCOTLAND, THAT Saturday morning, was at its brightest and best as Roper drove their hired car westward out of Dundee with Sheila sitting beside him with the road-map on her knee. At ten o'clock they were in Perth, at half-past ten they were passing through Comrie on their way to Lochearnhead.

Miss Pringle's arrangements had been perfect. The train had left dead on time from King's Cross at one o'clock yesterday afternoon, the hotel in Dundee had put up an especially late dinner for them, and the hired car had arrived on the hotel forecourt on the dot of nine o'clock that morning, just as Sheila and Douglas were finishing their breakfasts. And perhaps Miss Pringle had organised the traffic for them too, because the roads were all but empty so that they had all this moss-green moorland and mist-hung mountains almost entirely to themselves.

Reality came shortly before eleven o'clock, in Lochearnhead, in the shape of a sleek white Rover with the Tayside police-insignia on its doors, which was waiting for them at the junction of the A85, upon which they had travelled, and the A84.

Douglas pulled in behind the Rover, and as he did a mountainous sergeant and a constable who wasn't much smaller climbed out of it. Douglas joined them on the roadway and somewhat to Sheila's surprise, as she watched through the windscreen, it appeared that he merited a smart salute from the sergeant. They spoke together for a few minutes, then Douglas returned to the car and they set off again, following the Rover, but only for a few hundred yards before they stopped again, this time outside a grey fortress of a place that proclaimed itself to be the Inverkeld Guest-House.

'I won't be more than twenty minutes,' he said. 'Promise.'

'No rush,' she said. 'I'll have a wander around the village and take a few snaps.'

ROPER, Sergeant Mackintosh and Constable Murdo sat in the Murrays' well-appointed visitors' lounge. Deer-antlers and family shields hung from the dark oak panelling and a couple of beautifully basketed claymores were crossed gleamingly on the wall above the fireplace. Murray himself was a small, neat, balding man, sixty or so, sporting a wartime fighter-pilot's moustache and a tartan waistcoat under a leather-patched shooting jacket, a Scotsman down to his very bones. Mrs Murray was English, but had clearly lived in Scotland long enough to have developed just a trace of the accent. Both remembered Doctor Gribo.

'He arrived in a camping van,' said Murray. 'Yellow, with a buff stripe along the sides. I remember it because I saw him park it on the forecourt and I had to go out and ask him to park it around the back of the house.'

'It doesn't look well,' explained the trim and tartan-skirted Mrs Murray. 'Big ugly vans like that parked in front of the place.'

'We can give you the van's registration number if you like,' said Murray. 'It'll be in the register.'

'We already have it, sir,' came the slow, deep and sonorous tones of Sergeant Mackintosh.

Roper opened Miss Pringle's file and took out the newspaper cutting that showed Gribo about to fly to Crete to collect his wife's body. He handed it to Mrs Murray who glanced at it then passed it on to her husband.

They both agreed. The Doctor Gribo in the picture was definitely the one who had stayed at their guest-house on the night of Tuesday August 4th last. Mrs Murray found the relevant page in her register and held it out for Roper to see.

'I understand he made the booking by telephone,' said Roper.

Neither was certain, but Mr Murray was a methodical man who kept a business diary. He went away briefly and returned with it, opened at August 4th.

'Yes,' he said. 'He made the booking by telephone. At two o'clock in the afternoon. Said he'd be here by seven, in time for dinner.'

'But he arrived late,' said Mrs Murray, 'and we had to arrange a separate meal for him. I remember that particularly. And his curious name.'

'I seem to remember he said something about having to stop to change a wheel on his van,' said her husband.

'I know it's a long-shot, Mr Murray,' said Roper, 'but d'you remember if he mentioned where he was phoning from?'

'I presumed from somewhere locally, I suppose,' said Murray, frowning. 'Since he knew the name of the house, and we don't advertise in the Yellow Pages, nor are we in the AA guide. He must have got the name from somewhere.'

'Could have been a recommendation, of course,' suggested Mrs Murray.

'Yes,' agreed Murray. 'We get a lot of guests by word of mouth. And he was fortunate, I suddenly remember,' he added, looking at his diary again. 'Because a Mrs Jones had booked that room back in April and had rung in, only a few minutes before Doctor Gribo did, to cancel it. Had it not been for that we would have been full up and he would have had to go elsewhere.'

'April, you say,' said Roper. A lot of the Gribo's holiday arrangements had been made last April. 'How long did this Mrs Jones book the room for?'

Murray referred to his diary again. 'A week,' he said. 'Monday to Sunday. But I remember her saying something about her mother being taken ill and how she couldn't get up here.'

'Isn't that the woman whose deposit came back?' asked Mrs Murray, breaking in suddenly. 'Mrs Jones?'

'Yes,' said Murray, frowning again. 'I do believe it was. Strange that.'

'How strange, sir?' asked Roper.

'Well, in the light of it being an emergency,' explained Murray, 'we returned her deposit. Only the envelope with the cheque in was returned. Address unknown. We presumed she'd moved house in the meantime.'

'And how had the lady paid her deposit, sir?' asked Roper.

Murray went away again to look up that information in his accounts book. He was quickly back. Mrs Jones had paid her deposit by means of a virtually untraceable postal order, and given an address in South Wales.

'I presume you sent her a letter of confirmation, sir?' asked Roper. 'To this address in Wales she'd given you?'

'No, I didn't, in fact,' said Murray. 'When she first rang, she told me she was going abroad for a few weeks, but that she'd ring me soon after she'd deposited the deposit to make sure that it had arrived. Which she did, as I recall. So there was no need for a written confirmation. I still have the address here, if it's any use to you.'

He rose from the chair and handed Roper his diary, circling with his finger Mrs Jones' address in Glamorgan.

'Get it checked now, can we?' asked Roper, passing the opened diary to Sergeant Mackintosh. He nodded and without a word handed it on to Constable Murdo, who took it as he stood up and went out to their car and the radio.

In ten minutes, he was back again. According to the Glamorgan police, the street in which Mrs Jones had allegedly lived did not appear in either their latest gazetteer or their local electoral register.

So here was another false address, like the one M R Robinson had given to the Goldfinch Travel Agency. So it was more than possible now that Gribo had never come to the Murrays' guest house on the off-chance. It had been part of his grand plan, part of the itinerary that Roper no longer had any doubt had been devised by Alexandra Higgs, just as Mrs Gribo's Cretan holiday had been. Gribo had made sure that he was well remembered here. He had arrived two hours late and missed dinner so that Mrs Murray had had to prepare him a separate meal. He had parked his camping van on the forecourt, despite the prominent notice, fitted with a floodlight, which Roper had observed on his way in: *Private cars only. Vans and coaches to be parked at the rear of the premises, please.*

And how fortunate that Mrs Jones, who had probably been Higgs, had cancelled her booking only moments before Gribo had rung here to make his.

AND IT SEEMED that Sergeant Mackintosh too had had his doubts about Doctor Gribo as far back as the morning of Monday, August the 3rd last, which he ventured now as he and Roper stood among the trees just off the road that ran along the north-west bank of Loch Tay. A sign beside the

road read: *Ardeonaig 1 mile.* It was now midday of the
same Saturday.

'I arrived here before he'd got back from telephoning us,
sir,' explained Mackintosh. 'So I was able to spend a couple of minutes looking around. It had been a wet night and
the whole place was a morass. His van was parked just
here. Nose in, back of it facing the road. The nearside door
had been sprung with something like a crow-bar—door-
frame buckled, the window glass cracked. It all looked
very authentic.'

'But?' prompted Roper, because Mackintosh had obviously come across an anomaly or two.

'Well, whoever did it had to get to and from the vehicle, sir,' explained Mackintosh. 'And, so far as I could see,
someone had definitely sloshed about in the mud near the
door, but there was no trace of mud on the floor of the van
when he took me in there, and only his footprints and mine
in the muck round about.'

'Did you point that out to him?' asked Roper.

'Yes, sir,' said Mackintosh. 'And he suggested that as he
was wearing a fairly common pair of industrial welling-
tons, the thief might have been too. And the camera that
was stolen had been under the nearside passenger seat, so
all the villain had had to do was reach in for it.'

It was plausible. Just. Doctor Gribo, thus far, had
seemed to have an answer for everything.

They were in Killin village, at the southernmost end of
Lock Tay, soon after twelve-fifteen. Constantly in the air
was the murmur of water spilling over the nearby Dochart
Falls.

'And this is where I noticed the camper parked in the
evening of the third, sir,' said Constable Murdo, who lived
in Killin.

'Noticed it because of what?' asked Roper.

'It was parked on the grass, sir,' said Murdo. 'If it hadn't been the holiday time, I'd have moved him on. But in that season we tend to turn a blind eye to things like that, provided they don't hang around in the same place too long and make a nuisance of themselves.'

And it was Murdo again who had seen Gribo's camper on the morning of Tuesday the 4th, the van still parked where it had been the previous evening. That day had been Murdo's rest-day and he had been driving his wife into Crieff to do the weekly shopping. As he had driven past the camper, he had glimpsed a shadowy figure standing near the window, a towel around its shoulders as it scraped its face with a razor.

'Doctor Gribo?' asked Roper.

'I wouldn't know, sir,' said Murdo. 'I never got a look at Doctor Gribo.'

Which was a great pity. But all in all, it did appear now that Gribo had indeed spent those relevant two days in Scotland, which in turn meant that he could not have been on Crete killing his wife.

So the probability now had to be that Albert Haddowes had been M R Robinson, and that it was he who had flown to Crete and done the job at the behest of Doctor Gribo, doubtless for money, and possibly a lot of money, because nobody took a risk like that for nothing.

But what about Alexandra Higgs? Had her part in the affair ceased with her making the arrangements to put Mrs Gribo in the Ariadni Hotel? Or had she done more? Why had she been absent from work for the days in question, and absent on the strength of a lie, namely the funeral of an aunt who was still walking about? And, just as importantly, why had she had her hair cropped and dyed? To disguise herself, as Sheila had suggested? Very likely—but why? Where had Alexandra Higgs been during those few days, and what had she done? And why was she dead?

SOME OF THE ANSWERS were on Roper's desk when he arrived in his office at eight o'clock on Monday morning. Firstly a memo from Inspector Price. Alison Weekes, on Saturday morning, had located a car-rental firm in Weymouth which had hired out one of its vehicles, a white Ford Escort, to a Mr Derek Jewkes, or so his driving licence had stated. The vehicle had been collected at six-fifty a.m. on Monday, 3 August, and returned by the same Mr Jewkes at seven-fifteen p.m. that same evening. The mileage recorded on the car's odometer upon its return was 280.4, and Mr Jewkes, to the best of the counter clerk's memory, had been an exceptionally tall man with little hair, which was about as far away from the real Derek Jewkes as a description could get. But it was a very snug fit indeed upon the late Albert Haddowes.

And more, Derek Jewkes had been able to prove that he had been working all that day, helping to clean a block of offices in Dorchester. Mr Jewkes had also reported the loss of his driving licence at his local police station on Friday, 31 July last, which the station, having checked its records, had later confirmed. And Friday, 31 July had been three days before 'Mr Jewkes' had hired his car and Mrs Gribo had been murdered.

Secondly there was a telex from the Tayside Police HQ timed in at seven-thirty yesterday evening, at about the time he and Sheila were taking a taxi out of King's Cross on their way home. The camping van that Gribo had hired had been rented from a company in Glasgow. More interestingly it had been booked for him early last April, and by way of the Bristol branch office of the Wesco Travel

Agency, which office Alexandra Higgs occasionally visited in her role as Wesco's trouble-shooter.

And thirdly there was the memo from Dan Morgan, dated last Saturday afternoon. Morgan had established that a certain Martin Richard Robinson had died on 12 February last at the Eastern County General Hospital. He had been consigned to the hospital on the advice of Doctor Rex Gribo, of the Monksbridge Medical Centre, etc, and whilst Mr Robinson had been in hospital with his terminal illness, Doctor Gribo had attended him at least once a week. Mr Robinson had been forty-five years old, which was about the same age as Gribo, unmarried, and his only next of kin listed in the hospital records had been a female cousin who was a schoolteacher in Canada. Which would have fulfilled the requirements of a false application for a passport in the name of Mr M R Robinson to a nicety.

So now there was a discrete band of time during which M R Robinson's passport had been applied for, some time between 12 February, when Robinson had died, and the end of March, when Mrs Gribo's Cretan holiday had been booked. Because it was doubtful that holiday had been arranged before Gribo had been fairly certain about organising the illegal passport. And given those dates, the Passport Office's search for this particular M R Robinson would now be relatively easy.

But still there was no reply from the elusive Mr West, which was frustrating to say the least, because Mr West, according to the frequent stirrings in Roper's gut, would be a man with a story to tell. Because nobody stormed into and out of a funeral service, quite as Mr West had, unless he was somebody with an axe to grind.

Then, the memos read and digested, Roper sat down with a coffee and a cheroot and set about rearranging what he now knew and committing it to paper.

On Saturday, 1 August, Albert Haddowes had begun two weeks' leave. That was a fact.

On Monday, 3 August, Albert Haddowes, using the stolen driving licence of Derek Jewkes, took delivery of a rented car. Since he had returned that car the same evening, at seven-fifteen, he could not possibly have killed Mrs Gribo in Crete that same night. And hence, although Haddowes might have been the M R Robinson who collected the airline tickets from the travel agency, he was not the M R Robinson who had made the flight.

And the rented car had been returned to its owners with 280 miles on the clock, which represented an outward journey of 140 and a similar distance back again. Bearing in mind that he might have been carrying those airline tickets, what had been his likely destination?

It didn't take long to work that out. Gatwick airport. Using his spread fingers as a scale over the map on his wall, Roper found that Gatwick, give or take a few miles, lay within the 140 mile ambit.

So assume now that Albert Haddowes had ceased to be M R Robinson at the end of the outward journey to Gatwick. And then another M R Robinson took over, the one who was the applicant for the false passport.

Who was this second man?

At nine o'clock in the morning of that same August 3rd, Doctor Gribo had spoken to Sergeant Mackintosh up in Scotland. That was a fact.

And at eight o'clock on that same evening, Gribo's camper had been seen in Killin village. That was another fact, as was Constable Murdo's sighting of the van in the same place on the morning of the 4th.

What was not a fact, however, was that Doctor Gribo himself had been *in* the van. All right, so Constable Murdo had seen someone in the van shaving on the morning of the 4th. But had that someone been Gribo?

Had that someone even *been* a man?

Because anybody with a towel around their shoulders and scraping soap from their face with a razor would automatically be *assumed* to be a man. But supposing the razor hadn't had a blade? Supposing Sheila's idea that Higgs had had her hair cut and dyed to disguise herself was right on the button? And that it was she who had moved the van about in Scotland while Gribo had flown to Crete?

Having spoken with Sergeant Mackintosh early on the Monday morning, it would not have been so very difficult for Gribo to have reached Gatwick by midday, and thus give himself an hour or so to check in for his flight to Crete.

Perhaps Higgs' maroon Citroën had been in Scotland too. She could have driven him to either Glasgow or Edinburgh airport and he could have caught a Gatwick-bound shuttle flight. And likewise on the return journey. Time would have been tight, but it wouldn't have been impossible.

And then back to facts again: Mrs Jones—probably Higgs—telephoned the Inverkeld Guest-House at Lochearnhead to cancel the booking she had made earlier in the year and thus reserved a room in preparation for the arrival of Doctor Gribo. A few minutes afterwards, Gribo himself, with seemingly lucky timing, rang the guest-house and took up that same room. He could have made that call from anywhere, even Gatwick, perhaps having previously checked with Higgs that she had cancelled her booking as Mrs Jones. The timing of those calls to the guest-house would have been of the very essence lest a genuine chance-caller should slip in a booking during the meantime.

And then the last relevant fact: at nine o'clock on the evening of the fourth, Doctor Gribo in person had arrived at the Inverkeld Guest-House, which he left at nine o'clock the next morning, after which he dropped from the landscape until the Inverness police finally tracked him down at Loch Mullardoch and told him the news about his wife. By which time Higgs had driven back south and reported for work after attending the non-happening of her aunt's funeral.

And if all that jigsawed together as perfectly as it seemed to, then it was one of the most tangled conspiracies that had come Roper's way in many a long year. As plans went, it was shot through with a dozen possible holes, but it had almost worked, and would have worked perfectly had Spiridakis not got down to checking a few passenger-lists and pinned down M R Robinson as a possible suspect—and had Alexandra Higgs and Albert Haddowes still been alive.

That Higgs and Haddowes had been involved in the conspiracy was now almost beyond doubt, and now they were both dead because of it. Perhaps they'd suffered an attack of conscience and Gribo had had to somehow stop them from telling all, or they'd decided on a spot of blackmail, or they might have asked for too much money in the first place. The reasons for murder were many and devious.

'IT ALL SOUNDS a little far-fetched to me, Douglas,' proposed the ACC from the far end of the conference table, where he sat hunched over a photocopy of Miss Pringle's neatly typed transcription of Roper's earlier thoughts. The official Monday morning prayer-meeting was over and only the ACC, Roper and Superintendent Curley remained at the table.

'It seems to fit together a treat, though, sir,' said Bob Curley.

'Probably,' agreed the ACC waspishly. 'But can we make any of it stick? I mean, it's all so bloody complicated that we have to be dealing with a particularly clever man.'

'No, sir, I don't think so,' said Roper, from the other end of the table. 'I think the clever one was Alexandra Higgs. Gribo was just the mechanic, and when he took things into his own hands he made a right pig's-breakfast of it.'

'And you still haven't come up with a motive for Gribo killing his wife in the first place,' cautioned Curley.

'No,' agreed Roper. 'But I'm working on it.'

'So what's your modus op now, Douglas?' enquired the ACC.

'Mostly waiting, sir,' said Roper. 'I've got DC Weekes organising old passenger-lists from the shuttleflight operators at Glasgow and Edinburgh, although if Gribo used a different name in each direction that's not going to get us very far. And I'm also waiting for a telex from Crete about Alexandra Higgs, and I'm still trying to get in touch with a gentleman I spotted at Mrs Gribo's funeral service. And a return call from the Passport Office.'

'I see,' said the ACC, chillingly. The ACC was not at his best this morning. 'And how long will this waiting take, pray?'

But before Roper could answer, a tentative knock came at the conference-room door. 'Come,' snapped the ACC irritably, then: 'I hope this is *damned* important, Miss Pringle,' as that lady stole in with a quiet 'excuse me' and laid a telex in front of Roper as carefully as if it were a feather, then stole out again without another word.

'Well,' enquired the ACC peevishly, 'is it important?'

'Yes, sir, it is,' said Roper. The telex was from Spiri-
dakis, in response to Roper's of late last Thursday night:
ARIADNI HOTEL REGISTER SHOWS ALEXAN-
DRA HIGGS BOOKED IN ROOM TWENTY (20) FOR
PERIOD JULY 1 TO JULY 12 1983. UNCERTAINTY
ABOUT ROOM-KEY LEAVING WITH HER, BUT
POSSIBLE. HAVE CONFIRMED ALSO THAT MRS
GRIBO WAS BOOKED IN THIS SAME ROOM BUT
HAD IT CHANGED TO ROOM SIX (6) SOON AFTER
SHE ARRIVED. WILL TELEPHONE YOU AT MID-
DAY (BST) TODAY. REGARDS. SPIRIDAKIS.

'I see,' said the ACC, somewhat mollified now, when
Roper had finished reading the telex aloud. 'So I presume
that—oh, my God!' he exclaimed despairingly, shooting
out a hand to snatch up the trillingly demanding telephone beside him. '—No calls. D'you hear? *No* calls.' But
whoever the caller was, he or she was clearly persistent
because the ACC's silver eyebrows began to beetle and he
glanced interestedly across at Roper from beneath them.
'West, you say?...Yes, Sergeant, I'll put him on.' The
ACC cupped the mouthpiece. 'It's for you, Douglas. Sergeant Morgan's just made contact with someone called Mr
West.'

Roper joined the ACC at the head of the table and took
up the handset. 'Yes, Dan?...Yes, two o'clock'll be fine.
Did you manage to find out who he is, by the way?' Both
Curley and the ACC then watched something close to a
smile creep slowly across Roper's face at Morgan's reply.

'Now there's a surprise, eh?...I'll be with you in a few
minutes. And thanks, Dan.'

'If there's one thing I abominate, Douglas,' said the
ACC, acutely interested in the proceedings now, 'it's having to listen to one end of a damned phone call.'

'And if I didn't know you better, Douglas,' said Curley, as Roper laid the handset back on its rest, 'I'd say you looked downright smug.'

'I feel smug,' said Roper. 'I've just found out who Mr West is.'

'Who?' asked the ACC.

'Mrs Gribo's father,' said Roper.

THE CALL FROM Spiridakis came at a few minutes to noon, his tone at first accusatory.

'This room change made by Mrs Gribo at the Ariadni, Douglas, why was I not told of it at the time?'

'Would you have thought it was relevant?'

There was an apologetic pause. 'Well, no, perhaps not.'

'Nor did I,' said Roper.

'But now it is?'

'I think so,' said Roper.

A momentary silence. 'And who is this Alexandra Higgs?'

'A lady whose murder we're looking into. She was a big wheel in the travel agency where Mrs Gribo booked her holiday to Crete. And the lady's uncle's conveniently dead too. And from what I've worked out so far he could easily have been one of two M R Robinsons. I think the other one might have been Doctor Gribo himself.'

'So Doctor Gribo was not in Scotland?'

'Not necessarily,' said Roper.

'Ah,' Spiridakis exclaimed softly. 'This I must hear.'

'SO YOU THINK this Alexandra Higgs went ahead to reconnoitre the Ariadni so that Gribo would know exactly where to go. And that she perhaps stole a key to the room to make his entrance easier. Although Sergeant Stepanikis established yesterday that all the room locks at the Ariadni seemed to have an identical pattern, and the only differences in the keys is that of fair wear and tear. In which case the Ariadni must be the most insecure hotel in the Mediterranean. But, nevertheless, we are talking of long-term planning here, Douglas. Over a year, in fact.'

'So we are,' agreed Roper.

'She and Gribo were lovers, do you think?'

'Probably,' said Roper. 'At the beginning. They didn't finish up that way, though. All the signs point to Gribo having killed her. And most probably her uncle too.'

'But you say you still have no solid evidence?'

'No,' said Roper. 'Not yet. But it won't be long now. The one thing Gribo couldn't have faked was the photograph on the Robinson passport. Given a bit of luck, we'll be getting a copy of that some time today.'

'I wish you luck then,' said Spiridakis. 'And do not forget that when he comes out of one of your prisons then we shall probably extradite him in order to put him in one of ours. You will keep me in touch with events?'

'Every inch of the way,' promised Roper.

FIFTEEN

THE ELEGANT and elusive Mr West shook Roper's hand, then that of George Makins whom Roper had called in to take notes. West was still a very angry man. His eyes said it, his curt dry handshake said it and even the way he flung himself down in Roper's new visitor's chair spoke of a terrible volume of anger. He had also arrived five minutes early for the two o'clock appointment that Morgan had arranged with him on the telephone.

'Have we met before somewhere?' was his first brusque question. 'Your face seems familiar.'

'Yes, sir,' said Roper. 'I was at your daughter's funeral service.'

'Yes, so you were,' said West, scowling. 'I remember you now. So you obviously had your suspicions then?'

'Suspicions of what, sir?' asked Roper cautiously.

'Rex,' said West. 'Gribo. My son-in-law. The police don't usually attend funerals, do they, unless there's something suspicious about the death?'

'My interest was more personal, sir,' said Roper, still hedging. 'I was in Crete when your daughter died. Staying in the same hotel, in fact. It was me who found her body, unfortunately.'

'Oh, I see,' said West, both disappointed and taken aback. 'I didn't know that. Do you mind?' He held up a gold cigarette-case.

Roper shook his head and pushed his ashtray across the desk. The cigarette-case was tucked away and replaced by a gold lighter. A gold Rolex wristwatch too, Roper observed. There was a lot of gold about Mr West.

'Well?' enquired West, exhaling smoke. 'From what your Sergeant Morgan told me, I understand that you've been looking for me. I'm intrigued to know why.'

'Your behaviour at your daughter's funeral, sir,' Roper replied frankly.

'That's easily explained,' said West with an airy flourish of his cigarette. 'I simply wanted Rex to know that I was going to put up a fight.'

'A fight, sir? About what, exactly?'

'Money,' replied West. 'My business.' He extended an arm to flick an ash from his cigarette. 'I am not a poor man, Superintendent.'

OVER A STRONG black coffee served by Miss Pringle, West explained that he had spent the days since his daughter's funeral touring the wine-making districts of France, hence Roper's inability to make contact with him. He was a wine merchant, bottler and shipper, a supplier to several supermarket chains and had a dozen high-class retail outlets in the UK and on mainland Europe. It had been a family business for three generations, but it had been West himself who had grasped it by the throat and shaken it into the latter half of the twentieth century when he inherited the concern from his father in the early sixties.

'—and of course, it would all have been Susan's when the time came—in fact half of the business was already hers. Her mother divorced me, you see. Couldn't blame her, really, I'm not the easiest of men to get along with, and of course, since she helped me build up the business in the early days, she was entitled to half of it as part of her settlement. Mind you, it wasn't all that much at the time, but it grew. And then she died soon after the divorce, and

naturally enough she left her share in the business to Susan.'

To West's great disappointment, his daughter had had
no interest at all in the wine trade, apart from reaping the
rewards that had come her way at the end of each financial year. But on the other hand, to be fair, she had never
been reluctant to plough back some of that reward into the
business, as West himself did, so that it continued to expand.

But then Rex Gribo's shadow had fallen over her. In
1970, that had been.

'She'd contracted glandular fever. It was outside her
doctor's regular hours, so she had to phone for one of
those night-emergency people.'

And the emergency practitioner had been Doctor Gribo.
'She fell for the man, hook, line and sinker. A couple of
weeks later she rang me and told me she was engaged even
before she told me she was feeling better. About a week
after that, she brought him to meet me. Can't tell you why,
but I just couldn't take to him. Felt he was up to something. Didn't trust him. Didn't like his eyes. Money-
grubber, that's what I thought he was. Gave me the creeps,
in fact.

'Anyway, Susan was too bloody besotted to listen to
what I had to say and told me she was going to marry him,
and that was that. But I did manage to persuade her to
draft a contract, so that Rex couldn't lay his hands on any
of her assets if ever the pair of them divorced.'

'And what provision was made in the contract in the
event of Mrs Gribo's death, sir?'

'None, regrettably,' said West. 'But I'm not having the
bastard getting his hands on forty-nine percent of the
business I've sweated my guts out for these last thirty
years. I didn't mind Susan having it. But not Rex Gribo.'

'What kind of money are we talking about, Mr West?'

'A lot,' said West. 'Seven figures. Most of it's tied up in the business, mind, but if Gribo takes it into his head to sell Susan's share, which I don't doubt he will, I could find myself with a working partner instead of a sleeping one. And even if he doesn't sell, I should have to pay him a substantial dividend each year.'

So that was it. At long last West had come up with a hard and fast fact. Roper had at first thought that West was just another father-in-law with a long-standing grievance against the man his daughter had married—and there were plenty of those about—and had finally found a way to make trouble for him. Despite the depressed state of Her Majesty's coinage, a million pounds sterling, even if it was tied up in bricks and stock, was still a considerable amount of cash, and it might have been more than one million. But even if it was only the one, it represented a powerful motive.

And Rex Gribo, in West's eyes at least, had soon shown himself in his true light. Within a year of the marriage he had set himself up in a practice of his own, his surgery and equipment, so West alleged, paid for by his wife. As, later on, had been his share of the practice at the Monksbridge Medical Centre, and the lavishly appointed cottage at Nuncton Zelston, and doubtless too the grey Mercedes which had been bought new only three years ago. And then, for the last four years, there had been another woman in Gribo's life.

'Got proof of that, have you, sir? This other woman?'

'No, I haven't,' West admitted. 'But Susan had her suspicions. And she became very bitter. And then, about six months ago, he started smarming around her, which made her even more suspicious. Whenever he became the loving husband it was usually a preamble to his touching her for more money.'

But on this occasion Gribo asked his wife for nothing. His outward show of affection continued unabated and the upshot of that particular period was his suggestion that the two of them 'really get away from it all'. A trip to Scotland, hire a camping van, get out into the wilds of somewhere, just the two of them. Which only aroused his wife's suspicions even more because the last thing her husband had been was a latent Boy Scout. He had always liked his creature comforts far too much. He had also, around that time, purchased several fishing rods and all the equipment and tackle that of necessity went with them. Which, so far as his wife believed, was only another pretext for Gribo to go out on his own, perhaps to meet the other woman, because he certainly never seemed to catch any fish on any of his angling expeditions.

Surer than ever now that her husband was two-timing her, she finally faced him with all her suspicions, told him that she was thinking of instituting divorce proceedings, that all he had ever wanted from her was her money, that without her money he would have been nothing.

'And, as I understand it, that's when he suggested they took their holidays apart. Give her some time to think, so he told her. He even offered to pay for her holiday. A gesture of goodwill, you might say.'

'Who suggested she went to Crete?' asked Roper.

'I believe Rex did. He arranged everything, paid for it too, all she had to do was to sign a couple of forms that he'd collected from some travel agency or other. She didn't mind boats but she was absolutely terrified of flying, and she loathed going *anywhere* on her own. But then she decided that if he was paying she might as well get all she could out of him while the going was good. So he swanned off to Scotland and she flew to Crete and becomes a murder statistic.' West ground out another cigarette vindictively in the ashtray. 'And it wouldn't surprise me one iota if Rex were involved in Susan's death in some way. God knows how, mind.'

'He was in Scotland, sir,' said Roper expressionlessly. 'There are witnesses.'

'Yes,' agreed West acerbically, 'so I read in the newspapers. But then I'm one of those people who don't always believe what they see and read in the papers. Aren't you?'

'THAT'S DEFINITELY a man with a grudge, sir,' observed DC Makins when he returned to Roper's office to collect his jotting pad after showing Mr West back downstairs. 'Reckon there's anything in what he had to say, or was he just letting off a bit of steam?'

'A bit of both, George, I fancy,' said Roper. 'And he did give us the one thing we hadn't got. And that's a motive.'

EVENTS MOVED APACE after that. Makins had been gone only a few minutes when Dan Morgan rapped on the door. The Passport Office at Newport had just rung in. Armed with Martin Richard Robinson's full name and an approximate date for the passport application, they had quickly located his details and his photograph. If a despatch rider could be sent quickly enough, copies of the documents could be made available that day.

The passport had been applied for on February 25th last and issued on May 5th. And, as Roper had guessed, both the application form and the photograph on M R Robinson's index card filed in Newport had been countersigned by Doctor Rex Gribo, MD, MRCP, of the Monksbridge Medical Centre, which endorsements had been counter-checked with Doctor Gribo over the telephone, as was the routine procedure before passports could be issued. The fee for the passport had been paid by means of a Postal Order, which was virtually untraceable, as had been the spurious Mrs Jones's deposit for her booking at the Inverkeld Guest-House.

'How about the address the passport was sent to?' asked Roper.

'Six, The Row, Chumpton,' said Morgan.

'That was Haddowes' address.'

'Dead right,' said Morgan. 'But now we come to the bitter bit. The woman I spoke to gave me a description of the photograph. She reckoned the Mr Robinson she was looking at was wearing heavyweight specs and had a haircut like Friar Tuck.'

Which seemed like a setback, but surprised Roper not at all. It was still only two-thirty in the afternoon. Given a clear road, and with a good wind behind him, a motorcyclist from the Traffic Division could be in Newport well before five o'clock and back here at County by seven-thirty this evening. And after that there ought to be little doubt about who was the other M R Robinson.

ALISON WEEKES' enquiries of the shuttle-flight operators between Scotland and Gatwick had become a dead end. Because of the transitory nature of their services none kept passenger-records on their computers for more than a week after the flight.

But nothing was going to divert Roper now. Gribo had had one of the oldest motives in the world for killing his wife: greed. He had had the opportunity, arranged for him in the most meticulous detail by Alexandra Higgs, and had probably carried the means, namely a camera tripod, with him in his flight bag. The only snag to all the elaborate scheming might have been a delayed or cancelled flight somewhere along the way, but the gods had smiled on Gribo throughout.

Higgs had done all the planning and Haddowes had been the leg man. The one had probably done it for love, the other for money, but in the end they had both paid with their lives.

At five o'clock, with still nothing to do but wait, Roper went along to the squad office and told everyone to call it a day.

'But I want you all back here at six o'clock tomorrow morning. Sharp.'

The only protester was Inspector Price. 'But if Gribo's photograph is on Robinson's passport documents, we can pick him up as soon as the messenger comes back, can't we? We could be interviewing him by nine o'clock.'

'Tomorrow morning,' insisted Roper. 'Sorry if I've got to get you all out of bed early, but that's the way it's going to be.'

So Roper was surprised, when he went to draw himself a coffee from the machine soon after seven o'clock, to find Price out in the corridor with the same idea.

'Thought you'd gone home, Dave,' said Roper.

'I did,' said Price. 'But I got itchy feet and came back again.'

'Anybody else come back?'

'They never really went,' said Price, straightening up from the machine with a coffee in his hand. 'Dan Morgan slipped away for an hour to keep an eye on his kids while his missus went to the doctor's, but he came back about ten minutes ago. They're all hanging about in the canteen. Poised.'

'Restores your faith in human nature,' observed Roper.

'Yes, sir,' agreed Price. 'They're a good lot.'

'You've slotted in all right then?' said Roper.

'Hopefully, sir.'

'Good,' said Roper. Price had pulled up his socks over the last few days. He wasn't the most creative of thinkers, but he seemed solid enough and kept his paperwork up to date, and Dan Morgan had started calling him guv'nor instead of sir and that was at least a sign that the two of them had started to rub along together.

THE RETURN OF the despatch rider from Newport provoked immediate consternation.

'That photograph's never of Gribo,' said Morgan.

'I'd go along with that too,' agreed Makins, but then he had second thoughts as he held the photograph at arm's length and half-closed his eyes. 'Well, it's possible, I suppose.'

Weekes agreed with Morgan, and Dave Price wavered along with Makins.

'And that's why we nick him tomorrow while he's still half asleep,' said Roper.

AT SIX-THIRTY on Wednesday morning the three unmarked cars were parked quietly and discreetly in the vicinity of Doctor Gribo's cottage in Nuncton Zelston. The morning was breaking bright and sunny again, although there was a definite nip of impending autumn in the air and according to the weather forecasters there were likely to be scattered showers by midday.

Price and Makins stole quietly around to the back of the cottage, not that Gribo was likely to make a run for it, especially in his pyjamas, but he was a foolish man and who was to say that he would not be foolish now. Roper and Dan Morgan trod quietly and purposefully up Gribo's neatly flagged front garden path and tucked themselves under the thatched porch to hammer loudly on the cast-iron door knocker.

'Try again,' said Roper when there was no reply. 'Make it louder.'

Then a sign of life. A light suddenly gleamed through the lozenge-shaped window above the door knocker. The door was snatched open and there stood a surprised Gribo, still half-asleep, holding the door knob with one hand, the front of his dressing-gown together with the other, and so immediately unrecognisable that Roper could easily have passed him on the street.

'What the bloody hell's going on?' he mumbled thickly, then in a split second he realised what was, and tried to slam the door in their faces, but Morgan was quicker, shoving his shoulder against it and sending Gribo stumbling back down the passage.

'You're under arrest, Doctor Gribo,' said Roper while Gribo was still getting his wits together. 'For submitting a false passport application—among several other things. You don't have to say anything, but if you do it'll be taken down and may be used as evidence. Now get dressed, if you would, sir. Go with him, Sergeant. And don't forget your hair-piece, Doctor!'

SIXTEEN

GRIBO HAD AT FIRST tried bluster, then bluff, but both had run dry when Roper had faced him with his own photograph and his signature on M R Robinson's passport application. He had been given breakfast in a holding cell. Now it was coming up for nine o'clock in the morning and he was hell-bent on confessing all and concealing nothing.

'This key,' said Roper. 'I presume that's the key Higgs stole from the Ariadni last year.'

'That's right,' said Gribo. 'But it was the wrong room. I knew that as soon as I'd got in there and saw the suitcases beside the wardrobe. They were white. Hers were blue. I decided to abandon the idea then and go home.'

'But you didn't?'

Gribo shook his head. 'I locked the door behind me and started down the stairs. Luckily there was still nobody about. Then I heard Susan's voice. She was talking to someone. A woman. The two of them were coming upstairs. I backed up to the landing I'd just come from and watched them. They said good-night to each other. The other woman went into a room somewhere underneath me and I saw Susan go into her room and heard the key turn in the lock.

'I still thought that was the end of it. Then I thought of all that time and effort we'd spent making the arrangements, and I just knew that somehow I had to get into that room. And I looked at the key Alex had given me, and saw how crude it was.'

'And wondered if it would fit Room Six?'

'I thought it was worth a try.'

'Supposing somebody had seen you?'

'I thought I might have been able to brazen it out. I was carrying a bag. With any luck they would have thought I was a newly arrived guest who'd lost his way. I would have had to have smiled, said good-night and flown home.'

'But that didn't happen?'

Gribo shook his head again. 'I waited about ten minutes on the landing. Susan was a creature of habit, you see. She *had* to be in bed by eleven-thirty every night, she *had* to shower first, she *had* to check the windows, she *had* to read for exactly ten minutes. She was obsessive about it. Can you imagine *living* with a woman like that?'

Roper didn't answer. He was face to face with Gribo and sitting beside Dan Morgan. Price was sitting beside Gribo, and Makins and Weekes were sitting at the other table taking notes. Even at less than a yard away, it was hard to distinguish Gribo's grey-flecked hairpiece from the real thing.

'It just *fell* in. The key, I mean, I heard the water running. The bathroom door wasn't properly shut and I could hear her splashing about in there. I put my bag on the bed, unzipped it—'

'And took out your camera tripod?'

'Yes, that's right,' said Gribo, without a trace of surprise that Roper knew even that little detail. 'I went into the bathroom, pulled back the shower curtain. Her back was to me. She started to turn, but she skidded in the tray. I hit her. It was very quick. I don't think she knew anything.'

'What if she'd heard you come in her room in the first place and yelled her head off?'

'She wouldn't have screamed at the sight of *me*,' replied Gribo bitterly. 'She despised me. She was always telling me how weak and insignificant I was. And besides, she was wearing ear-plugs. Another of her unpleasant little habits. She put them in before she had a shower and kept them in all night. Do you know, in all the years we were married,' he confided to Roper then, 'I hardly ever had *any* kind of conversation with her between eleven-thirty at night and half-past seven the next morning? Can you believe that?'

'Then you set about making the whole affair look like a robbery,' said Roper.

'That was Alex's idea,' said Gribo. 'I couldn't get out of the place fast enough, but I had to do it because it was part of the plan. I locked the door behind me with Susan's room key and got rid of the stuff I took on the way back to Iráklion.'

'What did you do with yourself after the taxi dropped you off in Iráklion?'

'I found a public toilet where I managed to change my clothes. I dropped the old ones in several litter bins and spent the night wandering around the town, got to the airport early, had a shave and a meal there and flew home. Alex collected me from the shuttle at Glasgow and drove me out to the camper. She drove south to Monksbridge and I spent the night in the Murrays' guest-house.'

'In the room Mrs Higgs had reserved as Mrs Jones?'

'Yes, that's right,' agreed Gribo. 'We made the calls from the same booth before we left Glasgow airport. She cancelled her booking, and as soon as she put the phone down I made mine.'

'Were you still carrying the camera tripod?'

Gribo shook his head. 'I washed it off under the shower in the Ariadni, dried it on some toilet paper that I flushed down the lavatory and threw it into the sea before I left Agios Mateos. I tossed the two room keys after it. It's probably all still there.'

But everything had gone awry even before Gribo had flown to Crete to collect his wife's body.

'Albert Haddowes,' said Gribo. 'He rang me on the Saturday morning. We'd agreed not to do that, make contact with each other, I mean, not for several weeks. He told me he was a bit strapped for cash and asked if he could have his money that evening.'

'Blackmail, was it?' asked Roper.

'Sort of,' said Gribo. 'We'd already explained to him that it would be safer if we settled up with him after all the fuss had died down, and he'd agreed. But he insisted that he needed a few hundred pounds that day. I told him that I could just about manage two hundred, which was all I had about the house, and it was Saturday and the banks were shut. He said OK, that would do for now, and I told him I'd call on him late that evening.

'When I arrived, I could see he'd been drinking. Smelled of sweat and beer. He was most unpleasant. I gave him the cash. He counted it, then said he was sorry he had come so cheaply in the first place, and that he was thinking of doubling the asking-price. That's when I suddenly realised how dangerous he might be. And I couldn't take a chance on that, not after all the risks we'd taken.'

'So you decided to kill him?'

'Had to,' said Gribo. 'I really didn't want to, but I knew I had to. I pretended to go along with him. Told him I'd prefer to discuss it when he'd sobered up a little, told him I'd make us both a strong black coffee. I needed to get to his kitchen, you see. I'd come more or less empty-handed and I needed something heavy.'

'Which was ... ?'

'A wooden rolling-pin I found in his kitchen drawer—I did think of using a knife, but I decided that a knife was too messy. And besides, he was a big man and I'd have to do it from behind him and that wasn't going to be easy with a knife. Besides which, if I didn't get it right first time he could easily have killed me. So I settled for the rolling-pin. I stuck it in my raincoat pocket and finished making the coffee. I put my cup and saucer on the arm of the other armchair, stood his on the coffee table, went behind him to put the tray on the sideboard. And I hit him on the way back. I doubt he knew anything. For a little while, I thought I was going to have to hit him again, but after ten minutes or so he hardly had a pulse so I knew he was on the way out. I wrapped the pin in a Sainsbury's plastic carrier bag, washed the cups and saucers I'd used and put them back where I'd found them. By the time I'd done all that, he was quite dead.'

'Did you take back the two hundred pounds you'd given him?'

'No,' said Gribo, shaking his head. 'I didn't see where he put it, and I couldn't afford to waste any more time looking for it.'

Which doubtless accounted for the £200 wad of bank-notes that had been found in the pocket of Haddowes' jacket in his front room.

'How about the rolling-pin?' asked Roper.

'I took it home with me, scrubbed it—and the bag, and put them in the dustbin. Then I suddenly realised I'd have to phone Alex.'

'Because?'

'Because she was starting to fret over what we'd done and I thought she might take it into her head to phone Haddowes. And if she did, and he didn't answer, she'd be getting worried over that too and might take it into her head to go across and see him. And when she found him dead she would probably have guessed that it was me who killed him. And I couldn't risk that, could I?'

'No, sir, of course you couldn't,' agreed Roper.

'So, as I said, I gave her a ring as soon as I'd got back from Chumpton. I told her that I'd been along to see Haddowes and that he was getting a bit jumpy about things and that I'd given him a few pounds to take himself away for a few days. I told her he'd shot off to Blackpool.'

'She believe you?'

'Yes, I think she did,' said Gribo. 'And the next evening I thought I'd better go and see her. She'd been drinking too. She'd reached the maudlin stage, kept saying she wished we hadn't gone through with it. She was in much the same state on the Monday evening too.'

'And that got you worried, did it?'

'Of course it did,' said Gribo. 'And the following day I had to fly to Crete to collect Susan's body, and all the while I was away I kept thinking, what if Alex cracks up completely and goes to the police while I'm not there? Or any other time, come to that. That's when I realised that I'd have to kill her too. And besides, it wouldn't be long before she started asking awkward questions about her uncle. So she had to go. But I knew I couldn't kill her the same way I'd killed Susan and Haddowes, just couldn't do it *that* way, not to her. I'm not a brutal man, you see.'

'You mean not as a general rule, do you, sir?'

'Absolutely,' agreed Gribo readily. 'I loathe violence of any kind. And then on the Thursday night, after I'd arrived back with Susan's body, Alex rang again. She was getting jittery, she said, didn't know how much longer she could stand it. And she sounded *really* drunk and I realised that I'd have to move soon before she folded up completely. She drank a lot, you see. I'd always known that. And I came up with the idea of giving her something that reacted strongly with alcohol, but it had to be something she could have obtained for herself, so that it would look like suicide. I suddenly thought of those new tranquilliser tablets I'd been testing. They were stored in the hospital pharmacy, and Alex had free access there so the first thought would be that she'd stolen them for herself. I managed to take a handful. I didn't know how many except that it was more than enough. When I counted them later there were thirteen.

'I called on her around ten-thirty on the Friday evening. She'd been drinking again, looked a mess—I even wondered what I'd seen in her in the first place. She'd really gone to pieces since I'd last seen her. I gave her three of the tablets intact, and the rest in a cup of strong black coffee; I'd crushed those down in the surgery earlier on.'

Then had come a problem.

'—she just wouldn't bloody die. She was unconscious, flat out, thready pulse, and it was well past midnight and I was worried about somebody spotting my car parked round the corner. And I knew I couldn't leave her like that, so I dragged her into the kitchen and arranged her head on a cushion in the gas oven. I turned the gas on full and waited outside for about five minutes. When I went back in, she was dead.'

'And then you turned the gas down?'

'I had to,' explained Gribo patiently. 'I was frightened of it causing an explosion. I didn't want to hurt anybody else, you see. Then I left. I was beginning to choke on the gas myself by then. And that's about all there is to tell. Except that I turned on the television so that the neighbours would think there was somebody in the house, and went back to my car.'

'Leave empty-handed did you?'

'Yes,' said Gribo. 'Well, no, not entirely. I took her diary and gadget she kept her telephone numbers in. My number was in both, you see. Home and surgery. I didn't take anything else, though.'

Gribo had first met Higgs five years previously. He had been attending a seminar on the financial aspects of managing a medical practice and Alexandra Higgs had been one of the lecturers.

' . . . We just seemed to hit it off together.'

'And your wife never knew?'

'No,' said Gribo. 'Not specifically, not about Alex. It was all guesswork on Susan's part. I kept telling her she was wrong, but she wouldn't have it. And just before she went to Crete she said she was going to put a private investigator on to me. She'd been threatening divorce for several years, of course, but only in a half-hearted sort of way. It was her way of letting me know that I was dispensable. But it was only around last Christmas-time that I realised she actually meant it.'

'And that's when you decided you couldn't afford a divorce and decided to kill her?'

'Oh, there was a lot more to it than that,' countered Gribo. 'I wanted to make a new life with Alex—I really did love her, you know—' Roper quirked his eyebrows but passed no comment. There were still many vagaries of human nature that were totally beyond his comprehension. '—we were thinking of going to Canada and starting again there.'

'And for that you'd have needed money, of course.'

'I was going to sell Susan's share of her father's business back to him. After a decent wait, of course. He could have had it for what it was worth. I had no intention of swindling him.'

'But you had every intention of killing his daughter.'

Gribo's forehead puckered earnestly. 'There was no other way we could see. It wasn't an easy thing to contemplate.'

'I'm sure it couldn't have been, sir,' agreed Roper, who was beginning to wonder by now if Gribo's straight-faced rationale of his villainy was a portent of a plea of insanity when his case came to trial. But if Gribo thought he was going to get away with that after all those painstaking machinations, clumsily flawed though they had been, he was on a hiding to nothing.

'What made you choose Albert Haddowes as an accomplice?' Roper asked then.

'We couldn't think of anyone else,' Gribo admitted. 'Personally I never really trusted him from the very beginning. But Alex said that we had to use somebody we knew, and preferably a rogue who wouldn't be likely to go to the police. Firstly, we needed an address for the fake passport to be sent to, some place that couldn't be connected with me or Alex. So Haddowes agreed to be the poste restante. And then Alex thought it might be a good idea if somebody who wasn't a bit like me showed his face as Robinson when it came to organising the airline tickets in Robinson's name. And since we'd already drawn Haddowes into the scheme we decided to use him for that too. So he collected the tickets from the travel agency and brought them to me after the shuttle landed me at Gatwick.'

'Did he know you were on your way to killing your wife at that stage?'

'Oh, yes,' said Gribo. 'There was no point in pretending otherwise because he would have found out eventually. In fact, he offered to kill Susan for us—for a fee, of course.'

No, thought Roper, never in a thousand years. Haddowes was a braggart, a big talker, and to make himself look bigger still he might have offered to kill Susan Gribo, but he was really only a puff-ball, a petty thief, and when the crunch came he would never have gone through with it.

'Prepared to write all this down in your own words, are you, sir,' said Roper, 'and put your name to it?'

'Yes, I am,' said Gribo. 'Gladly.'

'Good,' said Roper. 'Thank you, sir.' He got up to go, reached the door and curled his hand around the lever—

'You know, Mr Roper,' said Gribo from behind him, 'I knew from the very beginning that all this wasn't going to work. And now that it's over, I'm quite relieved.'

'Yes, sir,' Roper agreed sombrely over his shoulder. 'Our sentiments are much the same.'

SEVENTEEN

'I'M SORRY I'M LATE,' said Roper, a Cellophane-wrapped bunch of flowers in one hand and a fragile and still slightly warm cake-box in the other, as he wiped the soles of his shoes on Sheila Carmody's doormat. 'I got held up again.'

'Don't worry about it,' she said. 'Tomorrow's Saturday and supper's a casserole.'

They kissed briefly in her softly lit hallway. Cupid appeared to have taken up permanent lodgings in County HQ over the last few days; Morgan and his wife had celebrated their twentieth wedding anniversary in a big way yesterday, and during the course of the week DC Makins and Alison Weekes seemed to have had a great deal of difficulty keeping their hands off each other; and earlier that evening, from his office window, Roper had observed Weekes slipping into Makins' car and wearing under her raincoat a daring little black dress which, had she worn it during the course of her duties, would have merited a serious formal caution on the grounds of a deliberate intent to entice and entrap.

And workwise too it had been a good week. That very morning Doctor Gribo had made his second appearance in the magistrates' court, pleaded guilty to the murder of Haddowes and Higgs and asked for the murder of his wife to be taken into account in order to avoid his later extradition to Crete. By eleven o'clock he had been remanded in custody again and the case committed to the Crown Court, and by one o'clock Roper had telephoned the central police headquarters at Agios Nikólaos and made Ioánnis Spiridakis a very happy man.

And the sun was shining again on Derek Jewkes. Late that afternoon, Miss Pringle had called into Roper's office with a photocopy, courtesy of Superintendent Curley, of a formal Withdrawal of Prosecution Notice served by Diamond Electrics Limited on the person of Derek William Jewkes. The charge of theft against Jewkes had been dropped and, according to a note appended in Bob Curley's hand, Jewkes had been given a stern warning and a second chance by Mr Wallis so he was still in work and feeding his herd of children, which was the sort of justice Roper much preferred.

In the warm and beef-casserole-fragranced kitchen, he half-filled a glass vase with cold water while Sheila snipped open the Cellophane wrapping of the flowers, at which point she raised the question of the flimsy white box that he had put on the table on his way to the sink.

'Cakes?' she enquired.

'Well, no,' he confessed, joining her with the vase. 'Not exactly. They're the reason I'm late. My ex-Super called in on his way home from evening classes. He's taken up cookery lessons.'

She cautiously lifted the flap of the box and they gazed down together at its gluey and overcooked contents.

'Oh, dear,' she murmured sympathetically. 'I see what you mean about them not being exactly cakes.'

'Old George Mower was dead tickled with 'em,' said Roper. 'It's the first time he's ever cooked anything.'

'Obviously,' she said. 'They're jam tarts—weren't they?'

'Allegedly,' said Roper. 'He wondered if we'd give an opinion. And he mentioned you specifically. "Your good lady", he said.'

'Can we lie?' she asked hopefully.

'I think we've got to, in the circumstances,' he said gravely. 'Don't you?'

Buried In Quilts

(First Time in Paperback)

Sara Hoskinson Frommer

A Joan Spencer Mystery

WHERE THERE'S A WILL...

Joan Spencer, violist and manager of the Oliver Indiana Civic Symphony, is busy with preparations for the group's performance at the hugely popular annual quilt show. But when the body of show organizer Mary Sue Ellett is found under a quilt, the competition takes on a sinister tone.

Joan suspects Mary Sue's death had to do with a missing will that the entire Ellett family has been circling like vultures to locate. But looking for cold, hard motives among the soft down turns up some surprising stitches—and the handiwork of a devious killer.

"Entertaining..."—*Publishers Weekly*

Available in June at your favorite retail stores.

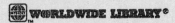 **WORLDWIDE LIBRARY®**

QUILTS

Down Among The DEAD Men

First Time in Paperback

GERALDINE EVANS

An Inspector Rafferty/Sergeant Llewellyn Mystery

A FAMILY AFFAIR

When rich and beautiful Barbara Longman is found dead among the meadow flowers, Inspector Rafferty doesn't believe it's the latest grisly offering by the Suffolk killer—though he believes her killer would like him to think so.

Rafferty and Llewellyn suspect someone close to home—someone among the descendants of the family's long-dead patriarch, Maximillian Shore. Everyone, it seems, had a motive: Barbara's weak, ineffectual husband; Henry, her ruthless brother-in-law; as well as Henry's bitter ex-wife. And the police duo discover that Maximillian Shore can wield his influence even from the grave—in a twisted legacy of murder.

"Competent…"—*Kirkus Reviews*

Available in July at your favorite retail stores.

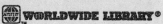

DARK SWAN

KATHRYN LASKY KNIGHT
A Calista Jacobs Mystery

THE RICH ARE DIFFERENT

Children's book illustrator Calista Jacobs is house-sitting in posh Beacon Hill and gets a peek into the world of wealth and privilege of the old-guard Boston Brahmins when she befriends neighbor Queenie Kingsley.

Unfortunately, Calista is also the one who discovers Queenie's lifeless body, a pair of garden shears protruding from her heart. Certain she can stand up to women called Bootsie and Titty, she enlists the aid of her teenage son, Charley, and Queenie's colorful brother-in-law, Rudy, and ventures behind the family's polished exterior.

And what she discovers are the ugly, dark secrets steeped in tradition...secrets worth killing for.

"Well-plotted..."   —*Booklist*

Available in June at your favorite retail stores.

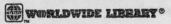 **WORLDWIDE LIBRARY**®

SWAN